THE LAST Super Chef

CHRIS NEGRON

HARPER

An Imprint of HarperCollinsPublishers

For the single moms, for all the moms . . . but especially
for my mom

ISBN 978-0-06-294313-2

Typography by Chris Kwon
21 22 23 24 25   PC/LSCH   10 9 8 7 6 5 4 3 2 1
❖
First Edition

know the exact amount of flour for the perfect cake batter. I'm able to tell if a steak is rare just by touching it. I can make a perfect piecrust without looking at a recipe. But I never quite recognize the ingredients that are going to get me into trouble until it's way too late. Tonight they're cupcakes, a culinary torch, and an undefeated high school basketball team.

We've arrived at the high school way early, but there are still plenty of pregame fans on hand, all of them staring at our foil trays and cooler. Staring at us—two fifth graders and a fourth grader—marching up the hallway, looking more than a little out of place.

This crowd is small potatoes, though. I'm talking red

skin or fingerlings, even. It won't be long before the gym and hallways are completely packed with tons of basketball fans. Which is perfect, because I'm actually counting on a russet-size crowd.

Tonight's idea started out small, with one simple fact that my best friend, Tre, dropped on me at lunch the other day: his brother Josh's varsity team, the North Sloan Eagles, have been straight-up crushing every opponent so far this season. High school basketball is especially huge in North Sloan. They even start the season early to squeeze more games into the schedule.

"Curtis, the gym's gonna be packed!" Tre told me days ago. "The whole town'll be there."

"Who are they playing again?" I asked him. I was kneading my tiny, doughy idea into some kind of shape in my brain. A baguette, maybe. Possibly a *boule*.

"Waxford. The Wolves. The Eagles've been away for almost two weeks. This is only their second home game of the season."

And just like that, my little idea got way huge, as if I'd put too much yeast into my dough and the carbon dioxide was releasing crazy fast. "Everybody, huh?"

On game night, Josh seemed almost nervous. He was so focused on beating the Wolves, he didn't ask us a single question. Not when we begged for a ride to his school, not when he picked up Paige and me alone in front of our apartment, not when Tre had to swing Josh's duffel bag into the front seat to make room for our cooler in the back.

We pass the kids at what must be the normal concessions table, two lanky teenagers. They've got some fresh coffee brewing behind them, and by the black and orange carafes I'm guessing one is regular and the other decaf. That's actually not a bad plan. But on their main table all they have are bottled waters and canned sodas arranged in color-coded rows. In front of those, a few cellophane-wrapped chocolate chip cookies looking as hard as rocks are piled beside a pyramid display of over-marshmallowed Rice Krispies Treats.

Amateurs.

"I still don't get why you need a lawyer for this," Tre complains.

I stop rolling the cooler. "What do you mean, lawyer?" My best friend falls silent. The distant squeak of sneakers in the gym tells me the Eagles are starting to warm up.

"I don't know," Tre finally says, shrugging. "You said you needed me to sue somebody."

"Not S-U-E sue, S-O-U-S sous!" I yell. He gives me a blank look. "I don't need a lawyer, I need a sous chef."

Tre smacks both frustrated fists against his hips. "You lost me, dude."

"You're Curtis's assistant, Tre," Paige says. "You do all the little jobs. Whatever Chef needs. At home, I usually do it."

"So you don't need me, then?" Tre's shoulders droop a little.

"We definitely need you. Paige has to take care of the cash box." My little sister dips her shoulders so her backpack will slide off them. She unzips it, revealing a vintage aluminum Wonder Woman lunch box. It rattles with loose change, most of which we found in the couch cushions. Unaccounted-for money isn't actually a thing in the Pith household.

"I can do that," Tre says, his eyes lighting up at the prospect of handling actual cash money.

"Oh, yeah?" I point out a nearby table. It's the perfect size, the one thing we couldn't bring that I was hoping to stumble upon. We each grab an end. "Tell me this, then." I grunt. This table's heavier than I thought. "If we're selling cupcakes for $2.25 each, three for $5.75, how much is it if someone asks for five?"

Tre's lips move silently as he tries to work it out, but Paige is way too fast. She shouts, "$10.25! $5.75 for the first three, then $4.50 for the other two—$2.25 apiece—for a total of $10.25. But!" She lifts a finger into the air. "You can get a sixth one for only $1.25 more . . ."

She's only in fourth grade, a year younger than Tre and

me (actually, eleven months, she always corrects me), but Paige Pith is hands down the whizziest math whiz in all of Sloan Elementary.

"Fine." Tre looks around. "What's my job, then?"

Paige grins. "You shout, 'Yes, Chef!' Like, a lot."

His jaw unhinges. "Seriously?"

We ease the table to the floor and extend the legs. "Any smooth-running kitchen needs a clear hierarchy," I preach, echoing one of my favorite TV chef's mantras. "Paige is on orders and money. I'm the chef. That means you get sugar and delivery. I'll show you what to do in a minute."

Once our trays are on the table and I've walked them through the plan a couple times, I carefully remove the foil to expose the first batch of cupcakes Paige and I prepped last night. The tops are all coned out, leaving an indent that's waiting for the star of the dish, not so much a frosting as a topping. I grab two chilled bowls from the cooler, one holding my signature pastry cream, the other a light meringue. A faint scent of vanilla wafts into the air when I peel back the plastic.

I fold the meringue into the cream—gently, don't want bubbles—and stand up a piping bag in a sundae glass. Before pouring my topping in, I need the coup de grace— that's, like, the ultimate last step that makes everything awesome—one of my go-to ingredients. I reach into the cooler a final time, my hand coming back with a single lemon and a microplane. Slowly, I grate just the right amount of lemon zest over the waiting bowl.

Paige starts organizing our coins into stacks of quarters and dimes and nickels. I have to say, my sister is an awesome sport, up for just about any of my wild ideas. She knows how much I love cooking, so at night when Mom heads out to her second-shift job at the post office, Paige helps me with whatever dish I try to master next. Because if I'm serious about becoming a great chef, I have to be sure to leave no culinary stone unturned.

And when I ask Paige for a few hours of her time at the high school, assure her that she'll be able to catch up on her precious homework in the morning before we chase the bus, she doesn't even stop stirring the risotto.

The only thing that seems to surprise my sister is my culinary talent. Whenever I drop some new technique out of the blue, Paige always says the same thing. "You know, I can't cook without burning everything, and Mom can't even boil water, so it's sort of amazing you can do all this."

Of course she doesn't understand, because Paige doesn't know my secret. She doesn't know who our father is. Mom never talks about *that* anymore. But years ago our mother let it slip to me. Ever since then, I've known who my dad is. Ever since then, I've understood *exactly* where my cooking talent comes from.

By the way, yes, of course I hate my last name. If you

don't know, the "pith" is that white section between the zest and citrus fruit—lemons, oranges, limes. It's the stuff you're supposed to stay away from if you don't want a bitter dish. Yep, the pith is the most useless "food" ever, the absolute worst name for a chef.

The crowd in the hallways has probably tripled when the first curious customer approaches our table. She's a teenager with long, straight red hair. She smirks as she waits for Paige to finish taping our sign to the front of the table.

CRÈME BRÛLÉE CUPCAKES
BY CHEF CURTIS PITH
$2.25 EACH OR 3 FOR $5.75

"Kinda steep, isn't it?" the girl asks. She points at the fuming teenagers at the regular table, no customers in sight. "Over there I can get three cookies for two bucks."

"Two bucks is a lot to spend for a chipped tooth," I say.

"Do your sales go to some kind of charity?"

"Definitely." I don't add any details. Our "charity" is the Pith family rent, a nip-and-tuck situation every month, but she doesn't need to know that.

The teenager narrows her eyes, and I can tell she's about to ask for more information, but Paige steps in and saves the day.

"I'm telling you, these cupcakes will make you rethink *all* your life choices." My sister's also my best sales rep.

"Really." The teenager peers more closely at our coned-out cupcakes. "To me they don't look finished. There's no frosting."

"Everything's made to order here." I nod at the other table. "As opposed to made last week. Or in some factory in China."

"First customer gets a free cupcake!" Tre shouts.

"Well, in that case, I guess I'll *have* to be your guinea pig," the girl replies.

I start to glower at Tre, but Paige catches my eye first. She shrugs. She and Tre are both right; we have to start somewhere. I grab my culinary torch and some gloves. After tossing one pair in Tre's direction, I wriggle my fingers into another.

I slide the small bowl of sugar toward Tre and ignite my torch, flipping the "continuous" button to on. With my other hand I take hold of the piping bag.

Tre's eyes get huge as he watches the torch's blue flame hiss. "Wicked," he whispers.

"Foil," I say, nodding at the table to refocus his attention.

"Yes, Chef!" Tre lays out a square of precut foil. Actual plates were going to cut way too deeply into our profit margin.

"Cupcake."

"Yes, Chef!" He removes the first cake from the nearest tray and plops it down in the center of the foil.

I pipe frosting—call it that if you have to, but this topping is *so* much more—into the indented cone, starting in the center and swirling it in the circular pattern I'd worked out would look best when I practiced with Paige last night.

"Sugar."

Tre dips his glove into the sugar bowl and throws clumps of crystals on top of my cream.

"Gently," I scold. "Evenly."

"Dude," Tre says. I send him my most chef-like frown, and it must work, because he fidgets and fixes his reply. "Yes, Chef." My new sous chef obediently pinches and sprinkles more sugar, slower this time.

I hit it with the torch, caramelizing the sugar like you'd do on a real crème brûlée, which I totally would've done if I wasn't worried about them holding up under the stress of travel and refrigeration. Cupcakes were definitely the safer choice.

The sugar works its way to the right color, a perfect caramel brown—not burnt, never burnt. I pull the torch back and look up at the teenager. "Please enjoy."

She inspects my creation—because that's what this cupcake is, a creation, the purest of culinary arts—from every angle before taking a huge bite, at least a third of the cupcake gone. Her hand flies up to her lips.

"OH-EM-GEE," she says. Her eyes grow wider with each chew. "This is . . . I want to marry this."

Her attention shifts to two more girls her age. They're pushing through the crowd toward us. Our first customer waves at them. "Madison! Soph! Get over here! And bring all your money!"

By halftime, our line has grown so long it stretches all the way to the school's front door. The people at the end are actually blocking the bathrooms now, leaving the diehards who waited until intermission fidgeting out in the hallway. The two long lines commingle, and before long some pushing and shoving starts.

I'm too busy to worry about it. I've had to stop to mix additional bowls of topping twice already, and we're on our last tray of cupcakes. Paige's lunch box has overflowed with bills at least three times, and my normally precise sister has had to resort to urgently stuffing the extra money into the front pocket of her backpack.

"What's going on out here? What's this line for?" I hear

someone who sounds extra angry shout, but I can't afford to look up. I've got caramelizing to finish. Not burnt, never burnt. When I'm done, though, when Tre delivers my most recent creation to our latest buyer, I sense a shadow looming over me. I peek up at the first person in a suit and tie I've seen all night. I feel all the blood drain from my face.

Mr. Ramirez. The high school principal.

"Is that a blowtorch?" he demands. "On school grounds?" He turns around, checking who's in line behind him, using his finger to point certain students out. "I see one, two . . . seven honor students in this line. Not one of you is thinking about fire safety?"

Several of the teenagers avert their eyes, examining the handmade "Go Eagles!" signs on the walls. What a waste of good butcher paper. "How old are you kids?" the principal demands of the three of us. "Where are your parents?"

A massive security guard appears behind him, folding his arms over his chest. His attempt at a disapproving stance isn't working, though, not with all that frosting on his mustache. See, Security Dude has budged his way to the front of our line twice in the past hour. He's $4.50 lighter and two crème brûlée cupcakes heavier since we opened up shop.

Tre thrusts a napkin toward the officer, then gestures at his own upper lip. "You've got a little—" he says.

The security guard snatches the napkin and wipes his face. He cuts his eyes toward the principal.

"Oh, that's just terrific. My 'security,'" Principal Ramirez says, making air quotes.

A new commotion erupts at the far end of the line, just out of view. Teenagers frown and grumble as someone else pushes their way through. "Coming through, coming through. You kids make a path, now. Coming through!"

I recognize the stern voice right away, then try to convince myself it can't be him. Not here.

The principal must be familiar with the demanding tone, too, because he quickly spins to us and starts waving his hands. "Put all this stuff away," he urges in a harsh whisper, gesturing frantically.

But there's nowhere to hide our mess, our ingredients and equipment. I stand still instead, watching the crowd parting, realizing how dumb I've been. Of course Mr. Arthur Pettynose, our landlord, the man who owns half of North Sloan, would be at the biggest game our school's seen in years. Where the rest of the town goes, Pettynose can't be far behind, shaking hands and kissing babies. I've heard rumors he's planning a run for mayor next election.

Pettynose uses his stocky girth to jostle the taller teenagers to the side as he surges ahead. He stops at our table. Looks down from behind that bulbous schnoz.

"Mr. Pettynose!" Principal Ramirez says in a tone that's

somehow already apologizing. "I assure you I had no idea this was—"

Pettynose cuts Ramirez off. "Curtis Pith. And with an open flame, no less. Fantastic. Just wonderful. And here your mother *promised* me your cooking days were behind you."

I can't speak. In fact, all three of us freeze for a few seconds. Tre's the first one to move. He reaches out and slides the "continuous" switch on my torch. The hissing flame cuts off abruptly, and the hallway turns even more awkwardly quiet.

Then my best friend whispers in my ear, as if somehow everyone else isn't going to hear his question amid the complete silence. "Uh, Curtis, you *sure* you don't need that lawyer?"

Here's everything you need to know about our landlord: Arthur Pettynose is *super* rich. So rich, in fact, our whole apartment could probably fit into his massive kitchen alone. I know, because I've seen it. He invited us into his mansion, across the street from our fading apartment building, the day Mom signed the lease a couple years ago. It had everything—convection oven, butler's pantry, stocked wine refrigerator, sparkling red KitchenAid. I remember having this desperate desire to cook just one meal in that kitchen.

Mr. Pettynose was a lot friendlier back then, before the . . . well, let's call it an accident. Seriously it was just a little kitchen fire. I mean, the firemen had the flames out in the blink of an eye. Ever since then, though, our landlord's gotten meaner by the day, constantly on Mom's case about my being in the kitchen. "He's too young, he'll burn my building down . . . blah, blah, BLAH."

As if Mom has any chance of slowing me down. Cooking—becoming a chef—is my dream. It gives me life, pumps blood through my veins. Not even principals or important townspeople can stop my march toward culinary relevance, though it seems they do have the power to put an end to unauthorized bake sales.

Most of the time I use my journal for recipes, but I keep other kinds of lists in there, too. In the back pages, like this one, summarizing the fallout of the epic fail Paige and I now refer to as Cupcakegate:

The Money. After all that work, we nearly lost every penny. Principal Ramirez tried to claim "no permit, no profits" and ordered Paige to start handing over all those crumpled bills. But then a few of those honor students staged a sit-in, chanting *We! Relate! To a great cupcake!* over and over. Tre's brother Josh, still in his sweaty uniform, came out and joined in. That held up the *whole* game. The Eagles' coach stomped into the hall after him and said if Josh didn't get back to the court, he'd have to forfeit, which convinced the principal and even Pettynose to relent. At home, our cash went straight into Mom's purse. And from there to the rent, which meant Pettynose would end up stuffing *our* money into *his* grimy pockets anyway. Life's pretty unfair when you're in fifth grade and completely powerless.

The Game. So North Sloan's previously unstoppable basketball team didn't forfeit, but they still ended up losing. Maybe because Josh only scored six points after halftime, which was a total bummer.

Mom's schedule. This happened almost every time I got in trouble, and it was always the worst part. Mom had no room in her daily agenda for parent-teacher meetings, but this "incident" was serious enough—and involved *both* her children—that the school wanted her to come in for an after-hours conference. Suspension was on the table.

"I don't have time for this." Mom whisks by, snatching Paige's coat off the carpet. She was supposed to leave ten minutes ago. "I do not have time for this," she repeats, hanging the coat near the door now. You can make it across our living room to the apartment's "foyer"—a two-by-two square of linoleum inside our front door, super fancy—in just a few big steps.

Paige is in front of the television, mesmerized by *Teen Titans Go!* There's about an hour every day, right after school, when she goes nearly comatose in front of cartoons. It's fine, though, part of our deal, especially on Wednesday nights. My sister takes control of the TV right after school so I can have it later. Eight p.m., to be precise. Because on Wednesdays at eight, *Super Chef* is on.

And DVR or not, commercials or not, I watch *Super Chef* live.

Paige once said I'd probably have a seizure if I missed even one second of my favorite show, but that's bonkers. I'd just faint a little or whatever.

"Your zipper again," I say, pointing at Mom's jacket. Its zipper is undone at the bottom, beginning to separate upward. Does it every time she wears it, but new jackets just aren't in the budget right now. She works in North Sloan's big post office plant, a behind-the-scenes mail-sorting job. At least she doesn't have to wear those awful powder-blue post office uniforms, the ones with the shorts and the dorky socks.

Mom frowns and tugs at the zipper. "Thanks, Curtis."

"Mom, I'm really sorry," I say. "I was only trying to—"

She cuts me off, meeting my eyes. "I know. Just . . . no more big ideas, though, understand?"

I nod. My gut's a giant flapjack flipped over too quickly, the same way Mom's schedule has been turned upside down by my most recent big idea.

Last night, when she thought I was sleeping, Mom got

on the phone with one of her close friends from work. She sounded worried. Out came words I've heard before, when she had other jobs. When she'd *lost* other jobs. *Layoff. Cutback. Downsize.* "I have to go to the school tomorrow," Mom whispered. "And it's definitely gonna make me late. Cover for me, okay?"

She hung up, and I snuck back into bed, pretending I'd been asleep the whole time.

"You kids take care of each other," she says now as she opens the door in a rush. "Curtis, make your sister some dinner, but—"

"Be careful," Paige and I finish for her in a chorus. Yeah, we know the drill.

'm staring hard into the cupboard. All I see are three tins of tuna. No linguine, only spaghetti. But the fridge does have a half a bottle of clam juice, and I think I can make out one little anchovy filet suspended in congealed oil.

"Your linguine and clam sauce is going to be more like spaghetti in tuna sauce, with clam juice," I tell Paige. "It'll be good, promise."

My sister, out of her cartoon trance, sits at the kitchen table doing homework. She shrugs and, without looking up, says, "I trust your creativity, Chef."

I pour what's left of the clam juice into my measuring cup, shaking out every last drop. Barely half a cup. I need a full cup normally. This is gonna be interesting.

• • •

"Last time on *Super Chef*," the disembodied, deep-voiced TV announcer begins. On the screen, this season's contestants rush around the kitchen, highlights from last week's episode. "The chefs were lost at sea as they teamed up in an all-seafood battle."

The theme music's starting, a low thrum that picks up pace as old black-and-white pictures of the Super Chef— first as a boy, then a teen in his earliest kitchens, always surrounded by food, clearly intrigued by every ingredient— descend toward a table, sliding over one another as they land.

The announcer pipes up again, repeating the same intro he gives us every week. "Growing up, his family moved all around the world. Japan, Paris, Dubai, London, New York. He's studied under masters, opened countless restaurants, inspired millions."

More images flash. Close-ups. The bottom of a pant leg, a spotless dress shoe. Hands straightening the cuffs of a crisp white shirt sneaking out the arms of an immaculate suit jacket. Next a wide shot: a figure standing alone in a glass elevator speeding up the side of a building that shines bright against the dark city night.

The screen changes again, the camera positioned at one end of a long hallway. The elevator doors open and the distant but familiar image of the Super Chef in his blue suit and tie appears. He strides down the hallway, also gleaming glass, lined with glinting knives and white chef's jackets. Directly toward the camera, the focus on his features sharpening with each step.

"Now, *he* is the master."

My pulse quickens. The Super Chef grows closer. His haphazard sandy-blond hair, spiked just a little up front, comes into view. Those hazel eyes, that signature smile. He unbuttons his suit jacket and hangs it on a passing hook without breaking stride.

"He is Lucas Taylor."

Now the star of the best show on the planet walks directly into the camera. Right before his chest is about to hit it, his hands shoot up. They rip open his white shirt, a button skipping away, tie flying off to one side. Underneath, his signature black-and-white chef's coat is revealed, the one with the diamond-shaped logo that hasn't changed since season one.

"He is . . . THE SUPER CHEF."

And he is . . . Curtis Pith's father.

Okay, that last one comes out in my head only, and it stays there, because I don't dare utter my big secret out loud in front of my little sister. If Mom wanted Paige to know who her dad is, she would've told her by now.

Like she told me.

It happened back in second grade, and it's still the only time Mom's ever mentioned it. Nothing before, and not a hint at this particular truth since, either. Sometimes I'm not even sure she remembers telling me at all.

I'd come home crying because Mrs. Moonworthy asked the class what we wanted to be when we grew up. Career day. I folded my arms across my chest, not completely sure why I was so opposed to participating, only knowing that I was. I was positive most of the class would join me in my silent protest, but instead kid after kid shouted out their answers like they'd actually been *hoping* someone would come along to ask them this very question.

"Police offer!" Kenny Simpson. "Computer Programmer!" Nate Evans. "Engineer!" Violet Johnson. "Dental hygienist!" Amy Stills.

Me: nothing. Complete freeze-up.

I knew most of them were just robotically saying whatever their parents did. Except Amy. Apparently she *really* liked going to the dentist. But for me, well . . . Mom was out of work at the time. Again. Besides, she'd had so many jobs before I didn't know which one to pick—waitress or janitor or bartender or—

What about my father, you ask? Good question, what about him? Up until then I'd kind of assumed he didn't exist.

That year was the same year the new *Super Chef* show debuted. Season one. Mom turned on the first episode but quickly lost interest, even started criticizing it. I couldn't understand why; everything about it was awesome. Contestants running around like crazy, trying things they weren't sure would work, forced to use foods they'd never even tasted, all under the watchful eyes of the Super Chef, who seemed to have done and tasted everything, traveled everywhere.

Sure, I was only seven, but I glued my eyes to that program every week. In fact, *Super Chef* was on again in the background when, through heavy sobs, I pleaded with my mother to tell me who my father was, what kind of work he did.

Mom bit her lip. I knew she was about to change the subject again, like she always did. Only this time, I wasn't going to let her. "Please tell me," I begged. "Please."

She averted her eyes. But she wasn't just looking away. Her focus moved to the television. To Lucas Taylor. A wistful smile crossed her expression, some memory passing in front of her like a fast-moving cloud. "Your father's a great cook. Super talented." Her eyes glistened, and she wiped one tear away.

I looked from Mom to the TV, then back again to her. A bunch of times, so my vision almost blurred. *Super* talented. Meaning . . . *Super* Chef? All at once, a bunch of stuff started to make sense.

How much I loved the show, how I hung on even the smallest movement of the Super Chef's hands. The excitement I felt watching him cook, the connection we seemed to have with each other, like I'd known him my whole life.

Mom stood suddenly, heading for the kitchen. Shoulders slumped, trying to hold it together in front of me. But I had heard enough, and, finally, I could see my own future. Finally, I knew what I would tell Mrs. Moonworthy.

Chef. I'm going to be a *chef* when I grow up.

As each episode aired, I started recognizing new resemblances between me and Lucas Taylor. Identical sandy-blond hair, even down to the little spike up front. Same hazel eyes. Sometimes I even think we stand alike.

Other stuff became clearer, too. Like why Mom didn't like his show, always tried to turn the volume down. It must've been because of whatever happened between them. But me? I only wanted to watch *Super Chef* more. Not just watch, either. I wanted to cook all the time. And suddenly I believed I could.

Mom had cried after she told me the truth four years ago. I never want to upset her like that again, so I don't talk about the Super Chef—not the *he's my father* part, anyway—and neither does she. It's our silent pact.

I've never told anyone else my secret truth, either. It just doesn't feel right, and it might get back to Paige if I spilled the frijoles to some friend like Tre. That's why my sister doesn't understand where my cooking talent comes from.

My father is the most famous chef in the world. Of course I can make a crème brûlée cupcake. Of course I can create a passable clam sauce even though I'm missing a ton of ingredients. Of course I'm going to be a chef when I grow up.

Without a doubt, I know that Lucas Taylor is amazing. I'm reminded of that fact every Wednesday at eight. But at the same time, I don't remember him. Like, not *at all*. I mean, he must've stuck around for *some* part of those eleven months between Mom having me and Paige being born, right?

What was baby Curtis thinking? How could he—I— not pay more attention? Lucas Taylor was *right there*.

Mom hasn't told me what happened between her and Chef Taylor, what caused their breakup, and now we have our silent pact, so I have no idea why they're not together, why we're not all together. Sometimes, when he's teaching me how to properly sauté a pork chop or poach an egg to perfection, I find myself trying to guess why. But that's pointless. And distracting. When I miss some important step and have to rewind, I remember what I'm supposed to do—skim the top. Discard the unnecessary scum.

Because it's kind of like making a perfect broth, isn't it? As it boils, the impurities become foam on the surface, and you have to be quick about skimming them off. If you don't get rid of that froth fast enough, it'll pollute your soup forever. So that's how I treat those thoughts, all that guessing and wondering about what happened. They're just unnecessary scum.

Let's face it, we've never received a single card from Lucas Taylor, not one letter or phone call. No mention on his big TV show of the two kids he has in snowy North Sloan. And Mom struggles to make rent every month while he sits on top of the biggest pile of money in the whole cooking universe. The Super Chef probably takes baths in hundred-dollar bills.

I thought there were laws and stuff about that, that dads had to give money to moms to help them take care of their kids, but for some reason Mom doesn't seem interested in chasing him down. Whatever happened must've been *really* bad.

In the end, there's no reason to wish the Super Chef will one day send us some magical financial parachute. If it hasn't happened by now, it never will. We're on our own. So I try really hard not to worry about who he is or what he has. Instead I focus on learning every single thing I can from watching him. If these distant TV lessons are all I'm ever going to get from my father, I might as well make the most of them.

On the screen, the latest episode continues. This season's *Super Chef* contestants line up at their stations with nervous smiles. They're waiting for the master to appear. The camera shifts to the front of the room, and the two huge doors featuring that same diamond-shaped logo separate to reveal three shadows. Out they march—the Super Chef and his two sous chefs.

To Taylor's right, Chef Claire Wormwood. Born in the United States, but she studied in Italy forever. She's been with the Super Chef almost her entire career, and she seems to be a calming influence in his kitchens. Whenever his temper flames up like an out-of-control flambé, Chef Claire is there with a lid to cover the fire.

To his left, jovial Chef Gabriel Graca from Portugal, lately just the comic relief of the show. I'm not sure I've seen him cook anything real since season two.

The intro music finally dies down, and the Super Chef steps forward. Something's weird, though, and it takes me a minute to figure out what. It's his chef's coat. Normally perfect, he's somehow messed up the buttons, making it look off-kilter.

Chef Taylor comes to a stop and surveys the contestants. I can't take my eyes off his messed-up jacket. "Welcome to the final five. We're going to get straight to the point. After all, a chef must always come to the kitchen prepared. Are you ready for your next challenge?"

The contestants shout in unison, "Yes, Chef!"

"Who can tell me what remains the most popular protein in America?"

"Chicken!" I yell along with the contestants.

The Super Chef points at the nervous cooks with one finger. "That's right, chicken. A whole chicken can yield more portions than the average cook at home realizes, making it a very cost-effective option for families. It's critical to know how to get the most out of it."

My heart starts to pound. No matter how many times I've seen Lucas Taylor break down a chicken, I always learn something new. And he always works with such speed and precision, a true master.

He steps forward and lifts the silver lid waiting at the display table. There it is, a gorgeous whole chicken resting on a cutting board, skin dimpled and fresh-looking, a knife and knife sharpener with it, all just waiting for his expert hand to separate the wings, the legs—

But Chef Taylor seems perplexed by the bird. He steps to one side. "Chef Claire, would you be so kind?"

Claire Wormwood's mouth drops open, but her jaw couldn't possibly be down as far as mine is. Even Paige notices the change. "Doesn't he usually cut the chicken?" she asks me.

"He always breaks it down," I correct her. "Yeah," I say even more slowly.

First his off-buttoned chef's coat, now letting his sous chef take over in this type of demo for the first time ever? The Super Chef has never acted like this before.

Something's definitely wrong.

Jenny from Seattle ends up getting eliminated at the end of this season's chicken episode. She actually forgets to separate the oysters from the thighs. I mean, seriously. Total brain fart.

I get so worked up I shoot off the couch, pointing and screaming, "The oysters! They're the best part!" This forces Paige to grab her furry blue earmuffs and slap them over her ears. She keeps them on the end table next to the couch for when I get too excited during *Super Chef*. So, basically every Wednesday at some point.

Poor Jenny's sobbing when Chef Taylor gives her the bad news. A lot of people cry when they get kicked off the show, which I always find unprofessional. Everybody knows you gotta have a strong backbone to make it as a chef. There's no crying in kitchens, unless maybe you're chopping onions. Even then, blink a few times if you have to. Sheesh.

The last part of the best show on the planet is always a preview of next week's episode, but I'm not too surprised when, instead of going to a commercial, the screen falls silent for a few seconds. Then a big, white "IN ONE WEEK" appears in the direct center of the black background, and the announcer says something brand new.

"Be sure to return next week for the most shocking reveal ever made on *Super Chef*. Chef Taylor plans to change the landscape of the cooking world *forever*."

After a few seconds, the dancing show that everyone but me seems to watch, *Feats of Feet*, replaces the white letters on the screen. I turn the TV off and fall back into my seat.

"What do you think it could be?" Paige asks. "His big announcement?"

"Has to be something to do with"—I wave my hand at the television screen—"all that."

All that is the weird way the Super Chef acted the entire episode. When Lucas Taylor headed back to the stage to join the whispered judging, he tripped up the stairs. At one point he even looked like he was limping. Another time, when he raised half a ravioli on his fork before tasting it, his hand kind of shook. Seriously, his left thumb was actually twitching.

"Is he nervous?" Paige asked when she noticed.

The Super Chef never, ever got nervous. He was always way too cool and calm for that. I inhaled. "I'm not sure."

The next day when we get home from school, we find Mom wearing sweatpants and her pajama top, the red-and-green one with the giant Christmas tree on the front. She's never gone to work looking like that before. Then she clicks a button on the controller and switches over to the Firestick, actually highlighting the row of new releases and not the free ones we've seen a thousand times already.

"Special surprise! Movie night!" She points at the kitchen. "Curtis, how about you make that Mexican popcorn stuff you guys like so much? I bought all the right ingredients."

Paige squeals. She loves my Mexican spiced popcorn. And the truth is, I haven't made it in a while. My mind starts listing the ingredients, the recipe auto-recalling into my head.

2 tablespoons unsalted butter
2 teaspoons chili powder
1 teaspoon ground cumin
2 cups . . .

But something's not right. No way can Mom afford to

stay home from work for a movie night. "What about the post office?"

"Jerry gave me the night off," she says. She kneels and puts her arm around Paige's shoulders. "*You*, sweetie, get to pick the movie."

I peer toward the kitchen. Usually Mom complains that her boss, Jerry, won't even let her take a full coffee break. Now he's giving her a whole night off? I want to try to figure it all out, but I spy a grocery bag on the counter and kernels pop around my head. "So you got the cayenne?"

"Think so."

"And the right kind of chocolate?"

"Curtis, go check. I'm sure everything's there."

"Cuuurtis," Paige whines. "Make me the spicy pop-cooorn!"

I head for the kitchen, shake the bag out onto the counter. There's cayenne, score one for Mom, but cardamom instead of cinnamon and the wrong kind of chocolate: just basic 40 percent dark, not the more expensive 75 percent Mexican brand I usually use for this recipe.

On the plus side, there is a bit of cinnamon left over in the cupboard, and if I find some chili flakes or nutmeg, I might be able to make this inferior chocolate sing. I roll up my sleeves and start blending spices.

Twenty minutes later, I'm balancing three bowls of warm, spicy chocolate popcorn as I carefully pace into the living room. Paige picked the latest Pixar, of course. It's paused on the title screen.

"See? You don't think I know your recipes, but I do," Mom says. "Had everything you needed, didn't you?"

I can't tell her she totally botched the ingredient list— no chili powder in sight—so instead I just nod and smile as I hand one bowl over to her, then another to Paige.

"Is it good?" I ask, watching them dig in.

Paige stuffs a handful of popcorn into her mouth, her cheeks puffing out like a chipmunk. "Terrible," she mumbles with a smile.

"Human bites," Mom scolds.

The movie starts and we fall into it, lost in the story, gathered up on the couch side by side under a heavy blanket. It's so warm and perfect, I start to nod off. But just as everything begins to go dark, the doorbell rings.

Mom clicks pause. She glances over her shoulder, then, smiling a secret at us, fixes a "shush" finger at the center of her lips. There's a shuffling in the hall, a loud knock. We slink under the blanket, huddling closer, trying not to giggle.

"Ms. Pith?" I'd recognize Pettynose's voice anywhere. But what's he doing here, snooping around? "I see your car's outside." Long pause. "On a work night. Are you home?"

I always *thought* he spied on us, the turd! He's probably trying to catch me cooking again. So what if Mom's car is home? That's none of his business.

Our landlord's shadow continues to darken the thin sliver of light coming from under the door for another minute or so, then we hear him stomp off.

"Whew," Mom says, fake-swiping her brow like she was sweating bullets. She pats both our knees. "Did not want to have to talk to that man right now. Tonight's for just the three of us."

She reaches for the remote, but I grab it first and hold it away from her, like I'm playing keep-away with Tre in recess. "What's going on, Mom?"

Mom's popcorn crunching slows down, then stops completely. "Curtis, I don't—"

"Why are you *really* home?"

"I told you, I have the night off. Can't I spend one evening at home with my kids, watching movies?" She hugs Paige closer. "Am I not allowed to do that?"

"Why are you hiding from Pettynose, then?"

"*Mr.* Pettynose," Paige corrects me before Mom has the chance. "I want the movie."

Mom's eyes narrow at me. "Let your sister finish her movie."

I hand back the remote, fold my arms across my chest, and scooch closer to the end of the couch, so there's a big gap between us. The blanket's only covering one of my legs now. It gets cold really quickly.

• • •

Mom wakes me up when she lifts Paige over one shoulder. My sister hardly moves. She gets that way around bedtime. Out cold, all floppy.

"Brush your teeth," Mom whispers when she sees me awake. "Then straight to bed. We'll finish the movie tomorrow." She carries Paige toward the back of the apartment. We only have one bedroom, which Paige and I share. Mom's bed is the couch. She lays a sheet over it, wraps a blanket around herself, and tosses and turns there.

When Mom comes back into the living room, though, I still haven't moved off her couch-bed. "Hey, I thought I told you—"

"Jerry doesn't give you nights off."

Mom's hands drop from her hips to her sides. When she exhales, it's like all the breath she has in her leaves her body at once. She deflates completely.

She sits on the couch next to me. "Okay, Mr. Smarty Pants. I was going to tell you in the morning. The post office let me go today."

"You mean . . . fired?"

Mom nods. Her lips are flat and her cheeks a little puffy and pinkish.

I feel myself breathing heavier. "You were late yesterday. Because of that stupid meeting at school. Because of me—"

"No, honey. No. That's not why. They were going to cut back anyway. There've been rumors about it for months. And I was the newest one there. That's how it works." Mom reaches back and twists her hair into a ponytail. She sighs. "It's so hard not to be the newest one, though, when you're constantly starting over."

"Is that what you're going to do? Start over?"

"Of course. I'll find something." She wears a smile, but it isn't her real one.

My head suddenly feels heavy; it droops down, pretty much on its own. Mom puts a finger under my chin to lift my face up again. "Hey, listen. I just wanted one good night with my favorite people before starting to interview again. Sorry to keep secrets. I'll tell Paige in the morning. Promise. In the meantime, I need your help."

I gaze up at her.

"We're going to have to make some cutbacks, and I need you to be brave about it."

"Okay," I say slowly. I'm not sure how much more cut back we can get.

She glances at the kitchen. "We're gonna have to call a timeout on the fancy ingredients."

"But—"

"Curtis, you know I love to see you cook." She snorts. "The only thing I probably love more is eating what you make." She grins and pats her stomach.

I lock my lips together, refusing to laugh at her joke.

Mom's smile fades until her expression matches mine. "But right now basic is better. We have to find ways to stretch our funds for a little while."

"But how am I going to become a chef if I don't practice?" I ask, panic bubbling up at the base of my throat.

"Honey. You can still practice."

My mouth drops open by itself. I puff out air loudly. She needs to see how shocked I am, how ridiculous what she just said is. "With what? Ramen noodles and string cheese?"

Mom frowns at me. "It's not a forever thing, Curtis. You know, lots of people aren't so lucky to be able to afford fancy ingredients sometimes, never mind all the time."

I nod like I understand. And I do, partly. I get how money works. And I'm pretty intimate with the difference in price between fresh Chilean sea bass and frozen tilapia filets. Still, if I don't have the right ingredients, I can't try the right recipes. My whole career's being blasted into oblivion, a giant mushroom cloud. Not a regular mushroom, either. More like . . . I don't know, a lion's mane or a *maitake* or something.

"You can do anything you put your mind to," Mom says, her smile starting to return. "You might just have to be a little more creative." She tickles my sides, and I squirm away. "Anything. Including . . . going to bed." She pushes me up to my feet. "Come on. Up, up, up."

I let her pull me toward my toothbrush, even though what I really want to do is keep arguing. Sprint into the kitchen, make some dough or start a stock or julienne some carrots. But I won't. I can't. I owe Mom and Paige that much. After all, I know Mom isn't telling me the whole truth. It *was* my fault she lost her job, it had to be.

And now here we are: no money, no job. Our lives, our *home* even, hanging by the thinnest of threads.

The Super Chef stands on the stage of his kitchen arena, a bright spotlight trained on him. His sous chefs have departed. Chef Taylor is alone, the complete focus of the camera's attention.

"It's time for a change," he begins in a serious voice.

"Curtis, I can't see," Paige complains behind me. I must be an inch away from the television.

A week has passed since Mom got fired. Sorry, "laid off." She's been home every night. Until now, anyway. Her other interviews have all been during the day, but tonight she had a second meeting at a restaurant in town. Paige and I are on our own for the first time since last week's *Super Chef* episode.

"Okay," I say. I step to one side, but with each word the Super Chef utters, I feel myself drifting back to the front of the TV. Tonight's episode ended a few minutes ago, when Jeff from Chicago bit the dust, leaving only the final three chefs. Then there were a bunch of commercials before the studio finally flashed back into focus and only Lucas Taylor stood before us.

This is it, his big reveal, the one they warned us last week will change the cooking world forever.

Chef Taylor gulps. "This season is nearly over. First, I want to congratulate all of our contestants. They've fought hard and cooked their hearts out. And I must say, I'm always so proud of our *Super Chef* competitors. These incredible cooks who accept the enormous challenge of competing on our show, in front of millions, they put their courage on display, front and center. But not only that. With each innovative dish and new approach they bring to our arena, they also show the world the very essence of food. They shine a stark, unflinching spotlight on the state of cooking today." He inhales. "I think that's been the greatest gift to emerge from this show, one I didn't expect when I started out."

The Super Chef seems to take a break. His eyes lose a little focus, his breath comes in measured beats. It's like he's summoning his own bravery. Finally he continues. "As you know, normally after each season of *Super Chef* ends, we take a break. We need the time off to return our focus to our restaurants, the rest of our businesses. But this year is different."

I glance over my shoulder at Paige. The earmuffs are off, and her eyes are wide. She's just as interested in what the Super Chef is about to say as I am.

"It's been a few years, hasn't it?" The Super Chef's smile at the camera seems sad. "I can't tell you how much I've appreciated everyone's support all this time. I've had a great run."

"He's talking like he's eighty and ready to retire," Paige says. "How old is he?"

"Forty-seven," I say without taking my eyes off the screen.

"Most of you know I'm not married. No children." That's the first time I've heard him say that out loud. It makes me feel so invisible my stomach clenches. At the same time, I'm glad Paige doesn't know the things I do. I'd hate for her to feel what I'm feeling right now.

"I've been thinking a lot about what we have here." Taylor peers around his arena, the same one he's used to film his show since season one. "About what the legacy of the Super Chef—all this work, for all these years—should be. And you know . . . it occurred to me that the Super Chef isn't just a single person. No, the Super Chef has become . . . well, more of an *idea*, one that should be used not just to demonstrate the present of cooking, but its future as well. If this show has to come to an end—"

The live crowd, previously silent, listening carefully, trying to understand where Taylor was headed with this speech, collectively gasps.

The Super Chef tilts his head, acknowledging their surprise but clearly unwilling to let it deter him. "As all good things do . . . I want our last winner to say more about the bright future of the culinary world than any winner from our previous seasons has. So we're not taking our customary break. We're staying right here for—"

Chef Taylor glances to one side, where a big TV screen waits. The *Super Chef* diamond logo appears in its center, quickly replaced by only the words:

THE SUPER CHEF

Then a big stamp graphic flies in, separating the first two words with a loud, clangy *ka-chunk*.

THE
LAST!
SUPER CHEF

The camera returns to Chef Taylor. The pace of his speech picks up with each word. "After this season's *Super Chef* champ is crowned next week, a new show will begin. *The Last Super Chef* will feature a new kind of competitor, never before seen in this arena. Kids. Each of the five contestants on our last season will be a child between the ages of ten and twelve, young enough, open-minded enough, with the right amount of eagerness, to be the ideal candidates to help us move on from *Super Chef* by showing the world's kitchens a clear path to cooking's future. The stark promise the culinary world holds."

Paige kicks me in the back of the leg. My knee buckles. But I don't turn around. I can't. She's excited. Of course she is. She doesn't know he's our father. She's not blown away by the idea of Lucas Taylor holding this contest in the first place, inviting a bunch of stranger kids to compete while continuing to pretend we don't exist.

And why? Why does there need to be a final season all of a sudden? Who's going to show me recipes like the ones I've learned from Chef Taylor and his team? Sure, there are other cooking shows, but none hold a candle to this one. There is no chef like the Super Chef.

Taylor continues. "The contest will also have a grand prize, to help the winner reach their dreams, strive for a future of their own. The winner of *The Last Super Chef* will start with $250,000 in his or her pocket, to do with as they see fit: start a restaurant, begin a fund for their own culinary education, maybe travel the globe. Perhaps the winner of the prize money will want to follow in my footsteps, start off by tasting the wonders of the world's cuisine. It will be entirely up to them."

The crowd murmurs when they hear the amount, more than double the winnings of any of the previous adult *Super Chef* competitions. I suck a breath in. It's also more money than Mom makes in . . . I don't know how long. Tons of time. It might be enough to buy an actual house for her and Paige. No more apartments. No more snooping landlords.

This is my chance to pay my mom back for all her sacrifices and hard work. To show both her and Paige there was a reason, some kind of outcome, for all my dedication to cooking these past few years. All the times they had to spend a whole Saturday on a long journey to some special out-of-the-way grocery or wait in a huge line for just the right cut of meat.

Because if there has to be a Last Super Chef—and I can't see any way to stop it, not from North Sloan—maybe all the competitors don't have to be stranger kids. No one else can possibly deserve to win more than Chef Taylor's own son, right? Well, of course it's right. I deserve that prize. Whether she knows it or not, Paige deserves it. Mom definitely deserves it.

"The Last Super Chef will be a kid who doesn't just love cooking. They'll need to live and breathe food." Chef Taylor inhales again. "Here's how it'll work. We'll be taking video submissions. The video you send in must demonstrate your unique cooking talents and show us why you deserve to be one of our contestants. You can find the full rules at thelastsuperchef.com. Once we have all the videos, we'll pick five kids to compete in a special shortened season of *Super Chef*. Only five!" he says, holding up his hand, with his fingers and that twitching thumb spread out. "The competition will last for a few weeks after that, and on Thanksgiving Day, we'll announce the champion. After our turkey and stuffing and pie, we'll get to find out who the Last Super Chef will be!"

Taylor waits for the hesitant applause from the live crowd to die down. "We're looking for kids passionate about cooking, kids who already have the talent to thrive and the drive to survive. Good cooks who want to be great chefs. Our online entry form will go live immediately after the show, and remain open to entries through midnight Saturday."

"This Saturday?" I yell at the TV. That's three days from now.

"Do you have what it takes to be the Last Super Chef?" Chef Taylor asks, as if he's heard my doubt and is challenging it. "Let's find out!"

Chef Taylor's image fades, and the black screen with white lettering returns, this time providing the URL to the rules and some fine print too small to read. As my straining eyes try anyway, I start to get one of those big ideas I'm not supposed to have anymore.

The moment *Feats of Feet* comes on, I power the TV down and turn all the way around to look at Paige. She's staring up at me like she's waiting for me to tell her what happens next.

Peering into her eyes, I realize everything I've ever wanted to be able to do for her, for Mom, is suddenly right in front of me. Forget working so hard to win first place in the church bake sale, never mind trying to help with the rent only a few dollars at a time. My days of sneaking into high school basketball games can be over—

"Paige," I say, my thoughts jumping around so fast I'm interrupting them myself. "How many cupcakes—"

"Is $250,000?" she asks. "At $2.25 apiece?"

I nod, and she sticks her tongue out of the side of her mouth. Her eyes roll up, as if they're trying to sneak their way into her brain to help it work the problem out on her mental whiteboard. Have I actually stumped her?

"I don't know, Curtis," she finally says. "Over a hundred thousand, for sure."

I nod, trying to stay outwardly serious and focused,

when inside I'm so excited and nervous and confused I can't speak for a second.

But finally I find my voice. "We need to make that video."

Paige nods back at me. "I know."

"That's the sixth place you've looked," Tre hisses at me as I set the potted plant outside Pettynose's back door down carefully. Nothing underneath but a few scrambling ants.

"So we try number seven." My words ride a cloud of smoke back to him. It's freezing out here, and that makes me want to get this done even faster. I spot a rock that might be fake near the gutter spout and drop to my knees to stretch around a bush for it.

According to the website of North Sloan's most popular home security company (it was easy to find, every expensive house in town has the same sign out front), the most common places to hide a spare key are:

Under the welcome mat.

Beneath a flowerpot.

Inside a false rock.

I memorized them before we snuck over here, storing the list in my brain right between "The Five Essential Ingredients for Baking" and "The Four Best Vinegars for Pickling."

"Come on, Curtis," Tre says. "What are the chances you're going to find a hidden key anywhere back here?"

"If he finds it on his seventh try?" Paige asks. "That'd be one-seventh, which is .14285 or 14.3 percent."

A commotion breaks out behind me just as my fingers have almost wriggled the rock free. I look over my shoulder in time to see Tre pawing at Paige's backpack while she squirms away from his reach.

"Cut it out!" she whines.

"Tre! What are you doing?"

"I'm looking for her off switch. She's a robot, right? There must be a way to shut her down." He reaches out for Paige again.

"Quit the noise!" I say through clenched teeth. I stretch again for the rock and grab it with my whole hand this time, working it free from the surrounding mud.

"I'm not a robot," Paige says in a wounded tone. "Tell him, Curtis."

But I don't answer, because in the dim light I'm noticing

the "rock" in my hand is an unnatural gray color and very . . . plastic-looking. When I turn it over, there's a black rubber flap I can pull out of the bottom. Once I do, a sparkling gold key drops out, falling onto the cement with a *ching*.

"Dude," Tre says, clearly impressed. "That's a fake rock."

I grin back at both of them. "Approximately 27.5 percent of homes use one."

"It was 27.52 percent," says Paige, who was looking over my shoulder when I did the security search. She takes a quick step away from Tre's reach, but he keeps his hands to himself this time.

I reach down and grasp the key between my finger and thumb, raising it up off the sidewalk slowly, as if I've unearthed a valuable truffle in the woods and I'm afraid I might lose it before I'm able to sell it for a hundred bucks an ounce.

"I don't know, man. You sure we can't make this video at your house?" I guess Tre never believed we'd actually find a way into Pettynose's kitchen. Now that it looks like we might, he sounds like he's having some big-time second thoughts.

"No way. Have you seen my pans? Our stove? The ingredients in the cupboards—as in, *none*—and all that peeling wallpaper? I'll never get a ticket onto *The Last*

Super Chef working from there. And you said your house is off limits, too, right?"

"For sure," Tre says. "The Dynamic Duo definitely do not need us cooking something over there right now." That's what Tre calls his parents. The Dynamic Duo. They're super involved in most of their kids' lives. Too involved, probably. Tre has three older sisters and two older brothers, including Josh, the star basketball player. Not just older, way older, as in all the rest of the family's in high school or college even. And every one of them is amazing in this sport or that music or such and such hobbies, so his parents are always driving all over creation supporting them. Must be cool to have such huge fans, even if they're your own parents. Or maybe especially when it's them.

So . . . not my house, and not Tre's either. But Pettynose's enormous kitchen, all those incredible pans, his stocked fridge and pantry? It's almost *too* perfect.

Paige and I agreed the best night for this caper would be Friday night. Tonight. Pettynose would be making an appearance at the Eagles game again—since the surprise loss during Cupcakegate, they'd returned to their winning ways, meaning our landlord would for sure be right there in the front row of the bleachers, intent on not missing a single dribble.

The second reason tonight worked was that Mom had scheduled another evening interview, at a restaurant in

Riverview this time. Besides ensuring she wouldn't be home for at least a couple of hours, it also tells us how desperate she's becoming. Riverview's way on the other side of town. Over a week with no job and waiting for unemployment to process means no money coming in, so she's chasing every lead she can find, even if it means driving forty-five minutes each way on a Friday night.

The entry video's due tomorrow at midnight. This is going to be my only shot at this. I slide the key into the lock of Pettynose's back door. Right before I'm about to turn it, though, I look back at Tre. "You did bring your phone, right?"

He pulls it out of his back pocket and turns his flashlight on, helping me see the lock better. "Of course."

Tre's my best friend, but I might not have involved him in this particular big idea if I didn't need to make a video. Paige and I have no way of doing it. If new jackets with working zippers for Mom haven't exactly floated to the top of the budget, smartphones or video cameras for kids haven't even cracked the very bottom.

I knew Tre had a phone, though. It's the way the Dynamic Duo keeps track of him when they realize they've been following high schoolers and college students to so many places they've forgotten where their only elementary school kid is spending his time.

The back door pops open. I cringe for a second, worried

about an alarm, but Pettynose didn't have one when we signed the lease last year. The house stays quiet. Still no security system. I breathe out relief, then look back at my best friend and my sister.

"We're in."

Paige unzips her backpack and slides out my chef's knives. Henckels. Not a complete, professional set, only what Mom could pull the money together for two Christmases ago. Still, they're mine, and I'm used to them.

Though, honestly, I'm not sure I'll need them tonight, not if I find the ingredients I'm hoping for. "What are you going to make?" Tre asks.

"Not sure yet," I lie. No sense announcing it till I know it's possible.

The fridge is stocked full with every kind of meat and vegetable imaginable. Perfectly lined up Evian bottled water, Fever-Tree tonic, and organic, cold-pressed orange juice. It takes me a minute to figure out if Pettynose has what I'd hoped he would. I thought I'd overheard him mention it to Mom once, but sometimes I think I hear food when the conversation's really about something else. Like that time Gabe Johnson was talking about the New York Yankees playing the Milwaukee Brewers, and I jumped into the circle to complain about Mom not letting me use beer in my Yankee pot roast.

The cool air from Pettynose's perfect-temperature fridge washes over me. There's a brief second when my heart falls because I don't see what I'm looking for. Then I push aside a carton of milk, and, magically, there it is—a beautiful hunk of gruyère cheese. I almost hear the angels singing and see the beam of light from heaven shining down on it.

"Yes," I say, pumping my fist and grabbing it.

Tre looks confused, but Paige gets it. She's seen me make this particular dish before. "Perfect! Want me to grate it for you?"

"You saw the rules. I have to do this by myself. No parents. I'm sure they meant no sisters, either."

"Okay," she says slowly. "So you're not going to use a sous chef at all?"

"Paige, I can't. I'm sorry. Just help Tre film."

Paige frowns a little, then slinks off to a corner. She'll feel different when I win. And I'll *be* different when I win. When I win *The Last Super Chef*, when I bank that money, I'll be able to give her and Mom anything they want. I picture Paige punching at the keys of a brand-new laptop, Mom enjoying a bubble bath in some giant claw-foot tub . . .

I blink. Priorities, Curtis. Work first, dreams of what to do with the folding stuff once it's safely tucked into your pocket later.

I finish setting out bowls and milk and flour and eggs and a bunch of other tools and ingredients next to that wonderful gruyère and some parmesan we also discovered. We shoot a few practice videos, testing angles, but we can't waste too much time. In only minutes, we're ready to start for real.

I nod at Tre. He taps the button on his phone. I'm on.

My voice sticks in my throat. I gulp to free it up. "H-hi, Ch-Chef Taylor. My name is Curtis Pith." Pausing a second, I imagine what the Super Chef must be thinking as he watches this in his office or studio. Do I look different to him? I must. It's been years.

This is it—my big chance to finally make my mission a reality. Maybe my *only* chance.

"I'm a huge *Super Chef* fan. The biggest, probably. I've been a cook for years now. I'm eleven years old, and I'm going to make something that might seem simple on the surface, but I'm sure you know is actually one of the hardest dishes to get right." I wave a hand over my waiting ingredients, and Tre pans his lens across them, just like we practiced.

"A classic cheese soufflé."

I wait two measured breaths, letting the drama of my choice sink in. I'm not making a BLT or whipping out a quick veggie stir-fry. This is a soufflé, a dish that requires a ton of technical precision. It's definitely a brave choice.

And that risk should be enough on its own, but it's time to ramp up the stakes way, way higher.

"Now," I say, "a lot of chefs in a contest like this would make several of these." I hold up one of the ramekin dishes we found in Pettynose's cupboard, pointing at three others on the counter. "Just to make sure at least one comes out perfect. That's the one they would present to you, my judges today. But me?"

I make a show of stacking the ramekins, leaving only one on the counter, returning the rest to the cupboard. When I come back in front of the camera, I lift the single remaining ramekin. "Well, I only have one chance to earn my way onto *The Last Super Chef*, right? So that's all I'm giving myself. One chance."

Deep breath. *Cook.* Eye on the prize.

Prizes, actually. Two hundred and fifty thousand of them.

The thing about a soufflé is it's mostly a waiting game.
"A great soufflé is all about timing and patience," I
narrate for the camera as I gently push my lone ramekin
onto the oven rack.

Hands up, I send another confident smile at Tre's camera, but inside my stomach is doing somersaults. I hope Tre
recorded everything to this point—all the egg separating
and butter melting and gentle whisking and careful folding. "If I have the timing right, it'll be about seventeen
min—"

Tre's phone starts to ring, interrupting our filming. He
lowers it, checking the number. His eyes go wide, and he

pauses the recording. "It's Josh," he says. He answers it on speaker.

"Quick game!" Tre's older brother shouts. "The other team only had six players, and one guy tore up his knee and the other got a concussion . . . anyway they forfeited! Everything was so chaotic I didn't see Pettynose leaving until he was getting into his car. He's on his way."

Paige stands up from her corner stool. The bag of marshmallows she found in Pettynose's pantry falls off her lap, but she snags it with one hand. "How far is the high school?"

"Twelve minutes at the most," Josh answers through the speaker.

Paige and Tre both look at me, expressions frozen with worry. I glance at the oven, my soufflé still raw. "I need the whole seventeen minutes."

"We have to stall him, then, don't we?" Tre asks, pacing back and forth on the other side of the kitchen island.

Paige tosses the bag of marshmallows onto the counter. "I think I have an idea."

All I can do is wait for my soufflé to cook. I'm trapped in Pettynose's kitchen until it does, alone with my thoughts. They're mostly about the Super Chef.

It's not the first time I've sat somewhere by myself in the past two days, worrying about my father, the man I feel like I've never met but I must have met, even if it was so long ago I don't remember it. The man who's taught me more about food and cooking than any other person alive. I can't shake my confusion, can't let go of the feeling something must be seriously wrong with him.

I'm not the only one who's concerned. There's been all sorts of speculation about whether Lucas Taylor is sick or depressed or maybe in some kind of financial trouble. All the food blogs and news channels have been trying in vain to guess the reasons behind this sudden and shocking announcement of a *Last Super Chef* competition.

But if anyone knows the answers, they aren't talking. Especially not Lucas Taylor himself, who had shouted "No comment!" to the paparazzi maybe a thousand times since he told the world about *The Last Super Chef.*

The media can't figure it out, and neither can I. I shouldn't be trying either. I should be concentrating on what I'm doing, crouching near the window next to Petty-nose's front door, watching Paige and Tre trying to start a tiny campfire in the front yard of our apartment build-ing across the street. They've got the wood stacked all wrong—I learned how to do it last year when I was deter-mined to figure out the fewest steps to creating the perfect campground s'more. But I can't help them fix it. I can't leave my soufflé.

I tiptoe back to the oven. Even though I know it's a myth,

the idea that noise makes a soufflé fall is still ingrained in my mind. Paige suggested I take my shoes off. I explained it didn't matter. Whether a soufflé collapses or not has a lot more to do with timing than noise.

So far, mine looks great, darkening to the proper golden brown. I glance at the clock for the thousandth time, counting the seconds, praying Pettynose doesn't come crashing in before I can present a perfect soufflé to my video audience. I sneak back to our landlord's front door.

The campfire's flames are dancing high now, and Paige and Tre have speared marshmallows onto the ends of long wooden sticks. They're just roasting the first ones when Pettynose's car pulls into his driveway. He opens his door and immediately peers back at my sister and best friend. Then he rushes across the street and starts talking to them. Talking that quickly turns into yelling.

They've done their job. Pettynose is completely distracted by the open fire in the yard of his apartment building. Now it's time for me to finish my part. I race back to the kitchen.

The clock above the fridge tells me I have four minutes left. The eye test, though, says it's a lot closer than that, and I trust my eyes way more than clocks that might be slow. Maybe I can get away with pulling it out in closer to three. I grab Tre's phone, hold it up like I'm taking a selfie, and start recording a new clip.

"Welcome back. As you can see, I'm just minutes from taking my perfect soufflé out." I angle the phone so the viewers can get a look inside the oven. "I can't wait to taste it."

Video off. Rush back to the front door. Pettynose is stamping the fire out. Tre has somehow ended up with both long sticks, flaming black marshmallows on the ends. He slices them through the night air like Fourth of July sparklers.

Now Pettynose points at our building. Paige and Tre dart in front of his vision, stalling as long as they can. Soon, though, they'll have to retreat into our apartment. Then our landlord will march up his driveway, storm into his house. Then he'll catch me in his kitchen. Then any chance I had of getting my ticket stamped for *The Last Super Chef* will be gone.

I can't let that happen. I scramble back to the oven, eyes darting around the counters for anything I missed when I cleaned up our mess. The place is spotless, exactly as we found it. I grab a potholder, set Tre's phone up to record myself again, and don't even check the clock. Time's up. The soufflé's either perfect or I'm dead.

"Hey there," I say, smiling at the camera like I'm not out of breath and going mad with worry. "Curtis again. Time to show you my masterpiece." I tug on the potholder, slowly pull open the oven, and ease out the soufflé.

It's the perfect color, the perfect height. No collapse.

"Looks good so far. Let's see how it tastes," I say to the camera before realizing I don't have a spoon. I try to joke around it, because my other option is sheer panic, which I already feel bubbling up in my throat. "What do you think? Should I use my fingers?"

Giggling like an idiot and leaving the phone propped up and recording, I rush to the other side of the kitchen, catching a glimpse of Pettynose halfway up his driveway, head down, mumbling to himself. I yank a spoon out of the drawer and hurry back to the camera.

"Consistency's very important in a soufflé, as I'm sure everyone watching knows." I'm talking a mile a minute. Deep breaths. I dip the spoon into the center. "It should be rich and creamy in the middle, soft and luxurious."

I turn the spoon over. The creamy soufflé filling comes out with it, and it's perfect. I stay quiet, letting my creation do the talking as I use the spoon to fold the center out of the soufflé, velvety and wonderful and exactly how it should be. I hold the first spoonful in the air, inspecting it with a suspicious eye like I've seen the Super Chef do a hundred times to contestants on his show. I cool it with a puff of blown air. Taste.

I've made gruyère cheese soufflés before. I botched the first couple, but since then they've all been pretty delicious. I have to say, though, this is the best one ever. I'm so amazed by my own work, I forget to speak for a second. "Maybe you won't believe me, but it tastes even better than it looks," I mumble through a full mouth of hot food.

I hear movement at the front door. If it's possible, I start talking into the video even faster. "Okay! This has been Curtis Pith with my gruyère cheese soufflé entry video for *The Last Super Chef.* I really hope you pick me. Bye!"

Stop button clicked. Kitchen lights off. Millions of thoughts running through my brain. What I should've said, how I should've smiled. Waved. Did I wave? And seriously, "Bye!"? I almost smack the potholder against my forehead, but there's too much to do.

There's no time to clean the ramekin, or the spoon either. I have to take them with me. I grab them and Tre's phone and start to rush for the back door just as I hear a key turning the lock in the front one.

At the last second, I remember the oven's still on. I rush back with my armload of kitchen tools. I squeeze one finger out of the pile and use it to jab at the cancel button. Then I hurry to the door, opening it at the exact same time the front one opens.

Kneeling outside, I set my stuff down on the sidewalk and pull the back door shut as quietly as I can. I'm hiding the key in the fake rock and burying it back in the mud when I see Pettynose's shadow stalk into his kitchen, that big schnoz stuck in the air, sniffing away.

Turd. The one thing I couldn't get rid of. The aroma. He smells the soufflé.

I regather the potholder and dirty ramekin and spoon. Pettynose heads for his oven. He pulls it open and peeks inside, one hand resting on the rack. He cries out in pain as he pulls his red fingers back, then tries to stand up too quickly, banging his head.

Tucking Tre's phone in my back pocket and the dirty spoon in my front, I take off around the house. I sprint hard, praying the whole time that our landlord doesn't see me running in the corner of his eye, hoping I didn't forget anything. Definitely trying not to worry that he might be the exact type of person to have his spoons counted and numbered, or about the fact the oven was still hot and the whole place smelled like melted gruyère.

The next morning, Saturday morning, our doorbell rings. It's followed by an urgent-sounding knock. "Ms. Pith? Ms. Pith, are you home?"

Pettynose. I swallow so hard I feel my gulp drop all the way down to my stomach. Paige lowers the volume on the TV, then twists toward the door. I shift in my chair, my history book suddenly feeling so heavy I have to set it down on the floor.

"Ms. Pith! Please!"

He's here to report us. The campfire for sure. After that, the soufflé. He's figured it all out. Maybe he had cameras. Or measured his milk with a black mark on the carton. Maybe the neighbors saw us, or maybe . . .

It doesn't matter how he knows. He just knows.

Tre's still working on the video at his house, stitching together the separate clips we recorded into one long file. I don't know what I would've done if my friend didn't have a computer and know how to edit video.

Now, though, I realize we're going to end up caught before our entry even gets submitted. Forget my chances of making it to *The Last Super Chef*, the odds of me being the first grounded-for-life fifth grader shoot to the ceiling like a smoothie with a loose lid.

Mom comes out of our bedroom wiping her hands on a towel. Another knock follows, more like a pounding. She arches an eyebrow our way before sighing and heading for the door.

Pettynose looks like he's been through a hurricane. His hair, thin at the top already, is scooped over to one side, like he used his hand instead of a comb. He's always in a clean button-down shirt, but today he's wearing one of those old-man V-neck sweaters. It's all rumpled and kind of tight on him.

"Do you know how to make a cheese soufflé?" Pettynose asks Mom as soon as the door's wide enough for him to take an uninvited step inside.

"A cheese . . . ?" Mom starts. I don't move a muscle. Not the twitch of a finger, not a shrug of my shoulders, not the hint of a frown or a smile.

"Miriam, she was my wife, you remember?"

"I do," Mom answers slowly. "Of course. You told me about her."

Pettynose was married? It never even occurred to me to wonder.

"It was one of her specialties. She made a fantastic cheese soufflé. A classic one, with gruyère. They were so creamy, and they never fell and . . . oh, they were just wonderful. Miriam did love our kitchen."

"They sound delicious," Mom says. I can hear the confusion in her tone.

"Last night," Pettynose says. He checks over his shoulder as if someone might be listening. "When I came home, I swear I smelled one."

Mom scratches her cheek. "I'm sorry, Mr. Pettynose, I'm not following. Smelled what?"

"Miriam's cheese soufflé! Right there in my kitchen. Her kitchen. Almost like . . . almost like she was there again. My Miriam." He lowers his voice to a whisper. "Even the oven was hot. And can I tell you something else? I keep a hunk of gruyère in the fridge. I can't make a soufflé, but sometimes I take it out to smell it. You know, to remember." He says it as if keeping cheese around just to smell it once in a while is a perfectly normal thing to do. "Last night, the kitchen smelled like a soufflé, a classic cheese soufflé, a gruyère soufflé, and that block of wonderful cheese . . . it was gone." These last few words come out in another stunned whisper.

Mom's neck muscles contract. I know why. She's straining to avoid looking back at me with her accusing eyes. "So what you're saying is . . . you lost your cheese?"

"I—no!" Pettynose runs a hand over his stubble. I've never seen him unshaven before. With that ratty sweater, it makes him look like a hobo. "No, I . . . I don't know."

"I see," Mom says. "But I'm still . . . What do you think happened?"

"Well, it's obvious, isn't it?"

This is it. I stand up. Maybe I can run. But to where?

Paige waves at me, urging me to sit back down. I do, slowly.

"It was Miriam herself," Pettynose cries. "She came back to my kitchen and made a soufflé. It's the only possible answer. The oven, Ms. Pith. It was *hot*." Pettynose looks past Mom, around our apartment. He spins around once, checking the hallway behind him again. "You haven't . . . She's not . . . You haven't *seen* my wife, have you?"

"Mr. Pettynose, are you asking if we have a ghost in the building?"

A ghost? No wonder I've never seen his wife. How does Mom know all this stuff?

Pettynose's shoulders slump. He runs a hand through his hair, a feeble attempt at straightening it. "No, no, of course not. That doesn't," he sighs, "it makes no sense, does it?"

Our landlord starts to chuckle and, after a few seconds, Mom adds some nervous laughter of her own. Paige starts giggling too. She eyes me. It takes me a second to figure out I should join in. Soon all four of us are chuckling softly.

Pettynose points at his temple. "Must've been all in my head. I do miss her so much. Maybe my mind decided to play a new trick on me."

Our landlord turns to leave. I start to breathe again, heavy puffs of relief. But in the hallway he spins around before Mom can shut the door. "One thing, though."

Mom widens the door again.

"Please ask your daughter and her little friend not to build campfires in the yard." Pettynose looks around Mom to the couch, where Paige has straightened, pulling her face from her hands. "As I told you last night, young lady, that's very dangerous," he says, shaking a finger in my sis-ter's direction. He shifts his gaze to Mom. "You know how I feel about fires, Ms. Pith."

This time our landlord leaves for good. Mom waits for him to round the corner before she shuts the door again. "What an odd, odd man," she mumbles to herself, her gaze distant.

When she steps toward us, her gaze clears up, and her eyes narrow. She looks from me to Paige. "Now what's all this about a campfire?"

• • •

All through the next week we're on our best behavior. Partly because Halloween's coming up, and being grounded instead of trick-or-treating is the literal worst. But mostly because, you know, *secrets*.

Thankfully, we survive, even if we're not entirely sure how deeply Mom has bought into our story that we had a sudden, irresistible urge to roast marshmallows Friday night. All we know is, the less we talk about it, the less chance she'll discover anything about the video or cooking in Pettynose's kitchen. And there would be no debate— that was definitely a big idea with a capital B and a capital I. Maybe the Biggest Idea I'd ever had.

And, I realize now, probably the dumbest. While I appreciated all the hard work Tre put into it, when I pop over to his house later that day to help submit our video, it looks amateurish. There's a ton of cutting and starting and stopping and skipped sections, plus Josh's phone call in the middle of one of the most important parts.

I don't look like a Super Chef at all. I only look like an overwhelmed kid running around like he has no idea what he's doing.

The week brightens when Mom gets a phone call telling her that her job-hunting efforts have finally paid off. Her new job's only temporary, at a law office helping them organize their files so they can move into a bigger space. Two weeks and then she'll be done. But Mom keeps saying if she impresses them, they might decide to find a permanent position for her. So she's been really focused on being on time every day and staying longer to do extra work if she has to.

On Wednesday Mom stumbles through the door at the latest time yet, eight o'clock. On the TV, the *Super Chef* theme music and intro is already playing: the glass elevator, Chef Taylor striding down the long hall, his smooth entrance into the arena. Like the complete opposite of the fabulous Super Chef, Mom trips on Paige's boots, throws her coat toward a chair but misses, and practically falls into the couch. She kicks off her shoes and starts massaging her feet.

"Oh, look," she says in a tired voice. "Your favorite show, Curtis."

It's this season's finale. Three chefs vying for the annual *Super Chef* title. The normal one. Mom dozes off every few minutes, bored out of her mind. The episode ends when a southern chef named Clifford Franks wins the season. His family's still celebrating with him in the background, confetti falling all around them, when Lucas Taylor addresses the camera. He has to raise his voice above the cheering.

"Before we go, I wanted to thank all the wonderful kids we've heard from in the past few days. Your submissions have been truly awesome. We received thousands upon thousands of them, more than we ever expected. So many of you are so talented it warms this chef's heart. I'm more confident than ever we're going to be able to show the world that the future of food is safe in your hands."

Thousands? Is someone beating egg whites into a meringue with a hand mixer or is that my head pounding?

"I've employed a huge staff to sift through all those videos and present the best ones to us for final review." The Super Chef gestures at Chef Wormwood and Chef Graca. "We expect to start notifying the winners next week, and we'll have a special way to do that. *The Nightly News with Brooke Morrison* has generously given us a five-minute slot at the end of each of their six-thirty airings. We'll use these live moments to announce our five winners, one per day starting Monday. We're moving fast on this one, so each winner will be given—in person—a one-of-a-kind, commemorative certificate to bring to New York, a mere two weeks after the final entrant is identified. This certificate will serve as their entry ticket to our final competition. The first step to becoming the last winner ever crowned in this arena, to being named the—"

Here the crowd joins in as he pumps a fist into the air with each word.

LAST!

SUPER!

CHEF!

• • •

We check out the rest of the rules at Tre's house that week-end. The website's really organized and the info is easy to find, even if some of the fine print is a little hard to understand. A lot of stuff about consenting to being filmed live and infrequent, monitored phone contact with family. The biggest one, though? The Super Five, as the media has already started calling the five as-yet-unknown contestants, must agree to leave school for a few weeks later in November.

"He did say the winner would be named on Thanks-giving," I say after reading it, trying to act like I'm not surprised the contest is scheduled to happen so fast.

"Yeah . . . but wouldn't it be easier to wait for summer?" Tre asks.

I lean in and read some more. "Well . . . there is some-thing there about helping us keep up with our school work."

"Us?" Tre grins. "You're already in, huh?"

My stomach groans. He's right. Do I really think it's going to be so easy to stand out among thousands?

But . . . actually, yeah, I guess I do. Because I have a secret weapon. I mean, doesn't it stand to reason that if the Super Chef's the best chef in the world, his son would have to be the best kid chef? Anybody judging those videos should be able to see that straight off.

Right?

"This is the life," Mom says as she settles onto the couch with her huge plate of nachos. Paige and I scoot over to make room, our own dishes of cheese-splattered chips raised over our heads to avoid any accidental dripping.

It's Monday evening. The first check from the law firm came home with Mom on Friday, so she bought the good cheese and the hearty tortilla chips needed for my simple yet classic nachos—ground beef, jalapeños, and cheddar. I might've also quickly searched for a nacho recipe I once heard of involving caviar. You know, in case soon we could afford such a thing.

Usually at this time of night Paige is watching her last

cartoon before homework starts, but tonight the national news has been on for the past twenty minutes. Mom, between scrolling through her phone and dozing off, hardly notices the change in programming. It's just that I figured we couldn't flip over right at 6:55 p.m. What if the first Super Five winner was announced early?

The final regular news story is about a recall of romaine in Arizona. When anchor Brooke Morrison finishes reading it, she turns to her right and says, "Now, Chef, your restaurants don't use that lettuce, do they?"

The camera pans wider, and Chef Taylor is really there, in the studio, sitting with his hands folded on the anchor desk. I sit up straight, matching his posture, as if he can see me as clearly as I can see him. "I'm sure our staff is checking on that as we speak."

He and Brooke laugh together, like old friends. When they settle down, she says, "And now we have something very special for our viewers. Or even, if I may say"—she nods at Chef again—"something *super*. Chef Lucas Taylor—the famous Super Chef himself—is gracing us with his presence tonight. Nice to see you, Chef."

"Great to be here, Brooke. And thanks so much for letting us use your show to announce our five winners this week."

"Oh, the honor is all ours. Seems like the entire world

is waiting to find out about the five kids who will have a chance to win *The Last Super Chef*. Was it hard to select them?"

Chef Taylor nods. "Very. For a little while, I thought we wouldn't be able to do it at all. Kids are so passionate these days. I wish I'd been as talented at that age."

"Now, Chef, I'm very sure you must've been." Brooke straightens a little and returns to her serious news face. "Before we get going, though, I do need to ask you the question that's burning a hole through every self-respecting *Super Chef* fan's brain these days: Why?"

Chef Taylor gulps. He shakes his head slightly. He doesn't answer.

Brooke Morrison presses on. "What I mean is, why the need to end your show? Why *Last* at all? You're not exactly retirement age, are you now? And why a kid? Why at this point in time, when you're at the height of your popularity?"

"That's a lot of whys, Brooke."

Brooke tilts her head in acknowledgment. "The world wants to know."

"I can understand that." The Super Chef pauses for a few seconds, considering. "But I can only answer one of your questions. The one about the kids. Why a kid? It's simple, really. Kids are the future. They always have been, every generation throughout history. And that's exactly what we want. What we're doing with our last season, trying to give our viewers a glimpse of how bright that future can be, it only works with kid contestants. Do you see? I really want to end the show on a shiny note."

Brooke nods but clearly isn't satisfied. "But why do you have to end it at all—"

"I'm afraid the rest of my reasons must remain private," the Super Chef cuts in, his upper lip trembling a little. I can't tell if he's nervous or angry. Maybe sad? "Besides, our focus should really be on the Super Five, shouldn't it? It's such an exciting opportunity for these kids, and we only have so much time. In fact, I believe one of my partners is waiting to introduce you to the first winner. I think we should check in with him, don't you?"

The newscaster takes a reluctant breath. "Yes. Yes, of course."

The Super Chef inhales as the camera zooms in on him. "Each night this week, one of the Super Five will be named right here in this segment. Not only named—our remote crew will visit them in person to hand out their *Last Super Chef* certificate. Now, these kids have no idea they've been picked yet. So I'm as excited to see their reaction as you probably are."

The Super Chef holds one finger to his ear. "Chef Graca, are you out there?"

The anchor desk disappears, replaced by a shaky camera

following Chef Gabriel Graca through some darkened streets. "Yes, Chef! I can hear you." He balances a black umbrella and lumbers ahead, turning to look over his shoulder into the lens. It's raining wherever they are, a gentle patter on cobblestone streets. "We're almost to the house. It's early morning here, so folks are just getting ready for the day."

There's an Asian man walking in front of him, pointing and nodding, leading the whole crew through streets lined with bamboo fences. The modest houses behind the fences are wooden and all kind of look the same—tan siding surrounded by darker trim. The camera crew and Graca round a bend, and a tall, narrow building shoots straight up into the sky, sudden and massive. It has five or six roofs stacked on top of each other.

"What a beautiful pagoda," comes Chef Taylor's voice from the studio. "Why don't you tell the audience where you are, Chef?"

"Yes, Chef," Graca, a little out of breath, says. "This is Kyoto, Japan. We're almost to the house we're searching for." A low-hanging tree branch grazes his umbrella, and he pushes it out of the way. For the first time I notice cylindrical-shaped white lanterns with black Japanese lettering hanging from the buildings on one side of the street. "There aren't many street signs here, so it's been a bit difficult to tell. But our guide believes our first Super Five winner lives"—he points, and there's a quick exchange with the Japanese man—"right here!"

I can't believe it. I expected people from all around the country to submit, not just little North Sloan. But Japan? That means those thousands of entries the Super Chef mentioned might have come from all around the *world*. My confidence and chances both shrink at equal rates, like when you cook up a big bag of leafy escarole and after it wilts all that's left is a tiny bowlful.

The Asian man nods and says something I don't understand as he steps to the side and points up some stone stairs. Chef Graca and the camera crew hurry up them. The door opens just as they reach the top. A girl my age, focused on adjusting the buttons of her red raincoat, comes out. I can tell by her knee-high white socks that she's probably wearing a school uniform underneath. She has a bright-yellow, square backpack fixed to her shoulders. She hears the noise of the group climbing the stairs and looks up, her eyes going wide.

"Kiko Tanaka?" Chef Graca asks her.

She doesn't speak, but Graca's voice must travel inside, because the door reopens and her parents appear. They recognize the sous chef right way. "Ah! Super Chef!" they shout and point, covering their mouths. "Super Chef!"

"That's right," Graca says, smiling. "Well, not me, but he is here with us." The Portuguese chef gestures at the camera. "Chef Taylor was so impressed with your beef Wellington, Kiko. One might expect a submission from Japan to be some manner of Japanese cuisine, but you were so outside the box I don't think you and the box were even in the same room! So . . . congratulations! You're our first Super Five winner."

Chef Graca reaches into his bag and pulls out a piece of paper. Not just any paper though, an official-looking certificate, the outer edges glimmering in gold trim. Both the traditional *Super Chef* logo as well as the new *Last Super Chef* one are prominently displayed at the top, and a #1 is bold and centered in the middle of the page. The camera zooms in, and I can see three pieces of information under the giant number.

DATE	TIME	PLACE
November 12	8:00 p.m. (sharp)	Super Chef Arena

"Your ticket into the contest," Chef Graca says as he presents it to her.

Kiko stares down at her prize, still in the sous chef's hands. He continues. "We'll be arranging your travel to our studios soon. You and your family will receive all the details, rest assured. What we need to know now is this: Do you accept your place as one of the Super Five? Do you understand and agree to the rules of the contest?"

Kiko slowly takes the certificate. She still hasn't said a word. She scans the paper with disbelieving eyes, reading it like she doesn't want to miss an important detail. "Y–yes, I do understand." She turns to explain to her parents in Japanese.

But it isn't just Kiko's parents behind her now. Her grandparents are there, too, both sets of them. They must all live in that same tiny house. The six adults of different ages erupt into rapid Japanese speech, only two recognizable words mixed in. "Super Chef! Super Chef!"

Kiko turns back to Chef Graca and bows once. Then she straightens and says, "I accept your challenge."

Back in the studio, the frozen image of Kiko Tanaka's determined expression appears over the Super Chef's shoulder. "So there you have it," he says to Brooke, "the first of our Super Five, all the way from Japan." Now a picture of a sliced beef Wellington replaces the still image of Kiko. Chef Taylor points at it. "Just look at the color on that Wellington. Even from six thousand miles away I could tell it was perfect. Kiko's going to be a tough one to beat."

I stand up off the couch, offering to take Paige's empty nacho plate back to the sink, realizing only now how sure I was that my name was going to be called tonight. My sister knows my expressions too well. "Don't worry, Curtis, there are still four to go," she assures me.

Mom was snoozing, her empty plate in her hands. As I reach for it, she jolts awake. "Just resting my eyes," she says first. Then, "What's that now? Four more of what?"

I don't answer. It doesn't matter if there are four spots left or forty. I mean, come on. A whole Wellington? All I made was one lousy soufflé.

I totally get it now. There's no way our chopped-up video of me basically blowing the biggest opportunity of my life is going to work like I thought it was. I've got no chance at all.

Super Five winner #2 is Pepper Carmichael from Boston. This time it's Chef Wormwood and another camera crew pacing up the crooked, hilly streets of Boston's North End to find the Carmichael family's condo.

"The incredible thing about Pepper there . . ." Chef Taylor, leaning his elbows onto the news desk, is telling Brooke Morrison a minute later. Over his shoulder, a tiny picture-in-picture version of Pepper, who has a ton of curly hair, is still jumping up and down with her arms pumping through the air. One of her hands clutches the gold-tinged certificate Wormwood handed her only a few seconds before. The only difference between Pepper's and the one Kiko Tanaka got is the big #2 in the center.

November 12, 8:00 p.m. sharp, Super Chef Arena. For the first time I wonder about my reaction to the show when it airs. The rules said it would be filmed live, unlike any *Super Chef* contest before it. Will my stomach allow me to watch a bunch of other kids compete in *The Last Super Chef* to win some of my father's money, without me? Or will I spend the whole hour bent over the toilet, puking my disappointed guts out?

The Super Chef's voice grows more animated. He's still talking about tonight's winner. "Pepper cooked *two* dishes in her video. At the same time! On one burner she was making a complex seafood gumbo—establishing a perfect roux like she did is no joke, let me tell you—and with her other hand, almost as an afterthought, she threw together a quick Jamaican Rundown. This talented girl made the whole process look so easy, I was surprised she didn't think to throw on a blindfold or ask someone to tie one arm behind her back."

"Amazing," newscaster Brooke says. "And only ten years old."

"What's a Jamaican Rundown?" Mom asks me from behind the couch.

"I don't know," I admit while refusing to pull my gaze from the screen.

Mom snorts. "Well, somebody call Guinness. Curtis Pith doesn't know how to make a dish." She paces toward the bathroom, shaking her head in amused disbelief.

"And she sells her spice mixes online!" the Super Chef almost yells. "You can try your hand at using them to make one of her recipes by visiting pepperspicesuptheworld.com."

"Amazing," Brooke says.

"Truly," Super Chef agrees.

Later I sneak Mom's phone out of her purse and find out a Jamaican Rundown is a fish stew cooked in coconut milk, garlic, onions, tomatoes, and about a dozen other ingredients. It's a good thing I have no shot at getting into this contest. These other kids are all next level. I'm not even remotely ready to cook alongside them, let alone *against* them.

I've never felt so far from being a chef. This whole time I've been imagining all the things I could give Mom and Paige with that prize money, but I think, deep down, I also believed that at least some of it would help me advance my cooking career. Now, though? I'm not going to make it onto *The Last Super Chef*. I'll never see that money.

I feel alone, lost on an island in whatever ocean's the farthest away from New York.

The next night, Wednesday, I almost mutter a curse when Bonifacio Agosto of Mexico City is located by Chef Jackie Gilmore, not one of the show's regulars but a frequent guest chef. I'm angry because the "perfect mole" Chef

Taylor describes had to have been made with a fantastic Mexican chocolate, nothing like the cheap stuff I've been forced to work with lately. What I wouldn't do for some of that chocolate right now.

"Let me tell you about this Mole Poblano recipe," Chef Taylor says, leaning back in his chair with a smile so wide you can't help but feel his amazement coming through the television. Bonifacio's entire body—not that there's much of it, he's super short—has gone limp. He nearly fainted when he saw Chef Jackie coming, and now the boy's mother is the only thing keeping him upright. Señora Agosto works hard to fan cool air onto her prone son's face.

The whole time, the third Super Five winner clutches his #3 certificate and keeps sleepily mumbling, *"Está bien, de acuerdo. Está bien, de acuerdo."*

"What's he saying there, Chef?" Brooke asks from the studio desk.

"He's agreeing to the challenge. The skill in this kid's fingers . . . it's stupendous. The recipe Bo used was handed down from his grandmother, and it dates back to generations before her. A mole done right is the kind of meal legends are made of, and this one was no exception."

"I'd love to see *that* video," Brooke says.

"Sorry, no time now," Chef Taylor says, smiling. "But here's a shot of the final result."

The screen changes again, showing a close-up of a deep, rich red sauce covering a simple chicken leg. When you make a perfect mole, it works on top of just about anything, and at any meal. Breakfast, lunch, dinner, doesn't matter.

"There were thirty-two ingredients in this one, Brooke. Thirty-two! And it took him three days to execute all the steps. He videoed them right along the way. Must've started working almost the moment we announced the contest."

"It seems like all three of your contestants so far are really amazing cooks," Brooke says.

"You're gonna have to be amazing to have a chance to win *The Last Super Chef*," Chef Taylor agrees.

Mom hasn't made it home from work yet, so tonight it's just Paige and I watching. "You're amazing, too, Curtis," my sister assures me.

I push up off the couch and stomp toward our bedroom. "Yeah. Obviously not amazing enough."

By Thursday I almost don't want to watch the Super Five announcements anymore. There are only two left, and I know for sure I'm not one of them. What was I thinking, making one little soufflé with less than ten ingredients? These other kids mastered dishes with thirty ingredients or more, or created two at the same time.

I start a list in the back of my recipe book.

The Super Five
Kiko Tanaka—Japan—A near-perfect beef Wellington.
Pepper Carmichael—Boston—A complex, rich gumbo while making a dish I never

heard of with her other hand. And she's already got a website.

Bonifacio Agosto—Mexico—the most incredible mole, handed down from his ancestors.

Ancestors?!? Mom's parents both died years ago; I never met them. And if I've ever spoken two words with my father, I don't remember them. He doesn't talk about his family much on the show, either.

Who was I supposed to learn all *my* recipes from? Who taught me? No one, that's who. I spent the past five years studying on my own.

Even though I'm not sure I want to be, that night I'm in front of the television again as Brooke Morrison wraps up talking about the aftermath of a bad earthquake in Asia. Mom isn't home yet, again, so I made easy turkey pesto paninis with mozzarella. Paige and I are finishing them on the couch, ready for the *Super Chef* segment pretty much only because Paige *ordered* me to watch it.

"Okay, you think it's not you," she said earlier. "But don't you want to know who else they picked? What they cooked? Where's that chef's curiosity?"

"Down the drain with the expired milk I just poured out."

And maybe Paige will be a teacher someday, because I swear the look she gave me is the same one I get from Mrs. Kadubowski whenever she catches me daydreaming in class. Dripping with disappointment.

"Fine. I'll watch."

"Besides," my sister continues now, "so what if you don't get in? Would it be that bad to have to stay here with Mom and me instead of going all the way to New York to win some dumb contest?"

"It's not a dumb—" But I stop speaking.

Because Paige doesn't get it. There shouldn't have to be a contest at all. Nobody should have to figure out which kid—which family—should get the last-ever *Super Chef* prize money, because everybody should already know. Lucas Taylor should be forced to tell the world about his children. About me, his *son* who *already* cooks. If he wants to go out on top—on a shiny note, whatever that's supposed to mean—why couldn't he do it by making a big show out of finally giving Mom the money he must owe her?

And if he won't, then I guess I should make sure to put myself in position to do the right thing in his place. Which makes getting into *The Last Super Chef* that much more—

"Wait. So you don't think I'm getting in either?" I ask Paige.

She opens her mouth to respond, but the *Super Chef*

segment starts and we both quiet down. Chef Graca and his camera crew pace through random streets again, but for the first time, they're not in some busy city. They've parked their vans and cars in a cul-de-sac in a suburban neighborhood. I can see parts of about five houses, and every single one of them looks as huge as Pettynose's mansion.

"Seems like they're in the same time zone this time, at least," Paige says.

She's right. The sky's the identical tone of dusk as it is outside our windows. There's even snow on the ground, though it's not piled quite as high as here in the streets of North Sloan.

"For Super Five #4, we're in Lincolntown, Illinois." Chef Graca gestures toward a mailbox. "It's this one right here—4975." He and the camera crew start up the driveway, but before they make it even a few steps, the front door bursts open and a dark-haired kid sprints out, arms waving in the air, yelling, "I accept! I accept! I understand the rules! I accept!"

The Super Chef chimes in from the studio again. "I see young Joey Modestino is our most excited winner yet."

"Wow, what did this firecracker make in his video?" Brooke's voice asks.

On the screen, Chef Graca is handing over the certificate and explaining the next steps to Joey, who doesn't appear to be listening. He's too busy flossing, his arms swinging back and forth at about a million miles an hour in the closest imitation of backpack kid I've ever seen.

The Super Chef answers Brooke. "Joey is our stuffed squid kid."

"Say that five times fast." She laughs.

"I really would rather not." A chuckle from Brooke. "It's not easy to clean and cook squid properly, but Joey seems to have been doing it since birth. His was stuffed beautifully, too, with swiss chard and oregano and pine nuts. Bread crumbs and fennel—he used the whole vegetable, seeds and bulbs and all—Joey definitely does not fool around. Plus anchovies and plenty of garlic, lemon, and onion. Classically Italian. My mouth is watering just describing it."

"Mine too," agrees Brooke.

"And stuffing it the way he did, I should add"—the Super Chef raises his hand—"makes it even harder to cook well. Yet one could see when he sliced into it that it was perfect."

There's a commotion in the driveway, and everyone has to get out of the way so a red Porsche can pull in. A large man, Joey's dad, I'm guessing, because they have the same wavy dark hair, climbs out of the fancy car. He's chomping away on what has to be half a pack of gum. He takes in the cameras littering his yard. "Kid! Ya did it?"

Joey finally stops dancing long enough to smile up at his dad. He shows him the gold-framed certificate. His father positively *beams* at him. "Of course you did! It's in the family, isn't it?"

As the large man comes around the car and lifts his son into the air, the scene switches back to the studio, focusing on the Super Chef's smiling face, and I realize with a certainty I've never felt before that my father will never lift me into the air like that. Chances are, if I don't get into this contest, I'll probably never even *meet* him.

The door opens, and Mom comes in just as I whip the last bit of my panini at Brooke Morrison's annoying grin. "Tune in tomorrow," the news anchor says, "for the final member of the Super Five!"

Mom yells, "No, I did not just see you throwing food at my television. What's going on?"

I fold my arms into my chest and fall back into the cushions. "Nothing."

"Nothing, huh? Well, you can do a whole lot of the same nothing in your room, mister. Now march!"

Friday night, I'm grounded for the last announcement. "If you want to cover my TV in food then maybe you can do without some screen time until next week," Mom said the night before as I cleaned my projectile panini off the carpet.

Suits me. I really don't want to see what spectacular German kid who makes his own strudel or Chinese girl whose grandmother invented Peking duck the Super Chef picks next. I'll just hang out in my room and be happy doing homework. Or staring at a blank wall with my arms folded across my chest.

Except Paige must still be curious because I hear Brooke Morrison's laugh, the one that tells me she's chatting with the Super Chef again, drifting into my room. I glance at my clock. 6:55 p.m., right on time. I almost rush out there anyway, my legs on autopilot, but then I hear Mom clanking dishes out of the dishwasher and remember I can't.

Then the doorbell rings.

I'd seen Pettynose earlier, when we were walking home from the bus, lurking around our building. He's probably here to check on us, make sure I'm not cooking. Or maybe I'm in more trouble. Which . . . of course I probably am, because life can't get any worse right now.

Good thing I'm already stuck in the bedroom. I mean, how much more grounded can I get? Still, I strain one ear in the direction of the door and the TV. "The final piece of the puzzle," the Super Chef is saying. "Winner #5 is maybe the most intriguing competitor yet."

And Mom says, "Oh my! Can I help you?"

And Chef Taylor says, "Let's go to Claire Wormwood right now."

And somehow Chef Wormwood's voice sounds echocy, like she's coming from both the TV and our doorway. "Thanks, Chef. Yes, ma'am, is Curtis Pith home?"

And steps thunder toward our room.

And Paige storms in, pointing behind her and gasping, "It's . . . the . . . with the . . . and the lights . . . and . . ." She takes a deep breath, and the rest comes out in a whisper. "They're here."

And I still don't believe her, but I follow her into the living room anyway. And even when I see the bright lights and the cameras and *the* Chef Claire Wormwood standing a foot in front of Mom, I can't quite make my eyes adjust to it all. I can't quite make it feel real. Because it can't be real. It can't be.

"Curtis?" Chef Claire asks, looking over Mom's shoulder toward me.

"Y-yes?"

She reaches into her bag, pulling out the last gold-trimmed certificate. It's the same one I've seen the past four nights, except this one—*mine*—has a big #5 in the center. "Congratulations, you're the final member of the Super Five. Do you accept our challenge? Do you still want to compete in *The Last Super Chef*?"

I stare ahead. Behind me, on the TV, the Super Chef is saying, "Probably the most interesting winner yet. His video showed us a real urgency, from the moment he committed to making just a single soufflé instead of several—the bravery of that!—to the way he cooked it throughout, in such a hurry. I can already see him handling the deadlines of the contest environment well—and every night in every restaurant in the world, too, I might add."

"Uh-oh," Brooke says. "I'm afraid our Curtis looks a little like a deer in headlights. He has to accept for this to be official, doesn't he?"

"Indeed he does," Lucas Taylor says.

I have to accept. Have. To. Accept.

"Curtis?" Chef Wormwood says. She sounds worried.

"Curtis?" Paige says. She sounds scared.

"Curtis?" Mom says. She sounds confused.

"I accept!" I blurt in Chef Wormwood's direction.

"You understand the rules?" she asks.

The rules. What were they again? Filmed live. Weeks away from school, from home. Limited contact with family.

I glance at Paige. She's holding her breath. I've never missed so much as a Memorial Day, never mind a huge holiday like Thanksgiving. But this year I might be too busy cooking on television in front of millions of people to make my famous oatmeal stuffing for my family. What will they do without me? Order from a restaurant?

I shiver. At the idea of my family ordering presliced turkey breast from some diner. At the fear I see etched on my sister's face. The same fear that suddenly seems to reach out and grab hold of my heart, too.

"What is this?" Mom asks. She blinks and holds a hand up to ward off the bright camera lights. "Accept what? What rules?"

I meet Mom's eyes. Take a deep breath. Throw on a grin that probably comes out a lot more like a grimace. "So . . . yeah. Mom? We should probably talk."

FROM CURTIS PITH'S RECIPE JOURNAL (BACK PAGES)

THE SUPER FIVE

Kiko Tanaka—Japan—A near-perfect beef Wellington.

Pepper Carmichael—Boston—A complex, rich gumbo while making a dish I never heard of with her other hand. And she's already got a website.

Bonifacio Agosto—Mexico—The most incredible mole, handed down from his ancestors.

Joey Modestino—Chicago—Italian expert, Dad drives a Porsche. Has probably worked with expensive ingredients I've never even seen.

Curtis Pith—Me—Oh man, ME. WHAT WAS I THINKING? In no time at all, I'll be on my way to New York. Then all I have to do to get that prize is beat all four of these Super kids. Right. Easy.

"**Y**our time starts . . . NOW!"

The audience lining the balconies surrounding Super Chef Arena erupts into applause and cheering. Up on the stage, the Super Chef stares at the big clock behind him for a long second, then looks out toward the five of us, standing at our stations. Left to right, Pepper, Kiko, and I have the front row, and Bonifacio and Joey work behind us. They've given Bo a little stepping stool so he can reach everything.

I should be starting already. Instead I stand frozen, waiting for Chef Taylor's gaze to rotate to me. He's ten feet tall up on that stage. We're just about to lock eyes when a lumberjack-size, bearded cameraman steps between us, blocking my view. The heavyset guy is two feet from my face, his bright light shining straight into my eyes. I'm about to put my hand up to block it when I remember the instructions the show producer gave us before we were guided into the arena.

"Don't pay attention to the cameras or the lights," the woman wearing the headset band in her mess of blond curls, Kari, said in a rush after collecting our certificates and handing out multicolored aprons. I got an orange one. Mel, the twentysomething handler assigned to me, helped tie it in back while I just about hyperventilated.

"Dude," he whispered as he cinched the straps tight. "You got this."

A brief surge of confidence lightning-bolted down my spine, but it disappeared quickly once I found myself directly beneath the scorching studio lights. They're not just hot; they sear the top of my head like the sun itself.

I guess I never realized that your whole face can sweat at once. I hope the camera isn't catching it. And that none of the viewers at home are noticing the way my hands are shaking.

Actually, I don't really care what anyone else notices. I'm only thinking of two people watching me right now. My mom and my sister. They're why I'm here, and if I know Paige, she's standing an inch away from the screen like I usually do.

I take a deep breath. I have no idea what I expected my first moments in this competition to be like. I guess I thought the five of us would get the chance to meet each other, and the Super Chef and his staff, too. Maybe I assumed we'd at least be given time to unpack.

Not in a million years would I have guessed I'd be doing mise en place in front of a giant crowd and a live TV audience less than an hour after I stepped off the private jet that brought me to New York.

After Chef Wormwood's visit to our apartment, Mom had gone through what Paige and I secretly labeled "The Three Stages of *Super Chef*"—first glad, then mad, finally sad. Glad had been when it seemed like her son had won something. Mad came the next day, when Mom gave us the third degree for how it had all happened, and we admitted to making our video in Pettynose's house, which meant admitting to cooking in his kitchen, which meant admitting to breaking in and lying to her about the reason for the campfire.

"But if he hasn't found out by now, he never will!" Paige assured her, and eventually Mom dropped it because she started to read the fine print that came with my golden certificate. The rules that told her I had to go to New York City by myself for weeks. That we wouldn't be able to talk much, just a few supervised calls. That I would almost certainly miss Thanksgiving with my family so I could compete in a contest I hadn't even told her I'd entered.

That's when the sad started. It lasted the whole rest of the week.

Every day Mom alternately burst into tears, then made another urgent call to the *Super Chef* offices to ask more questions. She was crying again when the limo pulled up at the precise time we'd been told it would.

"My baby," she kept saying, hugging me, letting me go, then hugging me again.

She might not have released me at all if it hadn't been for Mel. While the driver made a big show of opening one door of the limo and then stepping to the side, clearly hoping I'd hurry up and climb in without discussion, Mel came around the car with a wide smile. He reached Mom and gave her a long hug, like an old friend.

"I promise to take the *best* care of him," he promised her. "Curtis is one hundred percent my responsibility. I won't let you down."

Besides being a culinary student from North Carolina and a huge *Super Chef* disciple himself, Mel had a certificate in childcare from the Red Cross. We knew because Mom had asked him for a résumé about two minutes after she first received his name and email from the Super Chef people. Not only did he reply right away, he sent back a sparkling clean one. So impressive, she kept wandering into the room while reviewing it, giving us facts about him. "Do you know Mel got his undergraduate degree from Yale?" Now here he is, standing in front of us with a limo, looking just as polished in person as his credentials had promised he would be.

Mom kissed me about a hundred times and gave Mel about a thousand instructions and reminders before she let me go. By then Paige had made her way over to the limo. She was interviewing the driver about his car—gas mileage, time from zero to sixty, etc.

I tapped my sister on the shoulder. Mom was still focused on Mel, giving him some new reminder, number one thousand and one. Paige's face grew pop quiz serious as she turned toward me. "You're cutting a recipe that calls for one and five-eighths cups of flour in half. How many cups do you need?"

"Thirteen-sixteenths," I answered without missing a beat.

We hugged then, maybe the longest hug I had ever given my sister. I couldn't remember the last time we'd spent more than a few hours apart, never mind weeks. I closed my eyes and wondered how I was going to do any of this without Paige standing next to me. Without my sister reminding me about measuring and temperature and the rest of the scientific side of cooking it sometimes took longer for my brain to calculate.

"If I have to spend a month not seeing you," my sister said into my ear while we were still hugging, "you better win."

"I'll try."

Paige pushed back from me, grabbing my shoulders. "Do or do not," she said in her creepy Yoda voice that sounds a lot more like Rick from *Rick and Morty.* "There is no try."

As the limo pulled away with me sunk into the way-too-big back seat, Mel gave someone an update on his cell. I stretched toward the window to gaze out. I watched Mom grow smaller and smaller, hugging Paige to her side, wiping at the corners of her eyes. The whole week she hadn't mentioned or asked me about finally meeting my father. I figured it was because Paige was around almost every minute and she still didn't want her to know. Whatever the reason, I was glad she didn't bring the Super Chef up. I needed to stay focused on cooking in New York. Cooking and bringing that prize money home.

The limo guy picked up speed. At the last second I looked out the window on the opposite side. Pettynose stood on his front porch, a cup of coffee in his hand. His angry lips were locked together as his eyes followed the limo. Did he know about the soufflé? Was I leaving Paige and Mom alone to face the music by themselves? I tried waving to him, but he hardly moved.

Maybe he just didn't see me.

• • •

Mise en place means "set in place" in French. Basically it's another word for prepping ingredients, which, after turning in our invitation certificates, was what we'd been informed we'd be doing this first night on TV. We had thirty minutes to prep five artichokes, twenty onions, a dozen clams, and fifteen shrimp.

No one told us what was meant by "prep." We were expected to know. In fact, no one told us much of anything except that we weren't supposed to pay attention to the cameras. Good thing I haven't missed a *Super Chef* episode in . . . well, never.

Working fast, I use my knife to cut the top from the first artichoke, then trim off most of the stem. I start pulling the tough leaves away from the base, then scoop out the hairy choke in the center with a spoon before cutting the whole thing in half. Fill a glass bowl with cold water, drop in first the lemon halves, then my one finished artichoke. The lemon water will keep the artichoke looking fresh for the judges. "Acidulated," we chefs call it.

I prep the second artichoke the same way. Then the third.

Big inhale. Two more to go before I can move on to the onions. This isn't so bad.

The air in Super Chef Arena, already thick with tension, splits with the sharp and sudden trill of a whistle.

Chef Graca shouts, "Five minute mark! Chefs, you have twenty-five minutes left."

What? How could five minutes be gone already?

I glance over at Kiko. All her onions are diced and piled into plastic containers, filled to the top with not even a millimeter of room to spare. She's switched knives and started shucking clams. How did she do that so fast? Behind me, Joey Modestino has his tray of shelled and deveined shrimp complete. He's moved on to shucking clams, too. He catches me watching him with an open mouth and grins at me, then winks.

I thought it was going so well, but I must be in last place. I have to hurry. When I turn forward again, though, I jump, startled by Chef Graca standing right in front of me. He reaches up to his mouth and pulls his whistle out. "It's Curtis, isn't it?" His Portuguese accent sounds a lot stronger in person.

"Y-yes," I answer.

"Welcome to *The Last Super Chef.*" He presents his right hand. I forget to wipe my fingers on a towel, so when I drop my hand into his, a bunch of artichoke slime comes with it.

"Tell me, why did you choose to start with the artichokes?" he asks as, with a completely straight face, he wipes the slime away on his already food-stained chef's jacket.

I hesitate. Is he saying it was a bad choice? "I thought they'd give me the most trouble," I confess.

"Interesting. Well, we already know you don't mind a tough challenge. Don't we, Chef?" Chef Graca looks over his shoulder at the Super Chef.

Taylor waits for the cameras to swing his way. "That's right, Curtis here gives himself extra work when conditions are already difficult. Let's look at his road to *Super Chef*." He turns toward the big screen behind him. A video starts playing on it.

My video starts playing.

The one Tre had spent hours weaving together for me. My submission.

The video that shows me cooking in Pettynose's kitchen, plain as the suddenly twitching nose on my face.

If he hasn't found out by now, I remember Paige telling Mom, *he never will*.

Oh no.

Part of my mind keeps saying "that could be any kitchen" as my video plays on the huge screen. But suddenly I'm noticing tons of little details. The distinctive pattern and colors of Pettynose's tiled kitchen backsplash—maroon with green and gold diamonds. The big plaid P in the center of the clock Tre kept panning up to in order to show the time elapsing. Is there another kitchen in the world that has this same combination of décor?

But I already know the answer to that.

If he sees this video, Pettynose will no doubt recognize his own kitchen. My only hope is that he isn't watching, and that none of North Sloan's residents will let the wrong question slip. Something like "Hey, Arthur, didn't we see your kitchen on *Super Chef* last night?" followed closely by "Wasn't that North Sloan's own *Curtis Pith* in the same video?"

Will Pettynose march right over to our apartment? Nail an eviction notice to the door? Send Mom and Paige to homeless jail for *my* crimes? Do not pass go. Do not collect $200.

Thing is, we've been in homeless jail before. Close to it, anyway. It's no fun trying to find an apartment Mom can actually afford. You need a lot more than $200.

The whole time my video plays, I can't work. Pettynose must be squirming in front of his television watching me act like I own his kitchen, like I really belong there making his wife's specialty. Which I didn't know at the time, but still . . . I can't tear my eyes away. Definitely can't force my hands back to dicing onions.

Everyone applauds when my video, which feels like it was approximately one year long, finally ends. What are they clapping for? Are they impressed by how completely and totally I ruined a bunch of people's lives—including mine—all at once? Only when Chef Wormwood approaches Kiko, says a few words, then starts to play her Wellington video, am I able to move again. The feeling of dread that started in my feet has wormed its way up to my hands. They're working again, but they're going strangely slowly and making all kinds of mistakes. My onions aren't perfect like Kiko's. Only a few clams left, but the ones I've "finished" are a mess, shucked open but mangled where I tried to loosen the meat from the shell underneath.

A few minutes later I'm finally starting on my shrimp and Chef Taylor has Pepper giggling as he flatters her about her spice website. He calls for her video to play, and a giant version of her smiling face appears on the screen. The video zooms out as Pepper hurries from one burner to the other, somehow keeping two very different recipes on track. Distracted by it, I almost cut my palm trying to devein my first shrimp.

Concentrate.

Chef Graca blows that high-pitched whistle again on his way to Joey's station. "Five minutes remaining!" he shouts. This time I don't look at anyone else, I just keep working, but I know I must be way behind.

I can't help but hear little snippets of the other videos. Joey cooks because his father loves to eat. Bonifacio's grandparents owned everything from corner stores to taquerias, and he's always been surrounded by food. Kiko sounds a little bit like Paige; cooking is more of a science to her than anything else. Pepper already knows the names of the first seven restaurants she's going to open and the line of frozen health foods she's going to create.

I try to stop listening. I try to keep working. But I wonder what they heard in my video, because I didn't talk

about any of that stuff. Did they see the real me? A poor
kid who thinks he was born to cook because of the famous
father he didn't bother to mention? The kid who probably doesn't belong on the same chef-y planet as the rest of
them?

The final bell rings, and Chef Taylor shouts, "Knives
down, hands up!" There's still a handful of untouched
shrimp at my station, but I'm not allowed to fix it. During
a commercial break, we're asked to line up in front of the
stage while the chefs visit each of our stations and review
our prep.

The judges pace slowly, whispering to each other. I
sneak an occasional peek back to catch them checking over
a container of onions so closely they might as well be using
a magnifying glass or holding up shrimp for each other to
inspect.

The commercial must end, because all around the arena,
the red lights of the cameras flame back on. They track the
three chefs as they climb back onto the front stage to face
us. Chef Wormwood steps forward first.

"Our first challenge was mise en place." Her expression
is flat and serious. "Chef Taylor, who were your favorites?"

The Super Chef takes a step as well, so now he's even
with her. "Definitely Chef Kiko," he says. "The precision
of her knife cuts was unmatched."

Kiko straightens her shoulders with pride.

Last but not least, Chef Graca steps forward so the three chefs are even with each other on the stage. He waves at Kiko. "Congratulations! Please step to one side, Chef Tanaka." He glances up at the balconies and a smattering of applause rains down on us.

In traditional *Super Chef* fashion, Kiko takes two big sideways strides to her left, separating from the rest of us with a satisfied expression. She looks like she just got picked first for recess kickball.

"Anyone else?" Chef Wormwood asks the Super Chef.

"Most definitely. Points have to go to speed, too. Our fastest competitor was Chef Joey." Joey takes the cue to join Kiko. More scattered clapping, a few random cheers.

"These two contestants received the highest scores for this round." My gut feels empty as I realize they'll be the only two singled out.

"That means it's time to introduce you to our scoreboard!" the Super Chef cries, and the entire wall to our left lights up. There are five slots running down it. "From now until the last of our five challenges, this wall will be the lifeline for our competitors." New lights flash all around the empty slots, strobing and spinning. "Each episode can have only one winner."

Kiko and Joey breathe heavily with anticipation. "And tonight that winner is . . ." He pauses intentionally, just as he always does on *Super Chef*, causing the tension in the room to spike so high that if there were a skylight, it would probably shatter.

"Chef Kiko Tanaka!"

Kiko's name flashes brightly in the first slot of the scoreboard. To its right, a huge score of 50 lights up. She grins ear to ear. She raises her hand toward Joey for a high five, but he ignores her, his expression sour.

Chef Taylor either doesn't notice their exchange or doesn't care about it. "Each challenge will feature a prize. Normally, you'll know ahead of time what you're shooting for. Win the challenge, win the prize. Tonight, though, in this warm-up, we had to keep it a bit a surprise."

Earlier I'd gotten brief glimpses of the black-shirted helpers hanging around the edges of the arena, occasionally emerging to retrieve a dropped knife or wipe up a dangerous spill during the frantic challenge. One of those black-shirts approaches Kiko now, a box extended out in his hands. He reaches her and, after a hold-your-breath pause, lifts the top off. We see the insides on the big screen behind the Super Chef. Must be the same angle the viewers at home are getting.

Kiko sucks in a breath as the Super Chef officially puts words to what we're all looking at. "One Takamura Antoku chef knife!" he cries. "Perhaps you know them, Chef Kiko, as they're from Japan like you?"

Kiko nods, biting her lip. "This . . . it is the perfect

knife. All over Japan they are revered." She holds her hand close to her body, like she's afraid to reach out and touch it.

"All over the *world*, they're revered," the Super Chef says.

Kiko smiles, acknowledging his correction, and finally reaches out toward the box with a slightly trembling hand.

The crowd oohs and aahs. Joey drops his face into both hands. I'd be doing the same thing if I'd been that close to winning a knife like that. I've heard the brothers who make them put their heart and soul into every little detail of their products, all of it done by their family, nothing outsourced.

"Ah, he may have missed out on the prize, but young Chef Modestino wasn't far behind in the scoring," Chef Graca says. Hearing his name, Joey lifts his face out of his hands. "Let's see his second place score!" Joey's name slides in second with a score of 45. His despair fades into joy, and he pumps his fist so hard Kiko has to take a step away from him to avoid getting accidentally punched.

"The rest of you have some work to do to catch up after tonight," Chef Wormwood declares sternly, glaring at us with eyes as clear and stabbing as Mrs. Kadubowski on her best day. She glances over at the scoreboard again. "Let's see the complete results."

Bells ding and the rest of our scores light up the wall.

Kiko Tanaka	50
Joey Modestino	45
Pepper Carmichael	38
Bonifacio Agosto	35
Curtis Pith	34

As soon as my name shows up I glance at the Super Chef. Maybe it's my imagination, but it seems like he shakes his head slightly in disappointment. He raises his voice to announcement level. "Each challenge, this scoreboard will be updated with the latest results. At the end of the season, the young chef with the highest cumulative score will become . . ."

Now he looks up at the balcony, encouraging their participation, and all three chefs and the dozens of people watching shout in unison.

"The! Last! Super! Chef!"

For all the worrying from the media, the live arena crowd seems to have fully accepted the reality of this being the last season. They show how on board they are with the idea via their nearly deafening cheering. I hear all of it, but I don't see the people shouting and celebrating. All I see is the glowing 34 on that scoreboard wall.

All I see is the lowest score.

All I see is last place.

The cameras track the Super Chef and his two partners as they pace off the stage. Only when they're completely gone do the red recording lights fade. I've watched the show so many times I hear the closing music, see the credits rolling near the floor. But here in the actual arena there's no overlay of white names against a black background, and the only sounds are the orderly footfalls of the audience as they file out. The crowd laughs and smiles, as if what just happened was the normal-est of days at the office and not the most terrifying sixty minutes of our lives.

Kari the producer darts out a side door. She has clear-rimmed glasses that keep sliding down her nose as she half runs toward us. Those wild blond curls constantly threaten to escape the band of the slim headset, which so far seems permanently attached to her ear.

"Great job!" she cheers. "You guys are all naturals."

I'm pretty sure the rest of the Super Five are the same level of shocked as I am. Frozen in place, we stare straight ahead as her expression grows more serious. "Now. Your handlers are your go-tos for whatever you need while you're here." She points at a row of college-aged people, including Mel, standing off to the side. It seems each of the other contestants have their own "Mels," though I hadn't caught any names yet. "They'll come to me if they can't help with something. Please remember one of them will always be on duty upstairs. They're your overnight super-visors.

"Okay." Kari claps one hand against the back of her clipboard. "I bet you guys are super tired. Let's head up to your dorms."

Kari said "dorms," but the rooms we're taken to when we stomp up the stairs directly above Super Chef Arena aren't like any dorms I've ever seen. Not that I've seen a lot of dorms—or *any* dorms, actually—but I still feel like I understand enough about dorms to know *these are not dorms.*

The ceilings rise up so high my neck almost locks up when I try to see where they stop. The area we're standing in is cut neatly in half: one side a gourmet kitchen, the other a sparkling living room. We'd taken the elevator up to the fifty-fourth floor for the arena, so this must be floor fifty-five, accessible, as far as I can tell, only by stairs up from the studio below.

"Boys are that way," Kari says, pointing to a room on the left. "Girls on the other side. And that room." She points to another door in the back, closer to the girls' side. "Is where your assistant-handler will sleep each night."

This is different. Usually the regular *Super Chef* contestants get put up in a big house, and part of the drama is watching all the personal battles they have when they forget the cameras are recording their every move.

Then I remember: sometimes in an episode the Super Chef comes down to the arena as if he was waiting upstairs. "Isn't this the Super Chef's . . . ?"

Kari tucks her clipboard to her chest. "Chef Taylor originally built these quarters into Super Chef Arena for himself, yes, but as you're minors, we couldn't place you off site. So you'll stay here. There's a twenty-four-hour security staff downstairs." She glances up at shiny black cubes lodged into every corner of the ceiling. "And keep in mind, these cameras are always on."

"Where are our suitcases?" Pepper asks.

"In your rooms, of course. Sorry to take them from you and throw you to the wolves right off the plane like that." Kari barks out a nervous laugh. "It was the way Chef Taylor wanted to start things off. He is the boss, after all."

"Are our phones there, too?" Bonifacio asks.

Kari shakes her head. "No phones. As the rules warned you would happen, we took those downstairs for the duration of the competition. If there's an emergency, talk to the handler on call." She points at the back room again. "Or you can use that button"—now she gestures toward a glowing blue button that looks like a doorbell near the entry—"which will contact security downstairs. They *will* be here in *seconds*. And let me remind you: no internet here either."

"We can go to our bags, then? To our things?" Bonifacio wonders in a fearful tone. "Sí?"

"Sí, yes. Go ahead, unpack." Kari nods at the rooms to the right and left, girls and boys, then points to the kitchen and raises her voice as Bonifacio and Kiko are the first to head to the bedrooms. "When you're downstairs in the arena, you follow Chef's orders. But when you're in this space, you can do whatever you want. As far as meals go, the fridge is fully stocked. Chef Taylor figured you five were more than capable of cooking your own dinners. The on-duty handler will supervise and lend a hand as needed."

She starts to turn for the door, then seems to remember something. "Take note! Chef Wormwood will pay you a visit a little later to explain a bit more about the competition. So don't get too comfortable."

Once more Kari turns away, but again she gets only a step farther before whipping around. Each new announcement is made in a voice slightly louder than the last.

"Oh! And another thing. The handlers are *not* your servants. Please leave them alone unless you really need them. These folks are in college, graduate school." She nods toward the five of them, standing in a straight, attentive line. "They have quite a lot of studying to do while they're here interning."

Joey hears Bonifacio rummaging around the boys' side. The instructions and reminders apparently over, he races after him, shouting, "Dibs on the best bed!"

Pepper seems to realize he might have the right idea and hurries after Kiko into their room. I'm still standing in the huge common area, gazing around at the couch that looks more comfortable than any bed I've ever slept in, the gleaming kitchen, until finally my eyes fall onto the wall of windows leading out to a balcony I recognize. It's where a troubled Chef Taylor leaned at the end of season one, in turmoil over which of the two finalists should be declared the first champion. Outside now, just as they had that night, the New York City lights wink and blink and flash, as if the skyscrapers are alive and talking to each other.

From the corner of my eye, I catch producer Kari

clicking a button on a black remote. Automatic blinds start to descend over the tall windows, slowly cutting out the city lights. She holds the remote in the air, showing it to me. "This controls a lot of stuff around here." She makes sure I see her placing it on an end table. "You guys'll figure it out, I'm sure."

The hum of the motor fills the room. It seems to give Kari time to remember yet another item. "Everybody, listen up! One more thing. Some areas around here are off limits and locked. That balcony, for example." She locks eyes with me and I nod. "We can't have any accidents up here. Please be careful."

Mel paces over to the sliding-glass door and gives it a hard tug, confirming it doesn't budge. Meanwhile Kari inhales, and, still speaking loudly, finishes up. "Okay, Chefs, clear eyes, deep breaths. We're glad you made it this far. Mel here has the first shift."

While Kari checks her clipboard one last time, each of the handlers finds and hugs their assigned chef. Like Mel and me, they must have traveled here together and gotten to know each other on the plane. During our flight, he asked me a few questions about my mom and sister, any allergies I had, what kinds of foods I liked and disliked. "Although I think I got the full list of both from your mom," he joked.

Now he walks toward me again. I'm still staring at the blinds covering the windows. I think I might be in a little bit of shock.

"You okay, Curtis?" Mel asks.

I face him and nod, but I still can't find my voice.

His smile widens. "You had the blue suitcase, right? Spider-Man?"

I nod again.

He cuts his eyes toward the room that Bonifacio and Joey ran into, then tilts his head. "It's in there. Parked it myself."

From somewhere in their rooms, I can hear the rest of the Super Five crying out excitement over whatever they're finding. Maybe this is what camp is like: kids arriving to a new place, making interesting discoveries about this short-term home away from home, hours away from hovering parents. I have no idea; the Pith family could never afford camp.

Mel's right. I should check out my room, empty my suitcase. Mom warned me to do it quick so everything inside didn't wrinkle. When I'm almost to the door, I hear a whisper.

"Good luck, kiddo," Mel says.

At least I think it's him. When I turn around, though, he's gone.

• • •

The ceilings in the bedroom are just as tall as the ones in the common room were. Which means there's plenty of space for Joey to be jumping up and down on the top bunk of a bunk bed near the only window, another floor-to-ceiling wall of glass filled with the glow of the city.

"This view is completely amazing!" he cries.

Bonifacio is carefully emptying his suitcase on the bottom bunk, fixing any wrinkled shirts in his collection. Because that's what his shirts look like, a collection. Every one is a button-down with a slightly different pattern, as if he's spent a bunch of time hunting down one of each. It's *Magic: The Gathering*, the nerdy shirt edition.

"Can you see the Statue of Liberty?" I ask hopefully. I remember the Super Chef could see it from the balcony and this window is on the same side.

Joey jumps high one last time, turning to face me in the process. His leaping slows to small hops, then stops completely. "Yep. Snooze you lose." In a smooth motion, he drops down to his butt on the top bunk, bounces off it, and descends to the floor, barely missing kicking his bunkmate in the butt as his wild feet swing down.

Bonifacio lurches forward when Joey slaps his back. "We've got the bunks. Mo and Bo. Bo and Joe. The Oh-sters. Oh no? Oh yeah."

"Mo for Modestino?" Bo, rubbing his shoulder blade, asks him.

"That's what they call me back home," Joey confirms. He makes finger guns at Bo, then drops his thumbs like hammers. "Don't wear it out."

I lift my suitcase onto my bed, hearing Joey approach across the room behind me. "Your bed's closer to the bathroom, at least," he says in my ear. "Maybe keep you from peeing your pants like you did downstairs."

I do my best to ignore him while I struggle with my bag. It's pretty old, and it takes me a couple tries to get the handle to collapse, and even more effort to work the zipper loose.

"Are you not going to get your clothes, too?" Bo asks Joey.

"Someday." Joey's—Mo's—ladder creaks, and when I turn around he's returned to his side of the room, climbing back up to the top bunk. "Right now I'm gonna enjoy the sweet smell of victory. And this awesome view."

"I seem to remember the name at the top of that scoreboard being Kiko's, not yours," I say through clenched teeth.

Joey only sniffs deep through his nostrils, enjoying the scent of whatever his imagined victory smells like. "In time she too will fall. All of you will." He leans over the edge of the bunk. "Sorry, Bo. We can be total buds until then. But, you know, it *is* a contest."

I plop down on my bed. I'm only seeing three things

right now: my name lit up bright at the bottom of that arena wall, Joey's smug smile, and the Super Chef shaking his head slightly when my last place standing was revealed. For a second I tell myself it doesn't matter what he thinks. The fact he's my father is completely irrelevant to what I'm here for. But the Super Chef is something else, too. The main judge. So I guess I kinda do have to care about his opinion.

Not my father. Yes my judge. I've only been here one night and I already see how hard it's going to be to keep them separated.

"Attention! Line up!" A strong, deep, and female voice calls out from the common room. Chef Wormwood's command freezes me in place until she repeats it even louder. "Line up!"

Joey scrambles down his ladder. I burst up off my bed. He bumps me as he rushes to be the first one out of our room. I feel Bo close behind me as I follow, and see Pepper and Kiko emerge out from the other side at the same time. Chef Wormwood waits for us in the middle of the common room, still in her chef's jacket, her hands on her hips. Her expression is flat and stern.

We've all seen *Super Chef* enough to know the drill. We line up directly in front of her so that Joey, who got there first and took the center spot, is straight across from Chef Wormwood.

Mel peeks out of his door, sees Wormwood, and steps out. He leans against the wall, relaxed, watching the commotion with a smirk on his face. But when Wormwood shoots a glance at him, he snaps to attention, his arms glued to his sides. His lips flatten into a tight line.

Returning her gaze to us, Wormwood shakes her head while we organize ourselves, swapping spots with each other before shuffling to make sure our line is perfectly straight.

When we finally stop moving, she releases a disappointed puff of air. "Tell me just one thing. Are you guys good at *anything*?"

"I received a perfect score," Kiko protests. "My prep was—"

Chef Wormwood slaps a hand onto her forehead. "Perfect? Good Lord, I hope you don't think *that* was perfect. That would mean we have more work to do than I thought. Thank goodness we started with a warm-up."

"So we were not on the television?" Bo asks. He sounds relieved. He glances around at the rest of us, giving us all the good news he thinks he just heard. "It was only practice."

But Wormwood snorts. "I'm sorry, Mr. Agosto, that was most certainly *not* practice. At least, it wasn't supposed to be. And yes, from now on, you should assume you're *always* on television, including tonight."

The relief that had briefly crossed Bo's face fades into mild horror.

"Understand what I mean by 'warm-up.' I'm saying we were warming you up for the rest of the challenges. I'm saying you're heading for a lot more stress than a little bit of mise en place creates. I'm saying those of you who did well tonight—or *think* you did well, anyway—better not get too comfortable. Perfect scores are going to be a lot harder to come by going forward. And I am saying"—she paces to the end of the line, stopping in front of Pepper—"that if you want to win this competition, we better not see any more shells and veins on shrimp."

Pepper opens her mouth to respond but seems to think better of it. She keeps her face turned up, though, refusing to blink as she stares back into Wormwood's stern eyes. I never noticed how pasty Chef Wormwood is, like a person who's never been outside before, but it's super clear inches away from Pepper's dark skin.

Their mini-stalemate feels like it lasts forever, until finally the sous chef backs away, returning to the center position a few feet in front of Joey. "You understand the excellence we expect here, correct? You're supposed to be representing the future." She throws her head back, and what she says next feels like she must be quoting the Super Chef. "'A shining sign of what's to come.'" Looking down again, she continues. "If you think Chef Taylor is going to—"

"When do we meet him, by the way?" Pepper interrupts.

"Yeah, why are you here instead of him?" Joey adds.

Chef Wormwood glowers at them both. She tucks her
hands behind her back and straightens her shoulders. "I am
here because Chef asked me to be here. My job tonight is
to clue you in on what happens next." She pauses, waiting
to see if any of us will mention the Super Chef again, but
no one does. "So let's get to it, then, shall we?"

She starts to pace again. "Since each episode of the
show will air live, we want to spend as much time cooking as possible, so what I'm about to tell you will not be
explained again on set. I suggest listening closely." She
stops and looks down her nose at us. I try my hardest not
to fidget under the intensity of her gaze.

"Chef Taylor is purposefully keeping contact with you
at a minimum. He doesn't want his final selection to be
swayed by personal relationships."

What could be more personal than one of the Super
Five being your own son?

"We're not going to meet him?" I ask, wondering why
my voice sounds so concerned.

"Oh, you'll meet him." Chef Wormwood sends her
knowing grin toward me. "During the competition, each
of you will spend a single evening in a one-on-one session
with the Super Chef. He'll take you to dinner at one of his

favorite restaurants. You'll have a 'heart-to-heart' about your goals and dreams. Your vision for your own future, maybe. Outside of the raw scores of the challenges, this dinner will be your only opportunity to impress upon him why you should be the winner of *The Last Super Chef*. Competition points *will* be on the line."

A heart-to-heart? Why would we need that? *Super Chef* competitions have always been about food. I came here to cook. But I can see that Wormwood isn't kidding. So if this "Evening with the Super Chef" has to happen— and I'm not ready yet to surrender the possibility I might be able to get out of it somehow—then I have to keep it focused. Cooking talk only. No distractions.

"These meetings . . . they will also be on TV?" Bo asks. For a dude who submitted a whole video to be in a contest he knew would be on television, he seems awfully nervous to . . . be on television.

Still, now I can see Bo's concern, even feel an echo of it in my own suddenly somersaulting gut. Will I get to talk to the Super Chef before this evening? Or will my first conversation with my father happen in front of a world-wide TV audience?

"Yes, Mr. Agosto," Wormwood answers impatiently. "TV. The contest you entered is part of a television pro-gram."

"But if he finished last," Joey starts, saving Bo from

Wormwood's criticism. I look up to find him pointing at me. "Why's he still here? Aren't we kicking off one per episode like regular *Super Chef*?"

I gulp. So he rescues Bo only to throw me to the wolves? Definitely not cool.

"I'm in the middle of explaining that," Chef Wormwood says. "May I continue?"

Joey zips it and nods.

"All of you will go through this entire contest to its completion. Each episode will have its own score, and those scores will be added to your cumulative total. No one will get eliminated—*kicked off*, as you say—until the very end, when we pick a single winner. That means each of you is here for the long haul. I hope you're all prepared for that."

"Oh, I'm ready," Joey says, rubbing his hands together.

"I can't wait to meet the Super Chef," Pepper agrees.

"Tonight was your one and only warm-up challenge, a fifty point maximum episode. During all the other episodes, you will be able to earn a maximum of one hundred points toward your total."

"It's like the House Cup," Kiko suggests.

"Yeah, right. Total Harry Potter vibe," Joey agrees. He launches a fist straight up in the air. "Slytherin for the win!"

"I'm a Hufflepuff!" Bo announces proudly.

"Of course you are, bud," Joey says, rubbing one of Bo's shoulders.

"Gryffindor," Pepper chimes in. She looks to her right, at Kiko.

"Ravenclaw," Kiko answers, shrugging a little.

"One of each! What are the odds?" Joey says. He looks around Bo at me again. "You're the tiebreaker, Pith. Which house are you?"

"I—I don't know," I answer.

"You never did one of those quizzes? They take like two minutes on your phone."

"I, um, I don't have a smartphone."

Everyone is quiet for moments that seem to stretch out forever, until Wormwood finally breaks the awkward silence.

She glances at one of the ceiling cameras. "I swear, Lucas. Children. On *Super Chef.*" Shaking her head, she returns her attention to us. "It is not the House Cup," she says, uttering "House" and "Cup" like the very words are disgusting. "This is far more important than Harry Potter." With that, she turns and grabs a stack of printed sheets off the kitchen island. "This is *The Last Super Chef,*" she finishes, waving the pages in our direction.

"Chef Taylor believes there are certain keys to becoming and staying a great chef." Starting with Pepper, she paces down our line, distributing one sheet to each of us.

"Like you, there are five such skills. And so . . . besides tonight's warm-up, there will be five challenges, each one focusing on one of these qualities. After that, we'll have a final cook-off, *The Last Super Chef* finale. That'll be on Thanksgiving Day, as you've no doubt already heard."

"Knife work!" Joey shouts. "Tonight's key was knife work!"

"Again . . . tonight was *not* one of the five challenge episodes," Chef Wormwood says. "I did recommend listening carefully, Mr. Modestino."

"Entrepreneurship must be one!" Pepper shouts. "You gotta be an entrepreneur to—"

"I *also* suggest you refrain from shouting out future guesses. Part of each episode's score will be how closely you determine that night's theme. Fifty points for your performance, fifty points for the theme. All you're doing is giving your competition ideas, Ms. Carmichael."

The page Wormwood hands out is a complete schedule for the competition. I'm afraid to be caught not paying attention, so I only give it a quick glance, but it looks like the five challenges happen on every other day. The remaining, in-between days, and the weekends, too, all read simply, "OPEN/TRAINING."

The challenge days are numbered: Challenge #1, Challenge #2, and so on. No indication of the themes, of course, but the prizes are listed clearly. It's easy to see how they get bigger and bigger, too, right up until the last one, spending a week learning with Taylor in the kitchens of one of his most famous restaurants.

That last challenge, #5, happens the Monday before Thanksgiving. Then there's a two-day break before the holiday. That entry has a big, red GRAND FINALE slanted across it. I scan the prizes again, trying to recall every article I've ever read about the Super Chef, every interview I've ever watched. Has he given out such a list? His traits for being a great chef? I don't remember one.

Kiko's the first one to look up from the page. "No hints for the themes?" she asks with a wry smile, hope in her voice.

Wormwood glances at the schedule in her own hand, then meets Kiko's eyes. "I'd pay close attention to the prizes if I were you," she surprisingly offers. "There's more to them than might first meet the eye." She actually winks back at Kiko.

Everyone goes back to frantically reviewing the list of prizes. It's such an odd mishmash—a trip to Paris, an apprenticeship with a renowned pastry chef, a fancy stove, basketball tickets. My mind spins, and I hope everyone else's does the same, because I see no pattern at all.

Wormwood raises her voice again, forcing us to pull our attention off the schedules. "While you're competing, while you're doing the absolute *best* work you can do, make sure to be thinking about the theme. You'll have to submit your guess when the cooking is over. Do consider carefully. Some themes will be far more obvious than others. Now, questions?"

"What are these open days?" Pepper asks.

Wormwood shrugs. "We have some additional plans, but we're still finalizing the details. This all came together really fast. Basically these days will give you a chance to have the supervised calls with your families, catch up on your homework, and let you rest up before your one-on-ones with Lucas . . . Chef Taylor in the evenings. Among other things."

"Preparation! Prep! That was tonight's theme," Joey blurts.

"There was no theme tonight," Kiko moans. "She has already told us that."

"Any *other* questions?" Wormwood asks more harshly.

"May I call my mother?" Bo's request comes in such a low voice I almost don't hear it.

"Like I said, you'll get opportunities for supervised calls with your families on some of the open days." Wormwood narrows her eyes at us. "During these calls, there will be absolutely no discussion about the details of the competition. No unauthorized outside information should reach your ears at all. Any violation of this will result in your immediate ejection from this competition." She relaxes her posture. "Now, anything else?"

None of us speaks this time.

"Good night, then," Chef Wormwood says. "Make yourselves some dinner. I'm thinking you'll need the energy come tomorrow." She marches straight for the door without looking back, and slams it shut once she's through.

"Isn't she supposed to be the nice one?" Joey asks after a beat of silence.

"That's what I always thought," I agree. On the show, the Super Chef is usually first to show his temper, and it's typically level-headed Chef Wormwood who calms him down.

"So what now?" Kiko asks.

"What else?" Pepper says. She darts out of line and hurries toward the girls' side, calling over her shoulder when she's almost there. "Family meal."

THE LAST SUPER CHEF
COMPETITION SCHEDULE

Tuesday, November 12—Arrival—Mise en place warm-up

Prize: One Takamura santoku knife

Wednesday, November 13—OPEN/TRAINING

Thursday, November 14—*Challenge #1*

Prize: Two tickets to NBA All-Star Weekend

Friday, November 15—OPEN/TRAINING—
Evening with the Super Chef #1

Saturday, November 16—OPEN/TRAINING

Sunday, November 17—OPEN/TRAINING—
Evening with the Super Chef #2

Monday, November 18—*Challenge #2*

Prize: Family trip to Paris and the Louvre

Tuesday, November 19—OPEN/TRAINING—
Evening with the Super Chef #3

Wednesday, November 20—*Challenge #3*

Prize: Custom-crafted Molteni stove

Thursday, November 21—OPEN/TRAINING—
Evening with the Super Chef #4

Friday, November 22—*Challenge #4*

Prize: Apprenticeship with renowned pastry chef Madeline Dalibard, focusing on her specialty: layered pastries and cakes

Saturday, November 23—OPEN/TRAINING

Sunday, November 24—OPEN/TRAINING—
Evening with the Super Chef #5
Monday, November 25—*Challenge #5*
Prize: One week with the Super Chef in Taylor
House, his signature family-style restaurant in New
York City, working with him every night in its
kitchens
Tuesday, November 26—OPEN/TRAINING
Wednesday, November 27—OPEN/TRAINING
Thursday, November 28—THANKSGIVING—
The Last Super Chef GRAND FINALE

★Tentative schedule; subject to change

"It is *not* the House Cup," Joey says. He's wearing his sweatshirt backward, so it looks a little like a chef's coat, and his expression is eerily similar to Chef Wormwood's when she was standing right in front of us less than an hour ago.

"Stop it!" Pepper says. Mid-laugh, she risks a glance up at the ceiling cameras.

"Eyes on your work," Mel warns her.

Pepper jumps. "Party pooper," she says as her smile fades. She makes a show of giving her jambalaya another stir.

The fridge was so well stocked, we could've made anything, but when she came running out of her room with a bag of the Cajun spices she sells on pepperspicesuptheworld.com, we all agreed Pepper should make the first dinner. Now she waves her wooden spoon in Joey's direction. "But Mel is right. It's gonna be your fault if this burns, Joey. Let me concentrate."

In the short time he's been the only adult here with us, Mel's become a sort of kitchen chameleon—standing off to one side, arms folded across his chest, watchful eagle eyes seeming to catch every move we make. But it's weird, like you only notice him if you look straight at him. As soon as I start to laugh at another of Joey's jokes, I somehow forget Mel is there, as if he's found some new way to blend into the wall behind him.

Pepper uses a fresh spoon to taste her dinner. From stools on the other side of the kitchen island bar, Kiko, Bo, and I watch her nod, apparently pleased with the flavor. Joey's standing near the fridge, his temporary stage. He shakes his finger at us, still imitating Wormwood in a gruff, female voice that's not at all complimentary. "This is more *important* than Harry Potter."

His impersonation really is spot on. Next to me, Bo is suppressing a laugh as he sticks his index finger into the open bag, then licks the dust that comes back. Pepper used only half the package. She slid the rest toward us and challenged the group to name the ingredients. "Cayenne and onion powder are the most obvious," she said. "So you get those free because they're too easy. First one wrong has to make dessert."

"Paprika," Bo says after a few seconds of licking his lips.

Pepper spins around and thrusts her wooden spoon straight in his direction. Behind her, the jambalaya starts to hiss. "Come on, you can do better than that." She smacks her forehead, then issues her own imitation of Wormwood. "Good Lord!"

Joey laughs so hard he pig-snorts.

"No paprika?" Bo sounds traumatized.

Pepper straightens. "Actually, no, there's totally paprika. I'm just messin' with ya. Next!" She turns back to the stove and stirs some more.

Bo pushes the plastic bag toward me. I inspect the label first. At the very top it reads "Pepper Spices Up the World" and underneath, the name of this particular mix, "Spice Jam . . . balaya." A cartoon basketball player that looks a little bit like Michael Jordan flies through the air, as if he's about to slam-dunk. It's clearly a play on that ancient basketball movie costarring Bugs Bunny, *Space Jam*.

I turn the package over. There's no ingredients list. Then I wonder why I did that. Am I so intimidated I feel the need to cheat?

"How many of these do you have?" I ask as I dip my finger in the same way Bo did.

Pepper stays focused on her work, answering me without

looking back. "As of now? Seventeen. But I'm working on number eighteen, 'Lemon and Pepper and Everything Better.' That's the first one that'll have my face on the label. 'Cause, you know"—she dips her knees in a little curtsy move—"pepper. It's mostly for chicken dishes. First few tries have been too lemony." She glances back, meeting my eyes, waiting, I guess, for my reaction.

"How are you in business already?" Joey asks. "I can't even stay on top of my homework half the time."

"It's not that hard," Pepper answers almost immediately, puffing her chest out slightly. But something about the way her eyes dart toward her feet makes me think her words aren't completely true.

I don't say anything, though. I might be reading her wrong, and besides I'm too focused on not messing up in her spice contest. Bo already got his guess right. I can't miss on mine.

I flick my tongue against the roof of my mouth, making sure the flavor of the spices hits all my taste bud zones. Bitter on the back, sour and salty on the sides, sweet on the tip. "Thyme?" I ask.

"Very nice, Pith," Pepper says. "You got some game after all, don't you?" She raises her spoon high over her head. "Next!"

I start to slide the spice bag toward Kiko, but Joey shouts, "Gimme that!" and rushes between us, snagging it from my grip. A little pile of spice shakes out onto the countertop with his sudden movement. He marches away, back toward the fridge, taking a pinch out of the bag and tossing it into the back of his mouth.

Kiko narrows her eyes at Joey. She sighs. "I really cannot believe the chef would say *anything* is more important than Harry Potter."

Pepper rounds on her. "But it is more important. This is *The Last Super Chef.* There'll never be another one. Whoever comes out on top will be the most famous winner ever. That's why you're here, right? Win the money? Have everyone recognize you?"

Kiko shrugs. "I like the science of cooking. You experiment with the laws and rules people have figured out before you. Sometimes your own experiments make new laws and better rules for the next cooks. The work you do is part of a line that started here." She dips her finger into the pile of spices Joey left behind. "And goes all the way into the future." She runs the same finger along the counter as far as her arm will reach, pulling the spices along. They make a meandering trail, like a timeline.

"Also two hundred and fifty K is a fat stack of cash," Joey says.

Pepper frowns, almost like the money isn't what's important to her. She gazes hard at Kiko. "Okay, seriously, though. Answer the question."

A silence descends over the kitchen as Pepper and Kiko stare each other down. It lasts for only a few seconds before Mel speaks up again. "Pepper. I said eyes on the food. Or else I take over and you guys have to eat my dinner."

Pepper jumps again. She glowers at chameleon-Mel. "What are you, some kind of ninja?"

Mel only stares back, unmoving. I think about his threat and wonder if he's a good cook. I mean, he's a culinary student, right? So I guess he must be.

Doesn't matter, because his warning gives Kiko a chance to respond to Pepper. "I am here because I want to see if I could win, for sure. But I also have other things I wish to do, too, like be the first astronaut on Mars. Or maybe invent a new programming language."

For a second I imagine the conversation Kiko and Paige would have, and I almost shiver because I picture someone's head exploding. And it's definitely mine.

"But you can't," Pepper says. She sounds a little angry all of a sudden. I can tell she wants to turn around to face Kiko again, but she peeks at the glaring Mel first and decides against it. She yells her protest at the backsplash in front of her instead. "You can't be an astronaut or computer nerd or whatever, not if you win. If you win, you have to take advantage of it. Think about the opportunities! Chef Taylor's not going to give the big prize to someone who's not in all the way."

"Two hundred and fifty thousand big prizes," Joey mutters, echoing my thoughts as he continues swishing spice around his palate. Suddenly his eyes light up, and he shouts, "Oregano! There's oregano in here!"

"Correct!" Pepper confirms. "Next!"

Kiko spins off her stool and charges Joey. She snatches the bag from him and does the same tip-of-finger test. She stops, stands still, and stares at the ceiling while she licks her lips.

Bo leans toward me. "I did not taste the thyme," he confesses in a whisper.

I shrug at him. "Got lucky, I guess."

"You were not so lucky in the mise en place. Neither of us were."

"I was a little distracted." I can't tell him how much that video threw me for a loop, those shots of Pettynose's kitchen flashing away on that huge screen. I can't tell him how much I've been thinking about Paige and Mom since then, what kind of trouble I've gotten them into. I can't even call them to find out if I should worry or not. None of us have phones. We have no idea when the first supervised calls will come. Plus, Joey ran around checking the entire dorm as soon as Wormwood left, looking for some way onto the internet, but there was nothing. Not that the eviction of the Pith family would make CNN or anything.

Which means I better find a way to stop worrying about

my family, at least until I can find out if there's actually something to worry about. I definitely can't let myself get distracted during a challenge again, because I can already see that Distracted Curtis equals Last Place Curtis. And deep down, I know it's not just Mom and Paige drawing my attention away, either, so I also quickly remind myself again: that's not my father up there on the stage, at least not during this contest. It's just Lucas Taylor, the Super Chef. Just another judge I have to make sure sees how good a cook I am.

"Garlic powder," Kiko says sternly, like all of a sudden she's more focused on winning than before, which kind of scares me, because she's way ahead already.

Pepper doesn't reward Kiko's correct guess with any praise. All she says is "Next!"

So everyone guessed at least one ingredient correctly. I don't know a single person back home who could've done that, not even Paige. She helps me, sure, but she's not a cook in her heart, and her taste buds aren't that impressive. One time she complained I put too many jalapeños in the guacamole when I'd clearly used serranos.

These kids, though, they know all the same things I do. More, even.

Kiko walks the bag back to Bo for the second round. "How many ingredients total?" he asks Pepper as he accepts it.

Pepper turns off the burner, pulls on a potholder, and swings the pan of jambalaya toward the island. She starts to plate her meal on five clean white dishes. "You tell me." Then she yells, "Service!" as Bo dips his finger into the bag again.

While Bo stares down into the bag like he'll find the answers in there, Joey, Kiko, and I come around and grab Pepper's dinner. Together we walk the plates to the big table.

Behind us, silverware clinks as Pepper pulls a drawer open. "Bo," she says, gesturing over her shoulder with her chin. "Napkins? And the water?"

Bo stands up. He's still lost in thought as he reaches toward the napkin holder, adding a pile to the tray where the water glasses Pepper already poured out are waiting. "Sage?" he asks her.

Pepper reaches the table and makes a big buzzing noise. "Not bad, but I'm afraid I'm not a huge sage fan. You, sir, have the honor of making dessert."

"Flan! Flan! Flan!" Joey cries.

"I am not making flan," Bo says.

"Don't you know how?" Joey asks. "Aren't you from Mexico?"

Bo doesn't reply, instead passing the water and napkins out. His shoulders slump a little as he does it. I can tell he's disappointed to be on the bottom again.

Pepper raises her water glass in the air. The rest of us imitate her. I've never done a toast with anyone but Paige and Mom before.

"To our first family meal," Pepper says.

"Such an important step for any brigade," Mel agrees earnestly from back at the kitchen island, his glass raised too. This time, at the table, we *all* jump.

Pepper almost spits out her water. "Come on, man," she complains, wiping a sleeve across her mouth. "You have got to give us permission to put a cowbell around your neck or something."

The next morning I wake up still thinking about Pepper's amazing jambalaya, which no lie was the best Cajun dish I've ever had. As good as it was, though, dessert might've been even better.

Bo didn't try to dodge his guess-the-spice penalty. He dove into the fridge after dinner, finding some berries, which he washed and spread out in a pan. Followed by heavy cream, vanilla, and sugar, beaten together to make a quick Chantilly cream. He grabbed some packaged tortillas next, cut them into smaller rounds, and shaped them into cups inside a muffin pan.

"This is *not* flan," Joey complained as Bo walked around the table serving his curvy, crispy tortilla cups, fresh out of the oven and filled with berries covered in cream.

Then Joey tasted Bo's dessert. We *all* tasted it. "Are these berries roasted? Is that what you were doing over there?"

"And what do you call these cups?" Kiko asked, chipping at the edge of the tortilla cup with her spoon to test the consistency.

"Yes, roasted. And those are *buñuelos*. Not authentic, of course, only from a package."

I didn't think I was still hungry, but I devoured every crumb of what Bo put in front of me. We all did. Then, finally, came our first sleep in our new surroundings. And now, morning.

My eyes adjust to the lingering darkness here on the boys' side of the dorm. I roll until I'm facing the bunk bed. My roommates, Joey and Bo, are both still sleeping. I listen to their rhythmic breathing for a few seconds, thinking about what we learned yesterday.

I flick on the bedside lamp. The schedule Wormwood handed out is next to it. I slide it toward me and hold it over my head, reading with my arms out straight.

Looks like the "Evenings with the Super Chef" are scheduled mostly at the end of the open/training days between the challenges, though the sheet doesn't specify which of us meets with Chef Taylor on which nights.

And whichever night mine happens, what will the Super Chef ask me? My blood freezes thinking about the possibilities. So much so that I slap the schedule back down on the nightstand, facedown. It makes more noise than I intended, and across the room, Bo stirs, but he doesn't wake up.

My smallest opponent struck me as so timid at first, but then last night he made the most incredible dessert in such a short time. I can't be judging any of these books by their covers. It's almost like none of them have any weaknesses.

Joey rolls now, too, facing my direction. Even though he's across the room, I rush to flip my light off and turn away, hiding under my comforter.

That's when I hear Pepper scream out in the common room.

I jump out of bed and race for the door. When I rub the sleep out of my eyes and find her, though, Pepper isn't in pain like it sounded. She wears a huge smile as she pulls down a black-and-white chef's jacket from a clothing rack someone's rolled in to the center of our common room. She's holding it up to herself, checking the fit, as I skid to a stop a few feet from her.

"Look!" she cries. "They have our names on them!"

Kiko, Bo, and Joey skitter across the floor in socked feet, narrowly avoiding sliding into the rack in a heap. Their shocked expressions match mine. "What's wrong?" Kiko asks Pepper.

"Wrong?" Pepper says as she shrugs into the jacket and starts to button it up. "Nothing's wrong. Not with me. Not with"—she puffs her chest up and thrusts the left side out so we can clearly read the cursive, stitched name on her jacket—"Chef Pepper Carmichael."

"Wicked!" Joey says, tearing through the jackets, searching for his.

"I was hoping we would not have to use the aprons anymore," Bo says. "I do not like cooking in an apron." He, Kiko, and I sort out the remaining three coats. I realize I've grabbed Kiko's jacket at the same time she sees she has mine. We trade. The room is full of rustling as all five of us pull them on and button them up and scrunch our necks to admire our stitched names.

"Well, look what I found," comes an accented voice near the door. It's Chef Graca, wearing the identical style coat we are. The sous chef shifts his gaze downward, in the direction of Bo, who's still shifting his shoulders, making sure of the fit. "It's a little chef!"

I step around the rack. "Wait, there's two of them!" Graca cries. "Two little chefs."

"Looking sharp," Mel agrees from the doorway to his room. The duffel thrown over his shoulder tells me that he's already packed his things up, clearing out the handler room for our next babysitter. My disappointment must show on my face, because when we lock eyes, he sends me his trademark wink.

"It is these jackets . . . they fit so perfect," Bo says as he fidgets some more. For the first time, I notice his isn't long on him at all. Last night his apron practically touched the floor. My jacket is the exact right size, too. They must've figured out our measurements somehow; these are obviously custom-made. Maybe that's why we didn't get them before the first episode.

But there were no rulers or elderly tailors with straight pins in their mouths like I've seen in the movies, so how did they . . . ? I glance briefly up at one of the cameras in the ceiling, wondering how closely they're watching us. And who's doing the watching.

Eventually the rest of the Super Five finish buttoning our jackets. We line up for Chef Graca. "There's more than two!" he says, losing none of his enthusiasm. "There's one, two, three, four, five little chefs! Aren't you all fantastic?"

I'm guessing everyone else is as focused as I am on trying to avoid shuffling as much as we did for Wormwood.

"What is this? Picture day?" he asks, then gives us a big belly laugh. "Take it easy. You're the Super Five." I breathe out, relaxing my posture, and I feel Bo do the same on one side of me, Joey on the other. "Chef has decided you need some extra work on a few things before we get to the next challenge. So make yourselves some breakfast, get dressed and ready, and meet us downstairs in the arena. You have one hour." He taps the face of his watch.

"Yes, Chef!" we all shout together.

Graca heads for the door, turning to take one last look back at us when he reaches it. "I tell you what, you're all looking super."

We glance around at each other. We do look super, every single one of us. Grins are shared all around, and I can tell by the way everyone keeps looking at their sleeves that I wasn't the only one who dreamed of someday wearing a *Super Chef* jacket just like this one.

The door shuts. Graca is gone. And soon, so are our smiles. Because we might all look super now, but by the time this is all over, only one of us is actually going to *be* super, and we all know it.

"Have you seen these prizes?" Joey asks during breakfast. He's eating while standing at the island, his schedule spread out flat in front of him. "NBA All-Star Weekend? Man!"

I have to say he's right, the prizes, while in one way random, are also pretty cool. In fact, some might be almost too awesome, at least for me—it's hard to image the Pith family traipsing around France, harder still to figure out what we'd do with an expensive (meaning, huge) custom-crafted stove in our tiny apartment. But then again, maybe by the time it was shipped our way we'd already be living in the ginormous house I'm planning to buy.

"Do you think they could make any size for the

Molteni?" Bo asks. "My mother's kitchen is one big room at the back of the house. If I could put it right in the middle, it would be—"

"These trips are way, way better," Pepper interrupts, running her finger down her own copy of the schedule. "Especially Paris. What if I went global?" She stares up, her gears clearly spinning. "I could bring all my flavors, place them in French stores, maybe get a local spot on TV. Pepper Spices Up the World will be everywhere."

"No, Paris would be special because of the Louvre," Kiko says. "All that art and history in one place."

As they start up a debate on the best way to spend the grand prize money, from opening restaurants and taquerias to Super Bowl commercials featuring spice mascots, my eyes travel to the last prize, a week with the Super Chef in one of his most famous restaurants. So much time with him alone. I can't help but think of the stuff he could teach me—new techniques, skill refinements—but also . . . all the questions I could ask him. Like, why he left us, why he—

Suddenly, the door opens and Mel hurries through the dorm on his way to the handler's room in back. "Better get moving!" he calls out to us over his shoulder.

We all jump again.

"More cowbell!" Pepper shouts, pointing at him accusingly.

Mel's in too much of a hurry to be amused. "I'm serious. They're already waiting for you guys."

Minutes later, Mel leads us down the stairs toward a giant security guard dressed all in black except for the "STAFF" written in big white letters on the front of his shirt. The guard's standing silent next to producer Kari, his tree-trunk arms folded across his chest.

"Perfect! Perfect! Perfect!" Kari squeals as she appraises us, the newly jacketed chefs coming down toward her. She isn't wearing her headset, and a glance into the arena shows no cameras are waiting for us, either.

"We're not on TV today?" Pepper asks. We'd wanted to come down as a group but had to wait for her to make sure her every curl in the puff of her ponytail was tucked away successfully. As much hair as she has, it took a while.

"No TV," Kari confirms. "But let's have a little practice anyway."

She lines us up and shows us how to wait for our cue to enter the arena. We learn how to walk in a straight line, matching each other's footfalls. Or, at least, try to learn. At first we're all left feet. We mess up three times in a row—Joey flat-tiring my sneaker, Bo getting confused and stopping so suddenly Kiko nearly runs him over, Pepper halting in front of her sink instead of the burners so the faucet blocks her face—before we finally start getting it right.

We complete the final run-through to find Chefs Wormwood and Graca standing on the stage as we reenter the arena. We land back at our stations, same spots, three of us in the first row, Joey and Bo behind in the second. There's a black box right in front of each of us that wasn't there before. The lids are all closed. The Super Chef is nowhere in sight.

"Mise en place," Chef Wormwood announces when we settle into position. "I've talked to Chef Taylor, and he agrees this group needs a little remedial work on that particular topic." She rolls her eyes. "In my opinion a *lot* of remedial work."

Wormwood seems to notice Chef Graca looking a little surprised, but she ignores it, only raising her voice even louder. "You will find at your stations the same ingredients you worked with last night. We better see some improvement today," she warns us before pacing toward one side of the stage, where three steps allow her to descend to our level. "We stay here until we get this right. Trust me, I've got all day."

I open the box in front of me. There they are—the artichokes and onions, the shrimp and the clams. The instruction to start is given. Time begins to tick away. I get to work.

With no Pettynose video playing this time, I'm more focused on each step. Dicing onions, peeling and deveining shrimp, prepping artichokes. I work with my head down, not even checking the clock once. When I get to the clams, I think about how ridiculous it is to be asking us to shuck them. Most kids wouldn't know where to start, let alone finish in time.

Every so often one of the two sous chefs comes around to help us. Graca shows me I'm not holding my knife quite right. Wormwood explains how to tell when I've exerted just the right amount of pressure to pry a clam open. By the time the hour ends, I've actually completed everything. Surveying my station, I'm even pretty happy with my results.

I glance around at the others. Everyone is wearing the same look of satisfaction. The buzzer rings out on the clock in the front of the room, and that's when, for the first time, I notice the Super Chef standing behind it on the balcony, leaning forward with both his hands on the railing in front of him. Was he there the entire time?

"Again," he says in a deep, commanding voice.

Chef Graca sighs, but he doesn't look back to question his boss. "Again," the no-longer-jolly Portuguese chef repeats. Five black-shirts stream out of the pantry, each carrying a box identical to the ones we'd started from. They swap out old for new, wiping down our stations, clearing away all signs of the first round.

When I open the new box, it's like déjà vu. The artichokes. The onions. The shrimp. The clams. All exactly the same.

We spend another half hour trying to be perfect, this time aware of the Super Chef pacing around the balcony above, watching us. I try to concentrate, but now that I know he's there, I can't ignore the echoes of his footfalls. Even just listening to them, trying to avoid distracting myself by looking up, I can tell he has a weird walk. Eventually I can't resist watching it for a few seconds. He keeps sort of twisting his left leg outward, like it's trying to dance but the rest of his body isn't interested. Or like he's trying to step over something that isn't there. Wormwood passes my station, tapping her index finger on my cutting board. I refocus.

We finish another round. There's a beat of silence as we all look skyward at the Super Chef behind the clock once more, hands in his pockets. Almost like he might be relaxing, but he definitely isn't. Not if that intense gaze of his is any sign, anyway. His left leg bounces in place as he surveys our stations from afar.

I hold my breath, waiting for his verdict. Staring into his deep-in-thought face.

That's when it hits me. The Super Chef. That's him. Really him. Right here, in the same room with us. With me. And here I am, obsessing over his every movement and expression, the same thing I've been doing through the TV all these years. It's like I can't stop myself from wondering what he might be thinking. About our work, all of us, but especially about mine. About me.

But as his eyes flit about our stations, his expression turns from intense to flat. It reveals nothing, and Lucas Taylor doesn't even look my way before repeating his command. "Again."

I recheck my precise cuts, the same ones he didn't bother to inspect. How could he tell the quality of our work from way up there? What, is he too good to come down to our level?

I try to shoot a glare at him, but the Super Chef only starts his pacing again, in the opposite direction this time. Same twisty, clunky left step. Same inability for me not to notice.

And here they come. Five more boxes. Same exact ingredients.

Two hours later, when we're finally released upstairs after several more rounds, my hands are cold and shaking. My fingers feel locked into the position Graca taught me to hold my knife in, and I never want to see another onion or shrimp or clam or artichoke again.

The rest of me shakes alongside my hands. Not with cold, but more anger. It hasn't been enough for the Super

Chef to ignore me my whole life? He's going to fly me all the way to New York just so that he can prove he's able to continue ignoring me even when I'm right in front of him?

The five of us crash onto the leather sectional. We don't talk, not to complain, not even to celebrate that our first "open/training" day is over. We're too tired. Even though it's only midafternoon and I haven't eaten lunch yet, I fall asleep almost immediately.

Inside the arena, the crowd stamps their feet onto the overhead balcony in a chaotic, riotous beat. The noise slams into my whole body like thunder.

Kari crouches in front of us, glancing at her clipboard and mouthing out reminders. "Watch the person in front of you!" and "Smile!" and "Shoulders back!" Her headset looks at home again, nestled in her yellow curls.

We're waiting in the hallway outside the arena, in a single-file line. Wearing our *Super Chef* jackets, which must've been gathered up sometime after we all finally crawled toward bed. They'd been washed and pressed, then returned to us in sparkling new condition this morning.

Pepper is first in line. She nods at every one of Kari's

instructions, then takes a deep breath. After her it's Kiko, then me, then Joey, and finally Bo.

Kari raises one hand, five fingers, then starts counting them down, just like we practiced the day before. 5-4-3-2-1 . . .

Move, legs, move, I tell my lower half when Kiko starts to follow Pepper through the double entry doors and into the deafening arena. The crowd comes into full view. It feels like it's doubled in size compared with the last episode. Or maybe what's doubled is their sheer cheering volume— those stamping feet are joined by a ton of piercing whistles and even the occasional high-pitched scream.

This is it. The second episode of *The Last Super Chef*. We've had one day of rest since we arrived and were thrust into the mise en place challenge. If you want to call what we did in the last twenty-four hours "rest." I open and close my fist, making sure my hand has returned to normal. My right thumb cracks, I wince, and, even above the racket surrounding me, "Again!" echoes in my ears.

The Super Chef waits for us alone on the stage. The critical stare from yesterday is gone, replaced by his flashy, on-camera smile.

"Welcome back to *The Last Super Chef*," he announces proudly, and the cheering starts to die down. I glance around for his sous chefs, but my eyes can't find them.

"Let's get right to it. Warm-up is over. Today, the

competition starts for real, with Challenge #1! Please don't forget that the winner of tonight's competition will receive two tickets front and center for all the events at NBA All-Star Weekend in Los Angeles, coming up this February!"

The crowd gasps. I resist checking on Joey. I'm sure his expression is full of the same excitement and confidence that's been there since yesterday. He's been laser-focused on these tickets for hours. "NBA All-Star Weekend! Just me and my dad!" he kept spontaneously shouting in the dorms, as if he'd won them already.

"Let's remind ourselves of the scores from the warm-up episode, our mise en place challenge!" The Super Chef gestures toward the blank scoreboard. It flashes to life, displaying the same scores as last time, our names in order. Kiko first, with 50 points. Me, last, with 34.

"Tonight is also our first themed competition. So please remember, Chefs, to keep those thinking caps on while you compete." He taps his index finger on his temple.

"But before we can start, I think we're missing some key folks, aren't we?" The Super Chef puts one hand over his eyes like a seaman searching the horizon for lost boats. "Where are my sous chefs? Chef Claire? Chef Gabriel?"

To our left is a table I'm noticing for the first time. Something's on it, but I can't tell what because it's covered in black tablecloths. And anyway, my attention is pulled away when two booths light up, each no bigger than our tiny pantry closet back home. Chefs Wormwood and Graca appear inside them. Bulky, noise-canceling headphones cover their ears, and they're blindfolded, too.

"Well, *there* they are." Chef Taylor cups his hands over his mouth to project his voice. "Hey, Chefs! What are you guys doing over there?"

Their expressions don't shift a millimeter, not even when the Super Chef waves both hands over his head like he's stranded on a desert island, hoping to flag down a passing rescue plane. It's clear the sous chefs can't see or hear their boss at all.

"Sensory deprivation booths," the Super Chef announces with a knowing grin. "Four of them." Two more identical but empty booths light up. "Inside these, our contestants won't be able to hear a thing going on in Super Chef Arena. More on why we need such precautions later; suffice to say they're extremely important for tonight's challenge. Now, somebody get me my sous chefs back up here! I'm lost without them."

Wormwood and Graca are helped out of the booths. Once they're out in the arena again, they carefully remove their blindfolds and headphones. Chef Wormwood's rosy cheeks, clearly irritated by the tight equipment, match the annoyance evident in her straight-lined mouth.

Both chefs shake themselves back to their full senses. The booth lights flash off, dropping that side of the arena back into shadows. If you didn't already know the myste-rious capsules were there, you'd have a hard time locating them.

The sous chefs join Chef Taylor on the stage. He addresses us and the cameras and the audience above at the same time, alternating eye contact between all three as he speaks. "Two nights ago, our mise en place challenge involved some ingredients that can prove especially diffi-cult to prep, but can be equally daunting to actually cook with."

Two of the black-shirts fold back the first tablecloth. "Artichokes!" the Super Chef cries when several bowls of prepped artichoke hearts, surrounded by dozens more, huge and untouched by knives, are revealed.

"Onions!" he says next, and suddenly we see mounds of them, perfectly diced, again surrounded by tons of match-ing, beautiful, whole Vidalias.

Graca and Wormwood join in, yelling out "Clams!" and "Shrimp!" one after the other, more piles of the same components we worked with yesterday coming into view.

Terrific, I think, looking at ingredients I'd vowed only yesterday never to touch again.

"That's right, Chefs," the Super Chef says, "your chal-lenge today is to cook a dish using all of these ingredients, along with five more"—Wormwood and Graca each hold up five fingers—"that you select from the pantry."

"You'll each have one shopping minute," Graca adds. "Choose your ingredients carefully, then close your lid and head back to your station."

Kiko is first. She grips the edge of the counter in front of her. Her eyes fix on a single point in the distance, the entrance to the pantry. Her right foot is inches behind her left and stands up on a toe.

The Super Chef points back at the clock, waits for a new minute to start, then swings his finger through the air at the scoring leader. "And . . . go!"

Kiko races toward Pepper, slipping between her and the second row of stations, where Bo, standing on his stepping stool, looks on with a worried expression. A cameraman is hot on her heels as she nears the pantry, snatching up one of the shopping boxes just outside. The lid flaps open and closed as she yanks it from the rack. She darts to the right and disappears. The wall separating the pantry from the arena is frosted glass, so all we see is her shadow as she zips around in there.

On the stage, the Super Chef relaxes. All of the red camera lights in the room with us have winked out. The live television audience must only be watching Kiko now, through that single camera in the pantry with her.

I squint at her shadow, trying to guess what she might be selecting. Then I realize what a mistake that is. I have to focus on myself, my own dish. What should I make with these ingredients, and what else do I need to get from the pantry to pull it off?

Kiko emerges huffing. When she hits her spot, she heaves her closed box up onto her station. Another deep breath.

The Super Chef doesn't waste more than a few seconds, just long enough to track the second hand as it reaches the following half minute. He sends Joey into the pantry next.

One by one my competition streams behind the frosted glass. The camera follows their feet. My eyes track their shadows. And one by one they charge out, filled boxes in hand. Boxes that they lift up to rest upon each of their stations, lids closed. They shake out their legs.

I can't help but wonder if some of them have picked the same ingredients I will. But that's impossible to say, because I still don't know what I need. I've run through about a hundred recipes in my head in the last four minutes and settled on absolutely nothing.

"Chef Curtis!" the Super Chef shouts, and I look up to find his long, slightly shaking finger pointed straight at me. "Go!"

I cross the front of the stage. I don't bother looking up at the chefs as I sprint past them.

I guess my speed must surprise the lumberjack-y cameraman, who's even completing his look today with a flannel shirt. We do a little dance outside the pantry before he takes a huge step back, allowing me to slide past him.

It's my first time ever inside the *Super Chef* pantry. It looks the same in person as it always has on TV, from the pilot episode of season one. Brightly lit, everything beyond fresh, tons of options.

I freeze up. What am I making? What do I need?

I'm still not sure. I start to head left, then change my mind. The cameraman efforts to stay close, almost running into me a few times. I guess he wants to zero in on my face sweat again. By the time this is all over, I'm going to have the most well-known face sweat on the planet. Maybe I'll bottle it and sell it on a website, like Pepper does with her spices. *Fear by Curtis*. A scent everybody will want. Or probably more like absolutely nobody.

The essentials, get the essentials. If you have them, you can always find *something* to make. I head for the refrigerator case and throw it open. Grab a jug of milk. Snatch a carton of eggs. Protein, I need a protein.

I race for the butcher's block. Pork chops and pork loin and pig's feet, chicken legs and thighs and breast. And beef. There are ribeyes, New York strip, filets . . .

Filets.

When did I last cook such an awesome cut of meat? The rare times we eat steak at home, it's never a filet. Mom can barely afford the flank steak most times. Decision made, I wrap the best filet I see in some butcher paper and tuck it into my box.

I round out my picks in a huge hurry with a chunk of parmesan cheese and a bunch of asparagus. I race back into the arena.

"Congratulations," the Super Chef says when I hit my station. My breath returns to something close to normal again. "All of you. Now. Let's see what you chose."

The three chefs descend those same short steps and march toward us, reaching Pepper first. The Super Chef flips her box lid up and takes out her ingredients one at a time, setting them on her station. As he does, he describes them for the audience.

"Lobster. Excellent choice. Cabbage. Interesting. Brioche. Very good. Celery and dried apricots. Nice." He looks down at Pepper, who seems a little nervous. "If I had to guess . . . stuffed lobster?"

Pepper nods hard, smiling, proud of her selections. "You know, I might've enjoyed that," the Super Chef says, glancing over his shoulder at his sous chefs. Their grins seem especially devious.

Chef Wormwood lifts Pepper's box and holds it open for the Super Chef. He picks up the lobster, turns it over once to inspect it. With a frown he pops it back inside her box. The brioche gets the same treatment. Then the celery and apricots. Finally he meets Pepper's eyes again. "I suppose we can let you keep the cabbage."

Pepper's mouth drops open. Her gaze alternates from the head of cabbage in front of her, sad by itself now, to the Super Chef's evil-looking smirk. He starts to pace down the line, toward Kiko.

"I'm glad each of you came up with a great idea for a dish to make," he says in a louder voice, talking to us all now. "But this challenge wouldn't be worthy of *The Last Super Chef* if we just let you choose anything you wanted from our incredible pantry. Did you really think you were simply going to make your own dish and it was going to be as easy as that?"

I guess I kind of did think that. Except I wasn't feeling like it was going to be all that easy. In fact, I was already in pretty much full-strength panic mode. Now my heart goes from beating fast to downright thumping.

When the Super Chef reaches Kiko's station, he flips the lid on her box up in the same way as he did Pepper's. "You won't be able to keep your five ingredients. But you can have one." He lifts a single finger and smiles, like he's being generous. "And you won't be making five dishes separately, either." He takes a head of broccoli out of Kiko's box and turns it over.

"You'll be cooking one dish. Together."

After leaving Kiko with only a single slab of sliced pork belly, the Super Chef moves on to me. He heaves an impatient breath. "Now. Let's have a look at your selections, shall we, Chef Pith?"

Taylor opens my box and takes the filet out first. "That's a rather fancy cut of meat. Not really what I expected to find."

He doesn't waste time waiting for a response, instead continuing to pull ingredients from my box. The eggs, the asparagus, the parmesan, the milk. "Sort of an odd assortment. I can't even guess at what you were planning to make."

Don't ask me. Don't ask me. Don't ask me.

Because I have no idea. Because my father is inches away from me for the first time I can remember, for what feels like the first time ever, and I kind of can't breathe. Definitely can't talk. What if I open my mouth and something weird comes out?

He runs his perplexed eyes over my choices. "How about we let you keep the eggs?"

I nod like it's okay. Anything to get him to move on to the next chef.

A few minutes later, as the chefs return to the stage, each of us is left to stare down at the pitiful remnants of our frantic shopping.

Pepper has her head of cabbage.

Kiko, her pork belly.

I've got my eggs.

They leave Joey with a box of spaghetti.

Bo has one huge heirloom tomato.

"Of course you'll have as much of our mise en place to work with as you wish," the Super Chef says from the stage, pointing at the artichokes, onions, shrimp, and clams. "And the basics at your stations."

He pauses, letting the situation sink in. Letting our desperation sink in. I can see the remnants of everyone's ruined recipes weighing down their faces. It almost feels good not to have come up with a real plan back in the pantry. Like I have an advantage in a way, because the Super

Chef couldn't possibly ruin a plan that never existed in the first place.

"Which brings us full circle, to our sensory deprivation booths," Lucas Taylor says. The booths light up again, all four at once this time. "I said you'll cook your meal together, but I didn't tell you how." He hesitates, seeming to enjoy our collective confusion. "You will cook in the same order you shopped in, the current order of the standings, and each of you will be allowed six minutes. The rest will be waiting in our booths, with no knowledge of the other chefs' work. Every six minutes another of you will take your turn. You must continue the same dish the chefs before you started. Think of it like a relay race. Your dish is the baton."

The same order. It meant I would be last again. It meant whatever dish the others started, I would have to finish it. It meant if this whole thing turned out to be an epic failure, I'd be the last cook who touched it. I'd be the easiest one to blame.

After a quick commercial break, Kiko remains at her station in the center of the first row, our ingredients collected up and waiting with her. A single, glistening stack of thinly cut pork belly beside a lone head of green-white cabbage. A cardboard box of store-bought spaghetti leaning against a spongy carton of organic eggs. Bo's multicolored tomato, somehow looking the most vibrant and the most out of place at the same time.

The rest of us wait in line along the far side of the arena. One by one, we're led into our assigned booths. The blindfolds are tied tight, but not too tight. Finally, we're asked to pull on the bulky headphones.

As big as they are, they're still not perfect at noise canceling. I hear distant murmurs from the crowd and, for a second, I even think I make out the Super Chef's muffled voice, amplified by the arena's microphones. But then I sense the door clicking shut behind me. Not only is everything completely dark, but now there's no sound at all, and I know for sure there won't be.

At least not for the next twenty-four minutes.

I have twenty-four minutes to wait. Twenty-four minutes to think. I have twenty-four minutes, if I can make my brain do it, to plan.

What will the other chefs be working on when my time is up? Maybe a pasta dish with a seafood sauce? Or some kind of twisted cioppino?

Every time I think of a possibility, the dish I come up with is based on something I've made for Paige and Mom, and all of a sudden my heart is sick and empty, I miss them so bad.

The pattern repeats, dish after possible dish circling my head like they're on a conveyor belt, and in what feels a lot more like four minutes than twenty-four, I sense the booth door being thrust open behind me. A tap on my shoulder. Fingers untying my blindfold. It can't be my turn yet. I haven't even . . .

The world returns to focus before I can finish my thought. I blink about ten times to help my eyes adjust to the stark light. The rest of the arena flashes into view. Bo's at the station in the front row where Kiko started, frantically stirring something in a flat pan. Joey, Pepper, and Kiko are at the far end of the row, shouting at him.

I pull my headphones off. Sound erupts all around me. My hands instinctively shoot up to my ears to muffle it.

"Let's go, Chef." Graca encourages me to approach him with a wave of his hand. I try to will my feet to move, but they don't want to go. No, they want to run, to not stop until I hit the snowy streets of North Sloan and race into our apartment, dive under the blankets with Mom and Paige. Safe from crowds and pressure, from aching hands and the rumbling nerves in my gut.

"Ready?" Graca asks when I find myself standing next to him anyway. My feet must've moved on their own. Together we gaze down the row at Bo, working wildly, the rest of the Super Five shouting at him.

It feels like complete chaos. I've never cooked in these conditions before. Not even close.

No, I'm totally not ready for this, but maybe my numb stupidity bubbles to the surface and takes control of my body. Because, for some reason, I nod yes.

"In a second, they'll call for Bonifacio to stop working," Graça says close to my ear, nodding at Bo, who's moving faster than I've ever seen him go, up and down on his stool to reach for ingredients and put them to use.

On the opposite end of the row from where we stand, the already-finished chefs are still shouting instructions.

"Don't let the shrimp burn!"

"The pasta should be al dente!"

"The clams are done! They're dooone!"

The Super Chef never said anything about the other contestants shouting like that. But what else would've happened? There wasn't time to lock them back into the booths. And maybe this was part of the test, handling all that input when usually we cook on our own. Maybe it has something to do with the theme we're going to have to guess.

The theme! All of a sudden I realize I haven't been thinking about it at all. I glance toward the stage. Taylor and Wormwood are standing there, enjoying the turmoil playing out at the center station, like the insanity going on in front of them is exactly what they'd hoped would happen tonight.

Early options for the theme run through my mind. Flexibility? Staying calm under pressure? Ability to not completely lose your mind?

Okay, maybe none of those are the theme, but they're all things I'm about to have to do.

Chef Graca blows his shrill whistle, and I snap my hand over the ear closest to him.

"Your time's up, Mr. Agosto!" Chef Wormwood shouts. "Hands in the air!"

Bo's panicked eyes dart up. He thrusts his hands skyward. The wooden spoon he was using to stir drops to the floor with a clatter. He glances at me, hands still raised, and the hot panic in his expression quickly turns my blood cold. Why? Because, I think, he must know what they're making. He's probably just realized there isn't enough time for me to finish it.

I race forward as Bo, reluctantly, backs up to join Joey,

Pepper, and Kiko. I take stock of the situation. Pasta's boiling in a giant pot on the stove. The pan Bo was stirring has cleaned, whole shrimp and diced pork belly frying together. Pepper's cabbage is shredded on a cutting board but still raw. In a second pan, clams are simmering in olive oil with artichokes and onions. Nobody's touched my eggs.

"It's a clam sauce," Pepper shouts. "With artichokes! I make it at home all the time. Put it over the spaghetti."

"No!" Joey yells. "It's a carbonara. Shrimp and bacon."

"Sorry, Curtis" is all Bo calls out to me. It's somehow even less helpful than the other scattershot comments.

My eyes search the station, finding one bowl I missed. Sort of a dark, reddish sauce sitting by itself. I pull it toward me, find a clean spoon and taste. It's like ketchup, I guess, but not exactly. Similar, though, definitely some kind of tomato base. Somehow . . . familiar, too.

This weird sauce must've started with Bo's tomato, the remnants of which I see lying on a cutting board a few feet away. More than that. On second taste, I pick up Worcestershire and soy. Maybe a little sugar.

Why do I feel like I've used this sauce before?

I can't waste time. I push the bowl back, grab my eggs. Use the wooden spoon to give both pans a stir so nothing already going burns. I have to use these eggs; we're supposed to include all the ingredients. And I have to make one dish, even if it seems like the others have ignored this rule. By my eye, there are at least two dishes in front of me, maybe three.

Kiko's been oddly quiet, and I wonder why. Maybe she knows something that can help.

I find her standing behind the other three, eyes laser-focused on the bag of flour sitting untouched on the station. She redirects her gaze to my face, making sure our eyes meet, then moves hers to the eggs. I follow them. Next she looks at the strange sauce. Did she make it? Now the mayo. Finally Kiko meets my eyes again. Her mouth moves, but if she actually says the word, I don't hear it. Doesn't matter, though, because I read her lips, and I can tell what they say.

I can tell what they say, and I know where I've tasted that sauce before.

I can tell what they say, and it's flat-out brilliant.

"Okonomiyaki."

I use a clean fork to spin one of the strands of spaghetti out of the pot, blow on it, and sample it. It's starting to go from al dente to overcooked. Not a huge deal for what I'm going to use it for, but I should stop the bleeding, so I grab a strainer and pour it out. Then I drain the drippings from the pan of shrimp and bacon—pork belly, actually. Finally the clams and onions and artichokes. I line everything up next to the bowl of sauce and the shredded cabbage.

All the ingredients we were supposed to use, in one way

or another, are in front of me now. The mise en place from the other day, plus the pork belly. Bo's tomato is in the mystery sauce, Pepper's cabbage is shredded and waiting and Joey's pasta is cooked. Perfect.

I allow myself one second to stop, take a breath, and recalibrate.

Okonomiyaki is a popular kind of Japanese pancake. Not sweet like the breakfast pancakes Paige likes in the morning, swimming in syrup and filled with blueberries, but a savory one. Savory as in more like you eat it for dinner than breakfast.

They're Japanese, so it makes sense these pancakes always have seafood in them. Some kinds, like octopus and squid, I don't have here and can't use. But most of the time okonomiyaki has shrimp in it too, and definitely pork belly. I can make the clams work. And spaghetti might be a little bit weird, but some versions do use Japanese noodles.

After all, *okonomi* means "as you like it" if I remember right from that time last year when I got so excited to try this dish after seeing it on the NHK cooking show I sometimes watch before school. I did hours of research, watched a ton of videos on *YouTube*.

When I felt ready, I made Mom get the different seafoods, or at least substitutes when we ran across one out of our price range. And on a snowed-in Saturday, I cooked my version of okonomiyaki for the first time. Mom and

Paige sent all kinds of "yuck" faces my way as they chewed and forced themselves to swallow. They both pretty much hated it.

But I kind of loved it.

All *yaki* means in Japanese, basically, is "cooked." So this would be okonomiyaki "cooked" the way "Curtis" likes it—definitely, at least, the way Curtis *has* to like it, because I've got no other choice.

I get to work slicing everything into smaller pieces so I can mix them into my batter. As I chop, I wonder how Kiko knew I would understand how to make okonomi-yaki. She couldn't have known I'd tried it before. No, she just trusted me, and suddenly I wonder if that's the theme. Could "trust" be one of the Super Chef's five qualities of a great chef?

Joey starts screaming at me. "What are you *doing*? Keep the shrimp whole, doofus!"

I have only seconds, so I tune him out, concentrate on my knife work. Once everything is ready, I grab a big bowl and measure out my flour. Add a little baking soda. Some water. I'm working so fast my dry ingredients are flying out of the bowl. I know there should be dashi, but I can't worry about what's missing, only what's here.

I whisk until all the lumps are gone. It's starting to look more like pancake batter now. I sprinkle a little salt in, give it another turn. I should have that special mountain yam that makes it gooey, the one it took Mom so long to find in the Korean grocery back home, but I don't.

I start adding my ingredients to the batter.

The shrimp. Normally, they should be raw, not cooked, but I can't help that. The shredded cabbage. Some of the pork belly. The clams and onions, again they'd be better raw, and actually should be green onions, not Vidalias, but what can I do?

A pit opens up in my stomach. I was so sure this was the right thing to do when Kiko suggested it, but now I keep making excuses for substituting ingredients. Maybe this is going to suck. If this were normal *Super Chef*, I'd be sure they were about to send me home, but I can't even hope for that. "Each of you is here for the long haul," Wormwood had warned us. "I hope you're all prepared for that."

I'm pretty positive the only thing I was prepared for was dressing myself every day. Even that's questionable at this point, I think as I look down at my untied left sneaker, wondering when that happened, understanding I can't pause long enough to do anything about it anyway.

That's right—keep moving, keep moving, keep moving. Next, the artichokes—which honestly shouldn't come within five miles of an okonomiyaki, but I've got to use them. Every time I tell myself that, the pit in my gut widens.

I crack two eggs over the whole thing, then stir it all

together as quickly as I can. At least half my time must be gone. I hear screaming from all sides, but I ignore it.

The chunky batter starts to sizzle immediately when I form it into a round shape in the center of my pan— basically a big pancake, but not too big, this has to cook quick. I deal more of the pork belly onto the top, then use a brush to coat the surface with a bit more of the batter. It starts to really speak to me, searing and sputtering and crackling. If you learn how to listen close enough, food tells you how it's doing, when it's going to be done, and how good it's going to taste, long before you ever lift a fork of it to your mouth.

I might need about two minutes on each side, maybe less. I check the clock. This is going to be about as close as it can get.

While one side cooks I get another pan going, really hot, and ball up some of the spaghetti into a round shape about the same size as my pancake. I start frying the noodles so they'll stick together. It should be *yakisoba*, but "as you like it," right?

Or maybe more "as you pray to the heavens this will somehow work . . . it."

The next few minutes fly by in a blur. Flipping the pancake so the other side will cook. Stacking it on top of the pan-fried noodles on a clean white plate. Spooning Kiko's okonomiyaki sauce on top and spreading it thin. Swirling a spiral of mayonnaise over the whole thing. Graca's whistle blowing. Wormwood shouting, "Hands up!"

Everything done just in time, my hands shoot high toward the people in the balcony with all their crazy cheering. Like I've just been nabbed in a bank robbery, except I think my crime today has been committed against the cooking gods, or maybe the entire country of Japan. My breath comes in labored spurts.

I look down at the pancake in front of me. It barely holds together. Mayo drips onto the plate. The whole thing slouches a little, and I start to worry that I didn't cook it long enough.

Ugh. It's my dish, the same one I keep going between dreading the reaction to and being sort of proud of. Now I'm not feeling either of those. I just have one, lone, final thought as I watch steam drift off the top of this ugly thing on my plate.

It may be a mess, but at least it's a *hot* mess.

During the commercial break, the five of us, still breathing heavy after the past thirty minutes, reassemble at our assigned stations. When the red camera lights flare back on, the Super Chef doesn't allow even a second of dead air time.

"Well, Chefs, that was certainly exciting, wasn't it?" He looks down at the new table added to the stage, our clumsy attempt at the popular Japanese dish centered on it, as if he's surprised a dish for him to taste resulted from what he just witnessed.

"Okonomiyaki," he says, tilting his head. Is that admiration in his expression? "Who thought of this?"

I point to my left, at Kiko, and when I turn my head

to check her reaction, I see she's pointing at me. I look around. The other three chefs cast their eyes downward.

"It was not an okonomiyaki before Curtis," Kiko claims.

"Yeah, but Kiko was the one who told me to do it, and the sauce was already made."

The other thing that happened during the commercial is I had time to piece together what must've happened while I was in the booth. Kiko decided to make the pancake, and she started with the sauce, because she knew it would need time. We had no ketchup, so she had to make a quick version of that first, using Bo's tomato. Then she still had to combine it with the Worcestershire and soy to create an actual okonomiyaki sauce. One sauce to build another, really smart. Except all those steps probably stole most of her six minutes.

After that, the wheels somehow spun off. Either Joey didn't recognize what she was making or he just went his own way, and then Pepper did the same. By the time Bo got up there he must've been so confused he just floundered. Then it was my turn.

Had Kiko mouthed out "okonomiyaki" to the others? Or just to me? Maybe none of them knew what it was. Maybe she kept suggesting it until someone finally figured it out.

We lower our arms at the same time.

"Well, this was *someone's* fantastic idea," the Super Chef says. "How about we taste it?"

Wormwood and Graca come even with Taylor on the stage. Together they reach out with clean forks to carve out pieces of the savory pancake for themselves. The bonito flakes, one of the best parts of okonomiyaki—you put them on top at the end and the heat makes them dance like they're at a disco—are missing, but my swirl of mayo is nice and the pancake hasn't fallen completely apart . . . yet.

When the chefs have all taken their portion, they raise their forks to eye level and stare at our result, angling the pancake to get a better view of it from all sides. Finally, in unison, they bring their forks to their mouths to do something I only now realize I never had time for.

They taste what we made. Oh, man, how could I serve something to the Super Chef without tasting it first?

Wormwood stares up at the balcony, chewing, her face inscrutable. The Super Chef's head bounces from one side to the other like a confused bobblehead doll.

Chef Graca swallows first. "I'll admit, Chefs," he starts. "I haven't eaten a lot of okonomiyaki in my time, but this one is absolutely delicious."

The Super Chef covers his mouth briefly, swallows, then starts to laugh. "Chef Graca, I do believe I'm going to have to agree with you."

Wormwood casts the final vote. "This . . . was a phenomenal idea. One"—she heaves a deep breath—"I'm not sure I would've come up with myself. And it was incredibly well executed."

My whole body relaxes. So much tension leaves my shoulders and hips I almost fall over.

"Quite a dish." The Super Chef gives our pancake plate a quarter turn before looking up at us again. "Okay, Chefs. We warned you this was coming, didn't we? The time for you to give us your guesses on tonight's theme has arrived."

The Super Chef spreads his arms out wide, like an invitation, and more anonymous black-shirts rush forward again, each with an armful of blue plastic. They snap together the pieces on our stations so fast I can't tell how they fit, but I recognize the result. It's a temporary blue desk with walls on either side. Inside waits a black Sharpie and a white index card.

It's easy to figure out what we're supposed to do—write our theme guesses on the card. The little blue walls are just big enough to keep us from seeing each other's work.

The Super Chef and his sous chefs retreat to the back of the stage, forming a loose huddle, while a loud ticking starts playing on the speakers around the arena, accompanied by game-show-like music. I pick up the Sharpie. They didn't say exactly how long we have to answer, but I'm guessing it's not much time at all.

I run through my earlier thoughts. Flexibility, trust, a

bunch of others. They're all possible answers, but when I think about Kiko telling me what to do when she didn't have to, how easy it would've been to let me crash and burn, I'm almost positive the theme was something else.

I hurry to scribble the word down on my card.

"Before we get to our theme guesses," the Super Chef says, rubbing his hands together. "I want to remind our viewing audience of tomorrow night's special episode—'Evening with the Super Chef'—and announce who the first contestant to meet with me will be."

He hikes up the suspense for a few seconds by staring around at all five of us. I gulp. Tomorrow night, alone with the Super Chef. Alone for the first time with . . . my father.

Well, if you can call me, him, and millions of viewers "alone."

"This contestant and I will be heading to one of my favorite Italian restaurants in the city, Il Diletto, literally, 'The Delight.' And it certainly is that!" Chef Taylor inhales. "And that first chef will be"—again he scans the room with his gaze—"Chef Joey Modestino."

I turn around to see Joey beaming like he's already been named the actual Last Super Chef instead of just being picked for the first private meeting. And I can't help it, I'm a little jealous. Why does he get to go first? Then I realize I'm not remotely ready to be alone with Lucas Taylor yet anyway, and my jealousy fades into relief.

"Why don't we start with Joey's theme guess as well?" the Super Chef, pointing to the second row, suggests. "Please lift up your card and let us see what you thought."

Joey follows the instruction. His card says, "Grace Under Pressure."

Chef Taylor shakes his head. "While I'm sure each of you had to have plenty of that tonight, I'm afraid that wasn't the target theme of this episode. Let's stay in the back row." He shifts his eyes to Bo, who raises his card. "Leadership."

"Also incorrect," the Super Chef says. "Good guess, though. Leadership's always important. Front row. Ms. Pepper?"

Pepper bites her lip before holding her card out for the chefs to read. "Flexibility."

The Super Chef tilts his head but makes an oh-so-close face. "We certainly made you bend just about backward, didn't we? But I'm sorry . . . no."

"I'm getting a little concerned, Chef," Wormwood chimes in.

Graca shakes his head and smiles at Kiko and me. "Now hold on, friends. We have two more chefs," he reminds them. "There's still hope."

"We'll see," the Super Chef says. "Let's give Chef Tanaka her chance next. I really enjoyed your sauce, by the way, Kiko."

Smiling, Kiko raises her card high over her head. "Listening."

"That is a very interesting answer," Lucas Taylor says with a smile. "An underrated quality, for sure. Not just in the kitchen, but in life. I am sorry, though. Tonight, it's not what we were looking for."

Kiko's smile fades.

Four chefs, four different answers. It's amazing how we could all be challenged in the same way but interpret the exercise so differently.

The Super Chef turns to me. "Our final chance lies with Chef Pith here. Our okonomiyaki hero."

I don't want to raise my card. I don't want to feel the sting of that same look of disappointment he's sent the other four. But I've got no choice. I show him my guess.

"Teamwork."

"Well." The Super Chef looks to one side then the other, at his sous chefs. All three of them are smiling at each other, even Wormwood. I feel my face reddening more and more, right up until the point he speaks again.

"It seems we have a winner."

• • •

The episode ends with another quick huddle of the chefs, then a reveal of the scoring. After being last in the first episode, when the bells ding and the lights settle into place, I'm actually at the top this time.

Curtis Pith	90
Kiko Tanaka	75
Bonifacio Agosto	70
Pepper Carmichael	65
Joey Modestino	55

The next few moments are filled with a whirlwind of cheering. I feel so buoyed by the enthusiasm of the audience, I hardly notice the envelope brought out to me, not until my fingers actually close around it.

My eyes widen with understanding. I finished first in the challenge. The prize is mine. I stared at that schedule tons, the long list of rewards, but I still have to fight to recall which one I won. I remember when I picture Joey's face.

That's right. NBA.

I rip the envelope open and pull two oversized, sparkling tickets out. The sparkling words "All-Star" and "Weekend" glint back at me under the brilliant studio lights.

But I can't revel in my excitement too long, because the big screen flashes again, this time to show the updated totals after two episodes.

Kiko Tanaka	125
Curtis Pith	124
Bonifacio Agosto	105
Pepper Carmichael	103
Joey Modestino	100

In the blink of an eye, I've gone from very last to almost first. The show ends when the Super Chef says again, "Don't forget to join us tomorrow night for the first of our five episodes of 'Evening with the Super Chef.' Then be back Monday night for"—this time the crowd joins in without any prompting—"*The Last! Super! Chef!*"

As quickly as the lights fade, the chefs and the audience disappear. Kari pops out of some secret side door. She and her clipboard lead us back up the stairs into our dorms, where we crash around the big sectional sofa, exhausted. Tonight it's Renata, Pepper's handler from Italy, staying in the back room, hanging around us as silently as Mel did, supervising.

"Joey," Kari calls from the door. "In the morning we'll get you some more details about your dinner with Chef Taylor. It won't happen until the evening."

"The Super Chef said the next real episode will be Monday. So what's happening over the weekend?" Pepper asks her. "All the schedule says for the next three days is 'Open/Training.' You must know more by now."

Kari stops, a bemused expression crossing her face. She tucks her clipboard to her chest. "In fact I do," she says. "We've put you through quite a lot these first few days. Tomorrow will be easier. Only thing on the schedule is a chance to talk with the media a bit about your experience so far."

"Media?" Bo says, sounding worried.

Immediately after, Kiko starts to ask, "What do you mean by media?"

But it seems that's all the detail we're getting. "You'll find out more in the morning," Kari says. "Meanwhile, please get as much rest as possible. You guys have earned it."

The next morning I wake to the sound of Bo muttering in his sleep. It's hard to tell with his accent, but I'm pretty sure I hear him blurt out "Artichokes!" and maybe "Shrimp!" too. The slight panic in his voice makes it sound like he could be running from some life-size versions of the ingredients.

I blink my eyes open. When I glance at the bunk above Bo's, I notice Joey's sheets are bunched up, his bed empty.

I'm thirsty, so I get up and wander out to the common room for some juice. As soon as I open our door, I see Joey's sitting alone at the island with his schedule again.

I yank open the fridge. "Morning."

He grunts in my direction.

"Any news about the media thing?"

Joey furrows his brow. "How should I know?"

I don't answer that, just pour juice into a tall glass.

"Hey, who're you gonna take?" he asks me as I'm returning the jug to the fridge.

I don't get his question at first. I look over my shoulder at him.

"To the game. All-Star Weekend. Who are you taking? Your dad?"

"No." Doesn't he know about my family already? I bet he does. I know about his. He's just poking me, like he's done since we met.

"Listen," he says, scratching the back of his head. "Would you be willing to swap?"

"Swap what?"

"The tickets."

"Yeah, I know. I mean swap them for what?"

Joey looks around, as if he owns something valuable in this room he can offer me. "What if I win the next challenge? Paris, right? The Louvre? Bet you'd rather have that. You don't really seem like you're . . . you know. Into sports."

What's that supposed to mean? If he wanted me to say yes, maybe he should stop jabbing me about not having a father, about not being into stuff he clearly considers cool.

"I don't know," I say, taking a gulp of juice. "Maybe. Let's talk if you win."

"*When*," Joey says. "When I win. Listen, I need those tickets, man. My dad—"

Just then, the door opens. Kari, fully dressed and already wearing her headset, storms in, reading silently from her clipboard. When she looks up and sees only the two of us, her eyes go wide. "Are you the only two up? Oh no. No, no, no. People are already lining up for this press conference downstairs."

She reaches into her pocket and pulls out the same style whistle that Graca's been using. She blows into it so hard my ears feel like they're actually splitting.

And while I cover them and close my eyes, I keep hearing two words.

"Press" and "conference."

The buzzing in Super Chef Arena is constant and low, as if it were a swarm of bees out there waiting for us instead of a gaggle of reporters. From the waiting room, we take turns peeking inside.

The whole studio's been transformed—the cooking stations are gone, replaced by rows upon rows of seats for reporters and photographers. There's a long table set up on the stage where the Super Chef normally stands, with five chairs behind it, facing a mass of press, most of them murmuring while they wait.

Five microphones sit ready on top of the table, one for each of us. I pull at my collar. Our freshly laundered chef's jackets are so starched they're crisp, and my neck is super itchy. The coats crackle with every nervous twitch of our shoulders.

Kari runs up and down our line, repeating the instructions she'd given us a few minutes ago. "Remember, only answer the questions they ask. They know to stay away from certain subjects. If they cross any lines, trust me, I'll step in."

Someone must talk in her ear again, because her eyes seem far away. When whatever instruction she hears ends, Kari returns. She nods at us. "Okay, they're ready. Remember, stay behind each other. Even spacing." She steps out of the way and waves us on. "Go, go, go!"

Our training kicking in, we enter the arena in a straight, unbroken line. Shutters click as photographers snap what sound like thousands of photos of us.

For the first time I notice Chef Wormwood is waiting at the far end of the stage. She's holding a microphone. "Please welcome . . . the Super Five!" she announces.

A smattering of applause wanders toward us. We reach our assigned chairs, where a pyramid-shaped glass display in front of each microphone spells out our names.

"We're so glad so many of you have taken advantage of

this special opportunity to officially meet them," Wormwood continues. "But, as you can imagine, our young
competitors are very busy, so there isn't time for too many
questions. Please keep yours brief and to the point. The
chefs promise to do the same with their answers." For the
first time she directs her gaze at us, and her smile disappears. We've been on the receiving end of so many of her
glowers the past couple of days, I can actually tell them
apart now. This one says, *Do NOT yammer on like idiots.*

A bunch of shouting starts, a hundred questions at
once, and it's impossible to separate what anyone's saying.
Finally, the high-pitched voice of one short, dark-haired
guy sitting in the front row rises above the din. "Question
for all the chefs!" he says. "Do you miss home?"

By the way Bo had nearly fainted up in the dorms when
Kari described the press conference, I expected him to be
the last of us to jump in and answer the first question. But
he scooches to the edge of his seat and leans into his microphone. "Sí . . . yes. Yes, very much."

"What about Kiko?" a woman in the back yells. "She's
come the farthest."

I notice the reporter is Asian. Then I see that there's a
gathering of Asian reporters back there with her. I know
in baseball when a Japanese player comes to play in the
major leagues a huge group of their media follows him

from city to city for the first few months. I guess Kiko's getting the same treatment.

She clears her throat. "Yes, New York is a long way from Kyoto. And mise en place in Super Chef Arena is an even longer way from making soba with my grandmother in our small apartment kitchen."

That makes the reporters chuckle. As Joey and Pepper give similar answers, I wonder what Mom and Paige are talking about, watching this from our couch. Are they snacking? Please, not those veggie chips Mom insists on buying, when house-made chips are so easy to—

"Curtis?" Chef Wormwood says into the microphone at the same time Pepper elbows me in the ribs. I realize one of the reporters must have asked me something, and I just assume it's the same subject.

"My mom and my sister, Paige," I say, nodding. "I hope they're okay."

"Why wouldn't they be ok—" one reporter starts, but a louder and closer one wedges his question in first.

"What about friends? Starting with you, Pepper."

Pepper blinks. Everyone's staring at her. When she leans toward the mic, a piercing tone shrieks out of the speakers. Several reporters tilt their heads and stick fingers into their ears.

"Um . . . ," Pepper says when the spike of noise fades.

"Friends. Yeah, sure. I have lots."

"I bet they're rooting you on big-time back in Boston, aren't they?"

"Here's your chance to name a few!" another reporter shouts.

Pepper puts her hand on the microphone's base. She twists her fingers around it a couple of times. "Um . . ."

"Shout-out to my friend Tre!" I say, and I don't know if anyone else notices Pepper give me a tiny smile for rescuing her, even though I have no idea what I just saved her from. "He *better* be rooting for me!"

It feels kind of good to make a roomful of people laugh all at once.

Bo and Kiko list out some close friends, too. Joey must name half his school. He only stops when Wormwood clears her throat.

"Joey, tell us about your uncle Frank. He owns some restaurants in the Chicago area, doesn't he?" a mustached reporter in the middle of the room asks.

Joey nods. "Yeah, there's Vito's on second, and Violante's on East Superior, and—"

"Did he inspire you to start cooking?"

"Well . . . I would say I'm definitely here because of him," Joey agrees. "Uncle Frank and my dad are always cooking stuff together, and I've gotten to visit all the restaurants and help out in some of the kitchens, too."

"Bonifacio, your family's in the food industry, too, aren't they?" The mustached guy gets some dirty looks from the others for firing off his third question in a row.

"Sí, for a long time we have owned some groceries and taquerias, starting with my great-grandparents and now down to my mother and father." He stops and sighs heavily, then waves at the cameras. "Hola, Mamá! Hola, Papá!"

"I have a question for the young ladies," a tall woman with glasses and long, straight gray hair says from her position leaning against the wall. "Pepper, from the videos we've seen in your submission and on your website, it's clear you have a desire to be the best at whatever you do. Meanwhile, according to our research, Kiko has finished first in I can't count how many other competitions, from math to spelling to archery. As the only girls in the contest, have you found some common ground in the way you both excel at everything you attempt?"

Joey and I rock back in our chairs to give Pepper and Kiko a clear line of sight to each other. They lean forward to look at each other as they answer at the same time.

"We are staying in the same room," Kiko says flatly.

"We're becoming really good friends," Pepper counters.

Chef Wormwood's stern voice seems to slice through a sudden thickness in the room. "We only have time for one more question."

"Okay, okay," says a twitchy, skinny guy who seems

to be moving on fast-forward. "You can't pick yourself. Going down the line . . . if not you, then who do you think will win?"

"I think it will probably be Kiko," Bo says into his microphone immediately.

Kiko, sitting next to him, turns in shock. "Thank you." She hesitates. "But I cannot make such a prediction." She looks down the line at the rest of us before glancing at Bo again. "Everyone here is very talented. We are all trying our best."

"Yeah, like, why would I answer that?" Joey says. With a sudden movement, he turns to face Bo, and even though I only see the back of his head, I can imagine the eye daggers he's shooting at his little friend. Maybe their alliance will end before it ever had a real chance to start.

If I were going to answer the question, I'd probably be with Bo. Kiko seems to be the most talented of us, and she's already in first, even if she only has a single point on me. But I also admire her for other reasons, too, like the answer she just gave, so when it's my turn, I echo it.

"I agree. Doesn't seem fair to try to pick one."

And Pepper immediately says, "Me. You say I can't pick me, but that makes no sense. You want to know who's going to win, and I'm the only one here who's the best, so of course it's going to be me." She leans back, folds her arms across her chest, and surveys the room with a confused expression. "Was it supposed to be a trick question?"

Wormwood takes advantage of the short silence that follows. "Okay, I'm afraid that will have to be the last question. Thank you so much for attending. As Chef mentioned last night, Mr. Modestino's 'Evening with the Super Chef' will air tonight, and the second one is Sunday night, featuring Ms. Carmichael." Pepper's arms unfold and she sits up straight in surprise. "The rest of the competitors will next appear Monday night for the second challenge. Eight p.m. as usual."

When she finishes, Wormwood gestures for us to stand. We start to push our chairs back.

"Where is the Super Chef?" someone yells. By the time I look for the source of the voice, though, it's lost in the crowd.

A few other reporters nod. They start to stand, and it gets even harder to match question with face. "Yeah, why isn't he here?"

"This press conference is over," Wormwood repeats with a scowl.

But now the mass of reporters is surging forward, shouting about the Super Chef. "How often have you seen him? Does he give you pep talks? What's the biggest thing you've learned from him so far?"

The woman with the long gray hair and glasses stands

up on a chair, rising above her colleagues. She points at us with her pen. "These kids already look tired, just one challenge in. What are the working conditions like? Where is the Super Chef? This is his contest, isn't it?"

I notice Wormwood look over the top of us at Kari with a piercing glare, and the producer gets the message. She races out and starts to corral the Super Five into a tight circle. Our handlers rush forward, too, helping keep the reporters back. Soon the huge security staff join in. The reporters become a single-minded blob, pushing and shoving forward to get closer to us, continuing to rapid fire questions.

Kari barely manages to keep us together and guide us off the stage. She stays connected to the Super Five, leading our compact huddle all the way up the stairs and into the dorms. She slams the door shut, turns the lock, and leans her back against it for a few seconds, breathing heavily and hugging her clipboard.

25

"How do you think it's going?" Pepper asks, impatiently tapping a finger on her schedule. Joey's been gone for a couple of hours already.

The rest of us shrug.

Pepper refuses to accept that response. "You saw what he was wearing, right?"

Joey had come out of his room wearing the most extra clothes I'd ever seen on a twelve-year-old. Almost a tuxedo, with a bow tie and even a pocket square. His dark hair was slicked back with what must've been two handfuls of gel. When Kari and his handler, Craig, came to collect him, they both did a double take.

We knew the one-on-one meeting must be airing on

TV—live, Chef Taylor had assured his home audience multiple times—but that didn't matter. We had no TV. No internet, either. So while we desperately wanted to see what was going on between them, we couldn't. And it was pretty obvious why—we weren't supposed to overhear the questions the Super Chef would be asking Joey. That would give us an unfair advantage for our meetings, one he hadn't had for his.

Meanwhile, we'd tried to find other tasks to keep us busy. Made dinner, cleaned up first the dishes, then the dorms. Bo's handler, a big college intern from Wisconsin named Brett, supervised us the whole way. But now we aren't really sure what to do with ourselves. All we know is none of us wants to go to bed before Joey gets back. No way am I missing the chance to interrogate him about how his meeting went. I need as much intel as possible in order to develop a plan for keeping mine, whenever it ends up happening, on track. Cooking and food focused.

I don't end up having to wait much longer, though, because a few minutes later the front door bursts open and Joey storms back into the dorms.

"Take the L, losers," he yells out. Using the thumb and index finger of one hand, he sticks an L on his forehead. He grabs his belt buckle with the other, then starts kicking his feet out like he's in a rodeo. The "Take the L" dance from *Fortnite*. "I've got this thing . . . In. The. Bag."

"Your meeting went well," Kiko, sitting up, says more than asks.

Pepper twists in his direction. "What kinds of questions were there? Did you have to take a test?"

"It went awesome!" Joey shouts. He stops dancing and thrusts a fist into the air. "He loves me." He glances at Pepper. "I can't tell you the questions. You trying to cheat?"

Pepper turns back fast, facing forward again. "Fine. Be that way."

"Congratulations, Joey," Bo says, but Joey ignores him.

"Yeah, great," I add, because I don't know what else to say. I mean, not that I *care*, but it should be impossible that the Super Chef, who always said he built his empire from scratch, from totally modest beginnings, would have some kind of special connection with this silver-spoon-in-his-mouth Chicago kid. Joey must be exaggerating; he can't possibly be Taylor's favorite.

Mo or Joe or whatever they call him back home is still flossing when I quietly slip into the boys' dorm to brush my teeth.

We hit our first Saturday in New York, and the closest I've come to my father is the brief moment he stood in front of me during the Teamwork Challenge. Seconds before he stole away just about everything I'd picked out of the pantry. There was a time I guess I assumed part of the deal in coming here was going to be learning directly from him, but the reality is we've spent tons more time with Wormwood and Graca.

I know I'm not the only frustrated one, either. Every time one of the Super Five thinks we'll see the Super Chef—at the press conference maybe, or on a training day—he's either not there at all or far enough away he might as well not be there. Up in the balcony, looking down on us. Or pacing across the stage, camera people and sous chefs and black-shirts creating an impenetrable wall around him.

I'd caught Pepper complaining about it to Kiko last night. I'd come out for a glass of water before officially going to bed. Kiko was listening attentively to Pepper's rant, but when it was over, she only responded with "But they did warn us this would happen."

She's right, they did. Hearing about something happening and actually being in the middle of it going on, though, can be two really different things.

A bunch of maneuvering out in the common room wakes me up. I rub the sleep out of my eyes and glance over at the bunk bed. Empty, both top and bottom this time. Joey and Bo, at least, must be out there already. When the clock tells me I slept way in, I figure everyone else probably is, too. I scramble up and out of our room, propelled by the jumbo-size FOMO suddenly gripping my spine, steering me forward like I have a handle on my back. They're not all in the common room crowded around the Super Chef, are they?

When I race out and my eyes adjust to the activity, however, they find something even more weird. My new, brash Chicago friend is actually being charitable, dishing out breakfast to all the others. Never expected to see Joey volunteering to cook, let alone waiting on everybody.

Bo interrupts his chewing long enough to scold me as Joey pushes a slice of fluffy egg from a cast iron pan onto the plate in front of him. "You are missing the frittatas."

I sigh out a little bit of relief. At least I've only missed food and not Chef Taylor. My jealousy reports in for duty, making sure I know that Joey's upbeat attitude must be a result of his one-on-one really going as well as he's been claiming it did.

On his way back to the kitchen, Joey stops in front of me. He tilts his pan. There's one wedge of egg-y wonderment left. I can't help but smell it. My stomach grumbles.

"Is that lemon?" I ask, voice quavering.

"Yep, with leeks and goat cheese. You game?"

I scratch my head, feeling my hair pointing in all directions. For the first time I notice everyone else is dressed, too. I'm the only one still in pajamas. "Sure. Thanks."

"I'll get you a plate." He winks at me, and it's not even sarcastic like it usually is.

I wander toward the table and sit at the head of it. "Why didn't someone wake me up?"

"We tried," Kiko says after a swallow.

"You were out cold," Pepper agrees.

Bo gulps down another forkful. "I shook your leg. You kicked me in the stomach."

"Sorry." I glance up at the cameras. "What did I miss? What are we doing today?"

"It's Pepper's meeting tomorrow night," Bo says. "With the Super Chef." He sounds genuinely excited for her.

"I know. We heard that at the end of the press conference."

"Well, it's confirmed now." Pepper holds up a white index card.

EVENING WITH THE SUPER CHEF #2
SUNDAY, NOVEMBER 17
PEPPER CARMICHAEL
7:00 P.M.

"All I got was this," she complains. "We haven't seen anyone in person all morning."

"Super quiet," Joey agrees as he slides a plate in front of me. The frittata slice is in the direct center, and somehow it smells even more amazing than a few seconds ago. "The silence is startin' to freak me out a little, you know?"

I look at him. He's smiling at me like we're best friends. "Freaked out," I agree. "Yeah."

"It's the clam before the rainfall," Bo agrees.

"*Calm*," Pepper corrects him. "Before the *storm*." She picks up her empty dish and walks it toward the sink, then makes eye contact with me. "I'd eat and get dressed quick if I were you. You know how things are around here. There's basically two speeds. Waiting around and—"

"Pandemonium," Kiko finishes for her.

A half hour later Kari leads us downstairs, through the Super Chef Arena kitchens, into the elevator, and out the front door of the building. At first it feels good to breathe in the crisp November air. Then a car honks and a cab driver starts shouting at a truck driver, and I remember: Super Chef Arena might be a tough place, but out here it's 100 percent New York City and probably a whole lot more dangerous.

I feel more comfortable when I see Mel and the other four handlers approaching from down the block. For some reason, even though they're as much a part of the competition as Kari or Wormwood is, these college kids feel like they're on our side.

We pile into two vans idling at the curb, each of us wearing winter jackets with sweatshirts underneath. It seems about twenty degrees colder than it was just three days ago.

The drive—lots of waiting for pedestrians to cross and taxis cutting us off—takes maybe forty minutes. We pull to a stop, and a security guard yanks the side door open. The giant sign right outside the van tells me we've made it to a place called Leah Square Park.

"What are we doing *here*?" Joey asks, looking around at the trees and grass and benches.

Kari walks around the front of the van. She points to the far side of the park. For the first time I notice the black-white-and-red food truck parked there. The diamond-shaped *Super Chef* "SC" logo shines from one side. "You're doing *that*."

It takes a minute or two to march across the park to the food truck. Chef Wormwood is waiting for us when we get there, rubbing her hands together to ward off the chill. No chef's coat, just a heavy sweatshirt and jeans. My eyes find the Super Chef in the distance. He's dressed as casually as his sous chef, talking with some guys near the end of a long line that starts in front of the truck's service window and winds away into the distance, curling in on itself multiple times.

"I'll be around, okay?" Mel assures me in his usual

warm but confidential tone. He and the other handlers head out to help Taylor manage the crowd. I look up at the only adult left with us. Wormwood.

Behind her, the people in line wear ratty clothes and carry heavy backpacks. Some have dogs on leashes, a few drag giant black garbage bags along the ground. One or two push shopping carts filled with more bags and cans and blankets.

"Are they homeless?" Pepper asks. She takes a step back.

"Line up," Chef Wormwood warns. Pepper forces herself forward again.

Wormwood peeks at the line over her shoulder before turning her attention back to us and continuing. "Saturday mornings, Chef Taylor's food truck sets up in a local park to offer up a meal to those in need. This week you five are going to help." She begins to pace down our line, handing out blue plastic gloves for us to pull on.

"Is this part of the test?" Kiko asks. She looks around, probably noticing the same thing I am. No cameras.

Wormwood's serious expression doesn't change. "Everything's part of the test."

"Every Saturday he does this?" I ask as Wormwood stops in front of me.

"That's what I said."

"It's just . . . I've never seen it on *Super Chef* before."

"No," Wormwood says as she pushes gloves into my

chest. I have to reach up to grab them. "You haven't, have you?" As she paces to Bo next, she adds, "There are some things that aren't done for television. It isn't the point."

Inside the truck, we form an assembly line. Each burrito we make is the same recipe. Pepper warms the tortilla and passes it to Joey, who fills it with ground beef and some cheese. He slides it to Bo, who folds it, then pushes the completed meal toward Kiko. She wraps it in white paper.

I man the window, handing out a burrito and a bottle of water to each new person. I don't have to worry about taking money or making change. Everything is free.

After about a hundred no-charge meals, my bicep starts to grow sore from all the repetitive reaching. There's still no end in sight to the line. In fact, when I lean forward, I see more and more people arriving to join it at the back. The Super Chef's out there, too, traveling up and down, talking to the people waiting, laughing with them, hugging them.

Behind him are several black-shirts. They wear sweatshirts today, decorated with the same *Super Chef* logo. Chef Graca's with them, too. They're handing out other items—I make out socks, hand wipes, first aid kits, toothbrushes, toothpaste.

Chef Wormwood stays in the kitchen with us, stalking up and down our line. "A little less meat," she warns Joey.

"We have to get through as many people as we can."

"Can't we do something cooler? Elevate these? Is there any cilantro in here? A radish?" He raises his voice. "My kingdom for a radish!"

Wormwood shakes her head, but she doesn't scold him. "Save the elevating for the arena. A time comes when cooking becomes just that: cooking. Eating is simply eating. It's not about winning out here. It's about survival." She pauses a moment, and what she says next comes out quieter. "You guys are doing great."

"Thanks, kid," a gray-bearded man says to me as I pass him the next burrito. His frayed hood darkens his face. He can hardly steady his shaking hand long enough to take hold of the free food. When he turns to stumble away, Chef Taylor is right there to intercept him.

"How've you been, Sam?" Lucas Taylor asks the older guy.

"Had myself a good fall the other day," Sam answers. "Lucky I didn't break something." They talk some more, but it's only after they wander away. I don't hear the words, but I do see the Super Chef wrap a blanket around the bearded man's shoulders. I watch as Sam struggles to unwrap the paper from his burrito. The Super Chef reaches up with his own slightly shaking fingers. They work together to free Sam's burrito for him. It takes them longer than it should, but when they finally finish, Sam's able to take a hungry chomp.

"Curtis." It's Wormwood. "Pay attention."

The next person in line is staring up at me. I hurry to hand out another burrito, one more water. Then I lean over in Kiko's direction. She's in the middle of securing a new burrito inside more paper. "Not so tight."

She looks up at me sharply at first, then follows my gaze out the window. People are everywhere, sitting on benches or leaning against trees, standing in huddles to share warmth and, sometimes, half their burrito with someone who arrived late. She watches them work the wrapping off. Most do fine, but a few struggle like Sam had.

Kiko's fingers freeze. She nods back at me. "Yes. Okay."

The next burrito has an easy flap to grab hold of and unfold.

"**S**undays," Kari announces from the doorway the next morning, "are for catching up on your homework."

We make it to the common room just as she steps through the door. She stops quickly, tucking her clipboard close, to avoid a rushing Ashley—Kiko's handler, a tanned intern from Florida—and Brett as they carry chairs over to a new card table in the far corner. Actually, I see now all five handers are here, some setting up other tables, others organizing stacks of pages and worksheets.

Kari navigates around them all so she can deliver a big, flat box to the kitchen island. The curling pink script on the top and sides tells me it's from Cocoa and Hailey's Doughnut Shop, which I've never heard of, but this is New

York, after all, and there are probably a thousand doughnut shops better than anything we have in North Sloan.

"Homework?" Joey cries. I follow him over to the island. Straight to the box. "What, you think you can soften the blow with free doughnuts? I'm onto you, you know."

He flips up the box lid to reveal a kaleidoscope of frosting, glazes, and jellies. He quickly snags a long one with a chocolatey cream filling piped in a zigzag pattern straight down the middle. He eyes it before taking a huge bite. "Oh. Nutella. Wow," he says through big chews.

"Good choice," Kari says. "That's my favorite, too. And, yes, these doughnuts are most definitely a bribe." She tugs at the box as the rest of us eye it, trying to make a good choice. "No homework, no doughnuts. So should I take them back?"

"No!" Joey says, grabbing his side of the box and tugging. "There's another Nutella in there."

Kari lets go of her end. "You can keep them if you share," she says, her eyes boring into his. "And if you do your work. There isn't that much, you've barely missed a week so far."

"I'll trade this jelly for that Nutella one," Joey says to Kiko, and I'm guessing the fact that he's stopped arguing is about as close to an agreement to work on homework as our producer is going to get out of him.

"After breakfast," she continues, pointing around to the five pop-up stations around the room. "Find your handler. They each have the assignments your schools have sent along so you can keep up. They'll help you with them as much as they can."

Mel's waiting at one table with a little stack of papers in front of him. He waves and smiles just as, behind me, Bo says, "Hey, a passionfruit one. *Muy bueno.*"

An hour later, Mel and I are just finishing up my work. All that's left are a few math problems. I'm stuck on one. I scratch my temple and sigh, sinking my chin down into the hand at the end of one bent-elbowed arm.

"Math not your subject?" Mel asks me.

"I usually have help," I say, my words slurred because I'm too lazy to lift my head.

"Your sister?" he asks.

That makes me sit up. "Yeah. How'd you know?"

"Because the other day, in front of your building, in the ten minutes it took you to say goodbye to your mom, Paige asked me what the temperature was like where we were going, and when I told her it hadn't gotten above forty-eight degrees in the last month, she told me that was eight-point-something-something in Celsius, and that that was seven-point-something-something higher than the average December temperature in . . . hold on, I'll remember it—"

"Reykjavik. She wants to spend Christmas in Iceland someday. Apparently they have this tradition where they give each other books on Christmas Eve? And then spend all night reading them? In Paige's version there's hot chocolate. And my Mexican spiced popcorn. Reading all night is pretty much peak Paige." I point at the half-finished math. "This is about the only thing she'd think was cooler."

"There cayenne in that popcorn?"

I nod. "And chili powder. It only works with both."

"Interesting. I've only made it with cayenne."

I look up at him, surprised again to remember that he's probably an excellent cook. I keep forgetting he's in culinary school.

Mel gives my shoulder a little nudge with his. "Let's hurry up. If we finish fast, maybe you can tell me more about how the chili powder plays off the cayenne."

That evening, Pepper comes out of her room wearing a flower-patterned dress, all ready for her meeting with the Super Chef. Her hair is back to the way I first saw it on TV, curls everywhere. It jumps around on top of her head like it has a life of its own.

She may not have gone over the deep end like Joey, but

she definitely spent a lot of time dressing up and getting her hair just right. I start to panic. What am I going to wear to my dinner? I don't own these kinds of clothes.

Pepper fidgets while she waits for Kari to pick her up and take her to meet with the Super Chef. We wish her luck as she walks out the door. She turns and waves at us, finally smiling.

As soon as the door shuts, though, Joey stands up and faces the rest of us, like he's been asked to do some kind of presentation. "She didn't name any friends."

"What are you talking about?" Kiko asks.

"Back in the press conference. Friday. I keep thinking about it. She totally dodged the question about friends."

"That's crazy," I say, even though I kind of know it's not. It's just . . . it's not any of his business, that's all. "Those questions were being thrown at us so fast. Like you didn't get confused or hesitate?"

"Not about having friends, dude," Joey says dismissively. "You either have friends or you don't. It's not exactly multiple choice."

M onday morning, I'm the first one awake on the boys'
side. I slip out quietly into the common room to find
both Kiko and Pepper already there. Kiko's on the couch,
still in pajamas, flipping through a notebook that looks
kind of like my own recipe journal. Fully dressed, Pepper
is sitting at the stool on the island, sipping an espresso and
making a list.

"What's that?" I ask her.

"Nothing."

She brings up an arm to cover her pad, but not before
I make out the first bullet. "Teamwork." She's probably
trying to work out the next theme. I've spent some brain

cells on it myself. The NBA is to teamwork as the Louvre is to . . . ?

Yeah, I have no idea, and Pepper's clearly not sharing, so I wander over to the pantry, scouring the shelves for a good breakfast option.

"Well, we won't be needing any races into the pantry tonight, will we?" the Super Chef says from the stage that evening.

I sneak a glance to my side, at Kiko. She looks as bewildered as I feel.

"All the supplies you should require for this challenge are already right in front of you!" Chef Taylor explains with a shout, extending both hands out at the same time for extra emphasis.

The typical whirlwind of cheering and flashing lights and zooming cameras kicked off this episode, but now the commotion dies down. Our stations are back where they belong. Any evidence of the huge press conference just a few days ago has disappeared. The three chefs—Taylor, Wormwood, Graca—are standing in the same stage spots they're always in, as if red Xs marked their spots.

"Welcome to Challenge #2. Home cooks all over the country, all over the world, really, cook with the simplest ingredients every day. For them, cooking isn't about making something fancy. It's about feeding their families.

Tonight, it's your turn." The Super Chef looks eagerly at us, as if he expects us to understand what to do next from his expression alone. When we all just stare back, he waves his hands and says, "Well, go on, those boxes aren't going to open themselves."

Ten hands reach out to flip open the box lids in front of us. We start pulling out ingredients. They're stacked on top of each other in a way that really only lets you remove them one at a time. The Super Chef narrates as each item is revealed.

"A box of spaghetti. Jarred olives and pickles. Canned tuna. In fact, cans galore! Corn, peaches, green beans. Oh, and a box of instant rice!" His excitement picks up. "Dried lentils. English muffins. Pizza sauce. A loaf of plain sliced white bread. Cheese slices. Butter. Eggs. Milk. Sugar, both regular and confectioners'."

One after another the ingredients are set out on our stations. Everyday stuff, most of it canned or boxed or jarred. Nothing fresh, except the most basic of staples, like eggs and milk. It's the type of food you'd buy if you were on a strict budget. You can trust me on that—because it's the same stuff you'd find on any random day in the Pith pantry, too. On a lot of days, the *only* things you'd find in our pantry.

Behind me, Joey groans. I wonder if he's ever cooked without an expensive protein, at least a fancy cheese. I know he hasn't since we got to New York.

The Super Chef claps his hands to get our attention. I hadn't realized how hard I was staring at the groceries, already fixating on a plan. "These ingredients are the driving force behind the nightly meals in a huge number of homes throughout the nation. No filets or racks of lamb, no scallops or never-frozen fish, sometimes not even a fresh vegetable. Tonight, we want to see you take up the reins of the everyday hero of food everywhere: the home cook on a budget. You'll have only these ingredients and the basics at your stations to do your part."

I glance up to remind myself of those basics again: olive oil and vinegars and essential spices. My mind works even harder.

"You have forty minutes to make us an entrée and a dessert," the Super Chef continues.

"Dessert?" Joey mutters under his breath. Another thing I've never seen him cook: anything sweet. His dream of trading the Louvre tickets for my NBA weekend might already be evaporating into the rafters like hot steam.

"You're not obligated to use all these ingredients, but the more you employ in your dishes, the better. And remember tonight's big prize: Paris! The Louvre!" The big TV behind him shows images of the Eiffel Tower and the masterworks all throughout its famous Louvre museum. It lingers longest, of course, on the *Mona Lisa*. "Get ready,

Chefs." He stares up at the clock, waits a few quick seconds. "Your time starts . . . now!"

I see the tuna and the olives and the spaghetti, and I already know what I'm making for an entrée. I've cooked it before for Paige; it isn't that different from that time not so long ago I had to make her clam sauce but with tuna instead of clams.

That night, my sister told me, "I trust your creativity, Chef."

I remember the first time I made Mom a casserole using almost all canned ingredients. She'd been skeptical at first, but after eating it, she told me it was delicious. She told me something else that night, too. "Well, you certainly don't get all this creativity from me, that's for sure."

Outside the high school gym, just before Pettynose showed up, I heard some goth kids in the front of the cupcake line saying, "This is mega creative for high school concessions, isn't it?"

Then there's the Louvre, Wormwood's hint that the prizes are connected to the themes. Because, like Pepper says, for sure there's lots of history in that museum, but there's art there, too. A ton of art. A ton of . . . creativity.

And I know tonight's theme without having to consult Pepper's list of possibilities. Everything points straight to *creativity*, as if there's a lit sign above the Super Chef's head. The same Super Chef who's partially responsible for my having to be so creative all these years. But that doesn't matter right now. All that matters is cooking this entrée and dessert as perfectly as I can. All that matters is winning another challenge.

My hands start to move faster than they ever have.

By the time I walk my spaghetti and tuna up with my cinnamon rolls, my station is a disaster. But I've used as many of the ingredients as I could. The tuna and the olives, the spaghetti, a bit of the pizza sauce, the white bread and butter and powdered sugar.

The chefs take turns tasting my food. Wormwood takes a bite of one of my cinnamon rolls. "And how did you make these again?"

"With the white bread. You just cut the crusts off, thin out the slices with a rolling pin, brush both sides with melted butter, then make up some cinnamon sugar to sprinkle on top. Roll them up, bake them, and prep a glaze with the powdered sugar and butter. My sister loves them."

Wormwood chews her roll some more. She turns and shares a look with the other chefs. Then she meets my eyes again before saying, "Your sister's a smart young lady."

I almost faint.

Even though the other chefs bring forward some interesting dishes, like an everyday white-bread pudding and a tuna casserole somehow made with cheese singles and bread crumbs that started out as toasted English muffins, I know I did well. When the blue desks come out, I don't hesitate to write CREATIVITY on the white card in bold letters.

I guess the theme was easy for the others, too, because three of us get it right. Kiko, Bo, and I grin when Chef Graca confirms our guess is correct while Pepper (DEAL-ING WITH ADVERSITY) and Joey (COOKING WITH BAD INGREDIENTS) sulk some more. Then, like all the other nights, the scores flash. First for the challenge:

Curtis Pith	91
Bonifacio Agosto	88
Kiko Tanaka	84
Pepper Carmichael	79
Joey Modestino	70

I swear, I have to really stop myself from pumping my fist into the air. Stay cool, Curtis.

The envelope I'm handed for winning again is super thin. Still, I have to accept it with both hands because my nerves are jumping up my whole arm, wrist to shoulder. I might've started in last, but now I've won both Challenge #1: Teamwork, and Challenge #2: Creativity. My dreams aren't so far away anymore. They're not even right in front of me. They're actually in my grasp now.

During the moment I spend marveling at this latest prize, the running grand totals update on the scoreboard.

Curtis Pith	215
Kiko Tanaka	209
Bonifacio Agosto	193
Pepper Carmichael	182
Joey Modestino	170

I didn't have time to do the math, didn't think about it, actually. But now I try to channel Paige's powers to run the numbers in my head, in case what I'm seeing ends up being some kind of mistake.

First place. Not just for one challenge. *Overall* first place. Wait. Can I win? Will I really be able to buy Mom a house? I don't know how to floss or do the "Take the L," but my feet feel so light, I rush up the steps two at a time into the dorm, the rest of the Five not far behind.

In the common room, Joey tosses his chef's jacket at the sectional but misses. It hits the floor with a fluttering rustle. "Can't believe even he's ahead of me," he grumbles, gesturing toward Bo.

"Why don't you shut it, Joey?" Pepper says.

"Hey." It's Kari. We'd been led up to the dorms by Ashley. I didn't realize the producer had followed behind us, too. "There are three more challenges before the final. If you're mad about your current standing, do better next time."

Pepper and Joey sulk off to opposite ends of the sectional. Bo looks like he's about to cry. Kiko puts an arm around his shoulders.

Kari walks into the kitchen. "Curtis, great job tonight. Just in time for you to find out about your big day, too."

I'm still thinking about Wormwood actually complimenting my dish, about Paris and first place and new houses and . . . everything, so her words don't completely register in my brain until she's standing right next to me. I'm breathing normally right up until I see the same kind of white card Pepper got the other day waiting in Kari's hand. She sets it on the kitchen island. Slides it slowly in my direction, until it's close enough for me to read.

EVENING WITH THE SUPER CHEF #4
THURSDAY, NOVEMBER 21
CURTIS PITH
7:00 P.M.

She has another card for Kiko. Tuesday. Meeting #3. And Bo. Sunday, meeting #5.

"We've got the full one-on-one schedule ironed out, at least," Kari says with a smile. "Let me tell you, no easy task. Anyway, I think I promised to let you guys know as soon as we did. So here you go. And now you know."

Her attempt at a clever rhyme barely registers with me. I'm not next. At least there's that. Matter of fact, I have three whole days to prepare. But knowing the date and time of my meeting with Taylor makes it that much more real. So real, I suck in a rattling breath.

But wait. Why am I nervous about this? It's what I'm here for, right? Get as many points as I can, however I can.

I won the first two challenges. I'm in first place. I'm actually beating these other kids. The Super Chef can't possibly ignore all that.

29

Mom leans into the camera, as if she needs to be an inch from it for me to see her. "Are they feeding you? Is your bed comfortable? Are you sleeping okay?"

"Mommm," Paige complains, elbowing her way into the shot. "One question at a time. You're not letting him answer."

Off camera, on the other end of the table I'm sitting at for this call, Mel chuckles softly, immediately covering his mouth. It's Tuesday, a full week since we've been here. Time for our first supervised calls—twenty minutes with our families over Skype.

"We're feeding ourselves, Mom," I say. "And sleep is fine." I mean, sleep hasn't been *that* fine, but I'm not going to tell her about it. No reason to spark a full-blown Mom panic. "How are you guys?"

"We're feeding ourselves, too," Paige jokes. "It's been awful."

"Are you being careful in the kitchen?" Mom asks, gently pushing my sister away. "Mel! Where's Mel?"

"Right here, Ms. Pith," Mel says, leaning back in so the camera picks him up. "We're always on hand to help and keep things safe."

Paige interrupts again, and relief shows on Mel's face as he fades into the background once more. "Who's the best?" my sister asks. "Is it you? It is! You're so far ahead. It's so cool."

"No, they're all super talented. Some of the things they've cooked . . . Bo did this dessert, and Pepper made jambalaya. Oh, and Joey's frittatas."

"But you're the only one winning!" Paige sings.

Mom moves to block Paige away again. "Okay, honey, relax. Let Mommy talk to Curtis." Her expression brightens. "So! Huge opportunity for you coming up, huh? Your one-on-one meeting's Thursday, right?"

My meeting. The one I tossed and turned over for hours last night. I was supposed to keep it focused on cooking and food. But after winning those first two challenges, thoughts of Lucas Taylor actually recognizing my talent keep hopping up and down, waving for me to notice them.

The Super Chef wants to show the world the future of cooking? I wonder how he feels now that he can see it coming at him from straight out of his own past.

But I can't forget that Distracted Curtis is Last Place Curtis, and focusing on Lucas Taylor my father instead of the Super Chef the . . . well, the *chef*, is totally a one-way street to Distractionville. Every time I try to shove thoughts of impressing him, of finally showing him what he's been missing out on, back down, though, they pop right up again, like a mental game of Whac-A-Mole gone horribly wrong.

And now Mom's bringing it up? What, is she going to warn me about Taylor? Finally give me some advice, some way to approach my father? Does Paige know about him now? And I haven't even asked them about Pettynose yet . . .

"I'm sorry," Mel interrupts, squeezing back into the shot. "That one's out of bounds. No discussion about the upcoming schedule. Remember, there's information circling out there that these guys purposely don't know about. No discussion—"

"About what's next," Mom says flatly. "I got it the first time. No hints about the one-on-one evenings, either. Yes, yes." She rolls her eyes. "Your people have been very clear."

"Hey, Paige," I call out, changing the subject since I can

hear Mom's tone slowly growing angrier. "How's school?"

My sister's face jabs into view, angled in from one side. "School? Are you kidding me right now? I'm not going to talk about *school*. You're winning *Super Chef*!"

The rest of the twenty minutes goes by way too fast, Mom continuing to ask all sorts of logistical questions, Paige getting more and more excited about my first-place standing. Mel warns Mom time is almost up, but she tries to ignore him, keeps firing off reminders. "You take care of my boy, Mel! Be yourself, Curtis! Come back safe! We love—"

The screen goes black.

"Sorry about that," Mel says. "They're very strict about the time allowed for these calls."

He leads me out of the conference room. Kiko's waiting with Ashley right outside. Guess she's next. She seems a little nervous, shifting on the balls of her feet. We share a quick smile.

Maybe what Kiko was really nervous about, though, was her one-on-one. It happens that night, same exact time as Pepper and Joey before her. Like them, she leaves dressed up fancy, and like them, she comes back looking happy, but doesn't say much else. Which is pretty much how Kiko is most of the time. No reason to expect a flood of info from her now.

Besides, tomorrow's the third challenge. We're starting to spend a lot less time gossiping or trying to figure out what will happen next. Mostly we seek out as much rest as possible, because every day here is a little more exhausting than the one before it. I don't care what the schedule says, we haven't had an "open" day yet.

The next twenty-four hours pass by like a rushing train, and suddenly it's Wednesday, the night of Challenge #3. I'm standing in the center of the pantry while the rest of the Super Five race around me, scooping up ingredients, filling their boxes. I'm the only one who's completely lost, and my time is running out.

Three ways. *Three. Ways.* What can I make three different ways?

For about the tenth time I run through the cooking methods the Super Chef listed out to start this episode, hoping one of them—or three of them, actually, I need *three ways*—will spark some idea in my stagnant brain.

— Roast
— Grill
— Sear
— Sauté
— Fry
— Bake
— Raw prep

The idea is to pick an ingredient that can be prepared using three of those cooking methods. But . . . were there more than those? It seems like I'm missing one or two. And what does the custom-crafted Molteni stove prize tell me about tonight's theme?

Answers? No, nothing, and nada.

Chicken would be an obvious choice. Probably *too* obvious. What else, then?

The rest of the chefs are elbowing each other to get a crack at the pork and beef case, and that's when the answer leaps into my head and flops around like a freshly caught fish. Fish, of course. Because it's seafood I need.

I race for the fishmonger section, knowing I'll have it all to myself. The scallops couldn't be more obvious, right up front. I can grill scallops. I can use them in a ceviche, which is a raw prep. And of course, I can do the classical preparation: a picture-perfect sear.

I scramble for other ingredients, flavor profile ideas popping off in my head like fireworks. And, just as our pantry time is up, I hurry back into the arena, lugging my box.

The rest of the chefs are already setting up, and right away I notice three of them—Joey, Pepper, and Bo— pulling out pressure cookers. That's when that last item in the list, the one I forgot, shows up in my memory again. *Braising.* Sorry, buddy, but you're way late to the party.

Which is really too bad, because nothing brings out the flavors of a rich protein like a solid braise. Pepper has lamb; Bo, pork shoulder; Joey, some kind of beef, maybe a tenderloin. I steam past Kiko and notice her short ribs.

I want to kick myself but that won't help. Sure, I'm the only one with seafood. Maybe it'll send me back to last. On the other hand, I could stand out and take first again. Man, if I did, I'd have a big enough lead that they might cancel the rest of this competition altogether. I let myself dream about that for a second, picture myself standing alone in the arena with the Super Chef. No crowd, no sous chefs, no Super Five, just me and my father. He grabs my wrist and raises my arm into the air, like I'm some kind of MMA champ.

Hold up. Where's my gigantic ceremonial check? I shake my head, and the vision changes to what it's supposed to be. Chef Taylor disappears like smoke. All that's beside me is a huge pile of money.

Come on, Pith, *focus*. Stop worrying about the Super Chef and start remembering the two hundred and fifty thousand reasons you're really here.

It's no good, though, because I spend the next thirty minutes trying to cook while continuing to fight that same battle in my head. Constantly pushing away the wrong vision—me standing alone with the Super Chef, huge, proud smile on his face, patting me on the back—and replacing it with the right one—me standing with the money.

Focus.

Did I use too much cumin? I taste my sauce again, my tongue detecting exactly how much this war in my head has been distracting me. Because, yeah, there's definitely too much cumin in that sauce. I rush to fix it, but time is short.

And then it's up. My hands not only have to stop, they have to shoot skyward again, to prove I'm not still working. We're called forward to present our dishes. I hold my head high as I walk my three almost-perfect (that cumin!) scallops to the stage—one seared on a bed of sweat pea puree, the second in a tomato and lime ceviche with avocado and orange. My last offering is grilled and covered with a delicate ginger and way-too-much-cumin sauce.

The Super Chef and his two sous chefs taste my scallops. Without a word or hint, they send me back to my station. After another one of their quick huddles, they call for the next dish.

I end up being the only one to separate the three ways, and, waiting for the final verdict, I can't stop myself from thinking I made a huge mistake. The rest of the Super Five all find a way to combine theirs into a single dish. The most impressive is Pepper. Somehow she manages to stew, roast, and braise her lamb shank in thirty minutes. It seems impossible, but then I remember the snippets of her video from that first night, how she cooked multiple dishes at the same time, one hand working each. This challenge was made for her.

Also, can I just say that pressure cookers are amazing? I've been asking for one since I was eight.

Pepper presents her lamb shank stew with okra and carrots and a cilantro condiment drizzled on top. The three chefs try to remain stoic while they taste it, but I can see the faint smiles betraying their fixed expressions.

This is our fourth time on TV. Each episode goes faster than the last. I'm used to the applause and crazy cheering, the cameras in my face. But that doesn't mean I'm any more comfortable with these stressful challenges. In fact, it seems like the faster these hours go, the more exhausted I am at the end of them. I'm trapped in a totally different kind of pressure cooker.

I'm so ready for this night to be over, for the scores to flash and the lights to fade, but instead of the end coming, the black-shirts trot the blue plastic desks out, set them up again. They hand us another Sharpie and another blank white card.

The theme. Somewhere along the way, between the cumin disaster and my unnecessary daydreams, I forgot all about it.

Quick, what could a top-of-the-line stove that does everything mean in a challenge like this one? NBA, teamwork. Louvre, creativity. Molteni . . . ?

I can't come up with anything, so instead I try to think about Pepper, because I know she knocked this one out of the park. My eyes cloud with sweat, and I'm not seeing straight. I write down the best word I can use to describe her.

VERSATILITY

Unlike the first few challenges, though, my throw-the-dart guess isn't quite so lucky. Only Joey and Pepper land on the right answer, MULTITASKING. Of course. *Three ways.* With the right configuration on a Molteni, you can cook a bunch of things at once. In a ton of different ways. Heck, you can run a whole kitchen. That's exactly multitasking. And so is Pepper.

When the episode finally comes to its real end, when the bells ding and the lights flash, the new scores show up blurry. I wipe at my eyes to be sure I'm seeing them right.

Pepper Carmichael	92
Joey Modestino	88
Bonifacio Agosto	77
Curtis Pith	65
Kiko Tanaka	60

A representative from Molteni presents the award certificate to Pepper. "I hope you have room for our best, young lady."

"Oh, we'll make room," an overexcited Pepper agrees. "We'll turn our whole apartment into a kitchen if we have to."

Everyone laughs—the crowd, the Molteni rep, Pepper, the chefs on the stage. Everyone, maybe, except for me. I'm too busy inspecting the scores. I never imagined Kiko landing at the bottom of any challenge, but the chefs are right. Her attempt to combine baked, roasted, and smoked short ribs into a single dish was clumsy. She chose the perfect meat to braise, but, like me, hadn't bothered with a pressure cooker. Big mistake, and the only thing that prevents me from dropping back into last for this challenge. So much for those dreams of three wins in a row.

The lights flash again. The scores flip once more, rolling over into new grand totals.

Curtis Pith	280
Pepper Carmichael	274
Bonifacio Agosto	270
Kiko Tanaka	269
Joey Modestino	258

At least I'm still in the lead. Barely. My dream's still in my grasp, but it feels slippery, like I'm trying to separate the whites from some egg yolks using my fingers.

The only thing I take the time out to do before I fall into bed that night is write the list of skills we've learned so far. The Super Chef's keys to success. I'm growing as obsessed with them as I've always been with him, reviewing over and over the ones we know already, trying to guess what the final two could be.

But as much thinking as I do, I admit I have no idea which ones are left. I fall asleep hugging my journal, the page still open to the list I stared at until my eyelids felt as heavy as two bags of flour.

FROM CURTIS PITH'S RECIPE JOURNAL
(Back pages)

SUPER CHEF LUCAS TAYLOR'S
FIVE KEYS TO BECOMING AND STAYING A
GREAT CHEF

TEAMWORK
CREATIVTY
MULTITASKING

_____
_____

What's next?????

30

Cameras flash and click as the Super Chef and I make our way down a red carpet runner leading straight to a limousine waiting at the curb. My breath turns to clouds of steam as I take in the crowd, recognizing some of the same press and photographers who interviewed the Super Five the other day. They shout questions at both of us, but it's such a whirlwind of activity I can't hear their specific words.

I'm sweating, but I think it has as much to do with the bulky sweater I'm wearing as how nervous I feel. Mom found this pine-green, wool gem at Goodwill last year. The first time I wore it to school, Tre dubbed it the "green monster" because of the way it hung off me and made me look like Bigfoot covered in salsa verde. I have to roll up the sleeves a bunch of times to get my hands to make an appearance out the ends, but it was the only answer I had to Joey's tuxedo thing and Pepper's perfectly placed hair.

Before I left, I locked myself in the bathroom for a while. I needed to find a place in the dorm where I could be alone. Concentrate. Of course Joey had pounded on the door, suggesting his situation was an "emergency," but I shouted back that I wasn't ready yet.

And I was really getting ready, too, just not in the way he probably assumed. I guess you'd call what I was doing meditating, though I've never actually done that before, and I'm not sure I was even doing it right. I just needed to come up with some way to call a truce on the constant battle in my head, to remind myself that no matter what questions the Super Chef tried to ask me, I needed to keep this "heart-to-heart" focused on cooking and food. I couldn't allow other topics to seep in—the amount of time I'd been thinking about them these past few days aside. The cumin fiasco had already cost me part of my lead. I can't lose any more cushion. Eyes on the prize.

Chef Taylor's dressed in an amazing dark suit with a cornflower-blue tie that makes him look like the cooking version of Tony Stark. People swoon left and right as we sweep by them. I almost think I'm watching the old Super Chef as I hurry with him toward the car, huge security guys in STAFF shirts surrounding us, hands up, keeping the press at bay. But then I notice his halting steps, how he shuffles and twists that left foot, and, no, it's the new Lucas Taylor taking me to dinner, for sure. The awkward, stumbly one.

The driver holds the limousine door open for us. The Super Chef steps to the side so I can climb in first. He follows, the door slamming shut as soon as his butt hits the seat. Taylor unbuttons his suit jacket and shifts into a more comfortable position across from me. "I'm delighted we're getting our time together finally, Curtis. Just overjoyed. I could hardly wait for this night. It simply wouldn't come fast enough for me."

"Which restaurant are we going to?" I ask him, my first effort to keep the conversation on track. Besides, no one had told me yet, and I was curious. I even had a couple cross-my-fingers hopes on where he would take me.

And hold on. He could hardly wait? But . . . he *did* wait. For eleven years he's . . . Food and cooking, Curtis. You even meditated about this. Or stood in a bathroom, closed your eyes, and said a bunch of nonsense toward the mirror over and over again, anyway.

The cameraman who followed us out of the building settles into the front passenger seat of the limo. It's Mr. Lumberjack again. He pushes his lens through the window separating the front seat from the back. The red light flares on.

The live audience must be with us now. The Super Chef slaps the studio grin back onto his face. "We'll be announcing tonight's destination in a moment. First, I want to know how you're feeling, Curtis. How's the competition been going for you?"

My nerves jangle. I blink at him a few times to settle them. I should talk about the okonomiyaki. But that's not where my head goes. For some reason I skip that challenge and start with the creativity one. "I have a lot of experience with canned goods. You know"—I pause for emphasis—"obviously."

The Super Chef issues a slow, slightly confused nod back. The limo lurches forward, and we both put our hands out to keep from sliding around in our seats. "So that's been your favorite challenge so far?"

Behind me, I feel the camera adjust slightly, swinging from his face to mine. I wonder if Joey's and Pepper's meetings started out being filmed in the limo, too. I feel a little bit exposed, like the whole world's watching me over my shoulder. It's pretty close to true.

All I can do is nod back. This trip is rapidly turning into a nodding contest. It's because my words feel locked up inside me, behind a dam of . . . I don't know what. But seriously . . . how can he sit there and ask me these obvious questions, like I'm some kid he knows nothing about, who he's just meeting for the first time?

"Have you been to New York before?"

My slow nodding becomes an even slower, just as confused, shake of my head.

"First time, really? It's amazing here, don't you think?" Chef Taylor asks as he gazes out the window at the city lights. "Every kind of food imaginable is always right around the corner." He twists to face me head on again. "Tell me, do you like Persian?"

Nearly a year ago I made a killer tabbouleh for the Super Bowl. That's kind of Persian, maybe more Middle Eastern. Of course Paige told me she preferred regular salsa, that I'd gone a little "too far" in my experimenting. I love her, but that kid can be a real disappointment sometimes. That tabbouleh was one hundred percent the bomb.

"Sure, guess so."

The Super Chef's grin widens. "Not feeling too talkative tonight? You're not nervous, I hope."

Tell him about the tabbouleh. And that one time you made falafel. Food and cooking.

But somehow I can't. It's like . . . I don't know . . . all of a sudden I've decided he doesn't have the right to know the real me. To hear about the things I've done. Think about it. He had about one million chances to come to North Sloan before, and he did nothing with any of them.

Besides, are these questions even real? What does he already know? Do he and Mom ever talk? Secret conversations after we've gone to bed, like the ones I sometimes overhear her having with her coworkers?

If they did, if he cared enough to remember what they discussed, he should already know I've never been to New York. So did he really ask me that question because he doesn't know the answer? Or is he just asking things he figures the audience must be itching to hear? Is this even a real conversation?

The seeping frustration I've been feeling for days starts to smolder. The big, famous Super Chef wants to know if I'm nervous? Seriously? The question feels like a trick. Like some kind of lie.

I squirm in my seat, my insides swirling. A mini-tornado keeps touching down at different spots in my gut. I suddenly want to ask him all *my* questions. The father ones. Like, why leave in the first place? Why never come back? Why, now that I'm this close, feet away, right in front of you, are you *still* pretending?

Whack, whack, whack. I send all three moles back into their dark holes.

Still, I'm confused. The truce has failed; the battle inside me rages more fiercely than ever. My heart yearns to say all these things, ask these questions, but my brain has outlawed them.

Be yourself, Curtis. That's one of the last things Mom said before Skype cut her off. Is this what she meant?

Did she predict I'd turn myself around like this?

I still haven't answered him, and it's like I've beamed the confusion I'm feeling straight onto his face.

For a second, the Super Chef's smile fades.

For a second, he's the one who looks panicked. As if he's the one, not me, who's losing his grip on the big chance of his life, the whole reason he exists.

It's the same moment the brakes of the limo squeal as it comes to an abrupt stop.

31

Lavish curtains obscure the main doors and windows of Colbeh's Café. The valets outside brush them back for us, revealing an ornate set of double doors framed in gold. As we step in, I take in an immense circular bar with a floor-to-ceiling wall of wines behind it. The whole, dimly lit place teems with so many guests there isn't a single open seat.

A thin, slouching manager greets us—lots of smiling and clasped hands and bowing. He leads us in and quickly back, cutting a winding path around tables, every one packed with customers. They torque in their chairs and crane their necks to get a glimpse of the celebrity in their midst. Chef Lucas Taylor, the Super Chef, the most famous cook in all the world.

Finally we arrive at a private room in the very back of the restaurant. "We're so honored to have you choose Colbeh's for your special evening," the manager says to Taylor, bowing again. He pulls back another curtain, revealing a hidden section clearly reserved for VIPs. A round, raised table with a comfortable-looking booth covered in throw pillows sits empty, waiting just for us.

The Super Chef goes first, somehow not lifting his leg high enough and catching his foot on the edge of the step up. The manager panics, reaching out like he's going to catch the most famous chef in the world before he tumbles back. Captain Slouch is either picturing a lawsuit or landing his face on the front page of the *New York Times*. "Hero restaurant manager saves Lucas Taylor's life." He sighs relief when the Super Chef catches himself with one hand and lands successfully in his seat without further help.

When it's my turn to slide in, the manager repositions the curtain in his grip, as if maybe he hadn't held it open far enough the first time around. I climb into the booth without a problem.

Now that I'm sitting again, I feel my shoulders relax a little. I'd become super tense throughout the journey in the limo, and it grew even worse during the march through the crowded restaurant, the camera and all those eyes watching us so closely. Then the bearded guy finds a spot at the edge of the table where he can train his camera on either me or Taylor, as the situation demands, and I remember where I am. What's at stake.

I know it's just one lens, but I sense the millions of eyes behind it. All waiting to see which mistake I'll make next.

"Tell me how you fell in love with cooking, Curtis."

I always thought the Super Chef's hair was the same color as mine. His eyes, too. But now that I'm the closest I've ever been to him, both seem darker—his hair maybe more brown than my sandy blond. And if his eyes are blue, they're a dark blue. Almost black. Not really hazel at all.

Plus, that little spike in the front, the one that's always matched mine when I've watched his show on TV? It's gone completely. He's combing it flat now. Have I been seeing it wrong all these years? It doesn't seem possible. And besides, it's not what I should be worrying about.

I should be concentrating on his question. It's my chance to turn the discussion back to cooking. To get past some of this anger before I blow this meeting entirely. But I have to pick my words carefully. There's so much *you're-my-father* stuff wrapped up in any answer I can give for how I fell in love with cooking.

"My mom told me about my father. That . . . how he always loved to cook. How talented he was. Is. I was seven, and I guess . . . I started wanting to cook, too. So I did. I was . . . it didn't take long to understand I was born for it. Into it."

Super smooth, Pith.

I stare into his eyes, waiting for them to flash recognition of the truths I avoided for both our sakes. But, oh, he's good, because his expression betrays nothing. And, oh, I'm a coward, because I wanted to say so much more. I was so sure applying to come here was the right thing to do. Mom had no job. We needed that prize money. But now . . .

A thin waiter with puckered lips arrives and sets a dish of radishes, olives, feta, watercress, and mint down between us. He asks about drinks. Taylor orders something called sharbat for both of us.

The Super Chef must notice my confusion because he says, "Trust me, you'll like it. It's a delicious beverage. And very healthy."

The waiter's about to leave, but the Super Chef stops him and adds some appetizers. Mirza ghasemi, which I know is smoked eggplant with tomato and garlic; dolma; minced beef and rice inside grape leaves; some hummus.

"All sound good?" he asks me.

I nod mutely.

"You have a gorgeous kitchen, by the way," Taylor says once the waiter departs. "Not that it had anything to do with selecting you for the contest, but it was hard to miss all that fantastic equipment. Is that your family home?"

That question's *almost* about cooking, but I'm wary of a trick. Maybe he's trying to corner me into some kind of Pettynose confession. I'm definitely not taking the bait. I keep my answer short and simple.

"No."

The Super Chef gazes at me, his smile fading once again as he waits for my answer to extend beyond just that lone word. When all I give him is a matching stare back, he asks, "Is something wrong, Curtis?"

"What could be wrong?" I ask him. "What could possibly be wrong?"

Because I'm starting to feel like *everything's* wrong. Tonight, and for a long time now. Because winning some money for Mom suddenly seems like a tiny Band-Aid on a really deep knife cut. When what I really need are stitches, a ton of them.

"I don't know," Taylor says, sniffing a little in frustration. "I . . . this is our chance to get to know each other. I think you understand that."

The Super Chef continues looking at me with a flat expression. "You do get this meeting is the subjective component of the competition, right? If it doesn't go well, it will be that much harder for us to select you as the champion."

It's like he's begging me to bring it up. So, just do it, then. Say, "You're my father," and let the conversation spiral from there. But there's still a part of my brain with a mallet raised in the air, waiting to knock those words down again before they're able to pop out.

I inhale. "I thought we would be talking about food. Cooking."

"Yes . . . yes, of course."

Swallowing hard, I try my best to look friendly. Not the least bit confused. Or frustrated. I can tell by his single raised eyebrow it isn't working. He knows he isn't talking to the real me. That me, colorful, alive Curtis—bright Curtis—feels trapped, as if I'm back in my sensory deprivation booth, pounding the glass to get out, all while some black-and-white version of me is getting to talk to my father, botching it entirely.

Taylor sighs. "I've been *trying* to ask you about cooking, Curtis. All you give me are one-word answers." He leans back in the booth and inhales before reconjuring his studio smile from somewhere down deep. He pitches forward again. "Let's start over. How about that? Why'd you choose a soufflé to cook for your entry?"

Blood starts flowing back to my brain. I didn't want to talk to him about home, or Pettynose's kitchen, or Mom. I've been holding back from calling him out for being my father but never *really* being my father.

But here it is, finally, a question that's about food and only food. Exactly what I wanted. Isn't it? Sure, I should *want* to answer this one. I should want to talk about my soufflé. Even with him. Or maybe especially with him. It's all still mega confusing.

All I know is the colorful version of me breaks out of his cage and starts to talk.

"I wanted to prove I could do something really technical. Something simple but complex. To me, that's the secret of great cooking. Doing complicated things in a simple way. Making dishes that are actually super hard look like they're easy."

He smiles and leans forward, dropping his chin into his hand. "Tell me more about that."

After the waiter returns to drop off the appetizers, the Super Chef puts in a slew of entrée orders, and it doesn't take long for them to start showing up. Every time a new plate is brought to us, another one is ordered. We can't possibly eat all the food he requests, but we can at least taste each offering.

So that's what we do. A nibble here, a spoonful there. The dip of a radish into this sauce, a swipe of some flatbread through that hummus. As each new dish arrives, we discuss its qualities, tasting, savoring, agreeing, debating. What started as one of the worst nights of my life might be turning into one of the best. I'm sitting here with my father, the Super Chef, and we're talking food. Maybe it doesn't matter if we talk about anything else.

The meal ends, and the manager returns, slouching and bowing with his hands together like he's praying the food was okay, that the Super Chef said good things about it for the millions of live viewers that might soon become Colbeh's Café visitors. He leads us out again. The restaurant's tables have turned over while we were hidden away in back, so a whole new set of onlookers stare and marvel at us as we pass back through the dining room.

"Curtis, that was a great discussion," the Super Chef says once the limo begins to guide us back. "Your knowledge is impressive. But . . ." He sighs. "I'm just not sure I know *you* any better than I did before tonight. Maybe we still have time to fix that. You want to start by telling me a little more about home?"

Annnd we're back.

The joy of talking food with him fades. This time the knot that forms at the back of my neck is pure anger. It's as if the fact that it went away for a while makes its return that much stronger. I feel a scowl coming on, but I work really hard to keep my face straight.

But seriously   *now* he's concerned about home? *Now* he wants to hear all about it? *Now* he wants time to fix things?

"Home is North Sloan. I'm sure you know."

He nods. "I do. Of course. And you live there with your mom and sister."

"Paige," I say. *Your daughter*, I think. *You do remember her name, right?* "Yeah. The three of us. Just us three."

"Three's a good number."

What's that mean? "It's the best number, actually."

Chef Taylor twists his squinting face, like trying to extract secrets from me is harder than squeezing the last stubborn drop of juice from an orange. "Your little family seems very close."

"We are," I say. "Close, I mean. We have each other. It's all we need."

He almost looks like he wants to give up. But he still doesn't, asking a few more questions that continue to draw shortened replies from me. A determination to dance away from his probing jabs at my life drops over my eyes like a curtain. One I can hide behind.

Because he should have to earn these answers. All those years he should've been working harder to know me. One night of curiosity can't possibly make up for a decade of ignoring me.

Eventually the fire in my gut flares hotter than ever. I can't stand it anymore. He's in mid-question when I interrupt him with "Why there?"

"Why . . . where?" he asks.

"Colbeh's Café. Why there? You could've taken me anywhere."

"That's . . . well, that's true." He looks toward the roof

of the limo. "But remember, it's not just you I took there tonight." He gestures at the camera, again honing in on us through the limo window. I'm so used to it, I kind of forgot about it. Forgot this is going out live to every single one of the Super Chef's precious fans. That Mom and Paige have probably been watching us snipe at each other all night, sitting on the edge of Mom's bed-couch, exchanging worried looks.

Huge opportunity for you coming up, Mom said the other day. And my stomach sinks, because I quickly go from worrying I might've blown it to knowing I already have. Just as sure as we can't get back the years we lost, the years I spent fatherless, I can't take back anything I've done or said here tonight, either. All the stubbornness, the short answers.

Even after my amateur meditating, I still let the wrong daydream win. Too worried about this man paying attention to me finally. Forgetting all about the prize I came here to win, the one my family's waiting for me to bring home to them.

I wonder if my sister is thrilled I actually uttered her name. I wonder if she's mad that I didn't say more about her, especially with all the prying Taylor's been doing. But she doesn't know he's her father, so she wouldn't understand my reasons for keeping our life private, for trying to stay focused. Even though, in the end, I've failed at that, too. I'm more distracted and confused than ever.

My sister is bound to be wondering what's wrong. What if, if she hasn't already, this televised conversation forces Mom to finally tell her the truth? My throat catches as I picture it, my heart rabbiting with the knowledge I'd be missing it. That I would've been the cause of it. I know Paige would want me there with her if—when—she ever found out.

Instead I'm stuck in this stupid limo, sitting across from our father. Maybe, deep down, I thought coming here would help me to better understand who Lucas Taylor was. But it hasn't.

And now Paige might be needing me more than ever. But here I sit, available to her only through the magic of television. Which is the same as not really being available at all. I know that from my years of watching the Super Chef on the same dumb screen.

"We have millions with us," he continues. "I wanted to show them food from a region most haven't been fully exposed to. To explore new dishes with a fellow chef at my side. I didn't know you too well before tonight, and I still don't, but you seemed like the right chef for this particular journey. And you were."

It's probably a compliment. Somewhere in the back of my mind, I know my idol since I was small just said a lot of nice things about me. Made me sound like a peer and not an apprentice. But I don't hear them. Because I'm still consumed with the possibility of Paige feeling bad all those miles away, and even though I have no idea if it's really happening or not, I resent him even more for it. It's a resentment that partially deafens me. Only certain words get through to my ears, echoing in my mind again and again as I stare back at him.

I'm just not sure I know you any better than I did before tonight.

The limo pulls to a stop. I reach for the door immediately, push it open wide. "You don't know me?" I ask. "And whose fault is that?" I don't give the Super Chef a chance to answer. I leap out of the car and race past the reporters for the front door.

Behind me, I hear my father shout, "Curtis! Wait!"

A giant security guard barely keeps up with me as I storm into the building. I zoom up to the arena alone in the elevator. Once I hit floor fifty-four, I jump out, heading for the stairs and the dorms. I don't slow down. And I know Taylor will have a hard time climbing out of the car in his clumsy, awkward way. I know he'll never catch me if I don't let him. And I won't. I can't. Not tonight, maybe not for the whole rest of my life.

I race into the dorms and slam the door shut. I should have planned out my entrance like Joey. I should be pretending things went great, do the "Take the L" dance, maybe floss a little bit, but I can't. All I can do is breathe heavily and push my all my weight against the door, in case the Super Chef does follow me up here, unwilling to let our conversation end on the note it did.

But there's no noise on the other side. No one's stomping up the stairs.

"How did it go?" Kiko asks.

Everyone's staring at me. "I . . ."

I can't. I can't tell them the truth. I can't lie, either.

Shaking my head, I make for the boys' side. I wish I could say I get to sleep fast, that I immediately forget about this night, about the shock and disappointment and bewilderment on the Super Chef's shadowed face. But no, it's still there, like a photograph seared onto my forehead. And when our secret Santa rolls the laundered chef's jackets into our room around two a.m., I hear him loud and clear. Because I'm still wide awake, hiding under my comforter, replaying the entire Colbeh's dinner in my head over and over again.

Friday night can't come fast enough. I spend most of that day finding corners of the common room to be alone in, still in misery over what happened at Colbeh's. On the way to Colbeh's. Coming back from Colbeh's. Still seeing the Super Chef's shadowed confusion, wondering how much damage I did to my already-shrinking lead. Yearning for another challenge with a chance to re-earn the points I must've lost. Desperately wanting to get back to what I do best. Cooking.

The arena is almost unrecognizable again. Our stations, normally set out in two rows so that we face forward as we work, are turned sideways. We'll be looking at each other, three of us on one side, two on the other, if we cook in this setup.

Three elegantly decorated, round dining tables with crisp white tablecloths wait where the Super Chef normally stands. Each one has a colored flag in the center. Red, green, blue.

There's no room left for the chefs up on the stage, so Taylor and Wormwood wait near a new serving counter down on our level. There's been no sight of Graca so far.

I resist making eye contact with Taylor, focusing instead on the comfort the familiar tools in front of me provide. Pans and spatulas, knobs on burners, lights on the oven, spotless silver mixing bowls. But then he speaks, and I can't help myself. I look up, straight into his eyes.

"Welcome to the fourth challenge of *The Last Super Chef* competition!" Lucas Taylor declares loudly. Wormwood applauds next to him, joining the crowd above, who are as excited as usual. The Super Five are lined up single file on either side of the centralized stations, Kiko, Pepper, and me on one side, Bo and Joey on the other. We're waiting for the chefs to tell us what new craziness they've cooked up for tonight. Aware it could be . . . well, just about anything.

"We're honored to have some very special guests dining in the arena with us this evening." The Super Chef gestures toward the stage.

From offstage, a long line of men and women in formal attire pace toward the flagged tables in an unbroken, single-file line. Of course I recognize them immediately, because it's a who's who of every hot cooking show host and restaurant owner on the planet. Including Madeline Dalibard, pastry chef extraordinaire. Her appearance reminds me tonight's prize is an apprenticeship with her. "With a focus on layered pastries and cakes," I remember the schedule saying. Which makes sense, those are her specialties. Baklava, sfogliatelle, baumkuchen, napoleons, all of them different and time-consuming pastry and cake recipes from all over the world.

What makes less sense is what that tells me about tonight's theme. No point worrying about it yet, I warn myself. Let the challenge play out.

Graca leads the rest of the chefs forward, a total of eighteen of them. They wave at the audience and us. When they step onto the stage, they separate into three groups, six to a table. The crowd goes even crazier, as if at first they were stunned by all this star power collected in one place, and only now are they realizing the magnitude of what they're witnessing. Even stoic Kiko sucks in a breath, and behind me I hear Joey mutter, "Holy . . ."

Bo and Pepper are practically swooning, too, Pepper

especially. She's waving both hands, trying to attract some celebrity attention. I can't tell which one she's waving at. I'm not even sure she knows.

They're all so starry eyed. And me? I avert my eyes from the glittery, attention-grabbing entry, focus on the work we're about to do. My fingers itch with anticipation, ready to start slicing and stirring, flipping and mixing. Ready to get back to cooking.

Once all eighteen celebrities are seated and the applause dies down, Wormwood steps forward to explain tonight's challenge. The Super Five will be working together to deliver a three-course meal to these special guests. In the first challenge we teamed up to cook a single dish, but tonight will be the first time we'll be operating as one unified kitchen.

The waitstaff will drop the tickets off at the new serving counter where Chef Wormwood, tonight's expediter, will coordinate the meal from the spot known in kitchen-speak as "the pass." She'll be calling each of us up one at a time to work alongside her. We'll have to pay close attention to make sure the dishes go out to the customers exactly as ordered.

"One second, Chef," Chef Taylor says, interrupting her.

Wormwood turns quickly, a puzzled expression on her face. "Chef?"

"No, everything you've said is right, precisely as we agreed," he assures her.

Chef Wormwood furrows her brow. "Exactly. So if I may continue—"

"But as I stand here, I realize I want to switch things up." Some of the guests onstage, watching their exchange closely from their seats, start to whisper to each other. Only a few seconds in, and there's already an irregularity. It's peak Super Chef. "How about I expedite, and you work the kitchen?"

"Chef, I . . . I'm not sure that's a good—"

"It'll be *fine*," the Super Chef says, cutting her off. He steps toward the pass and slaps it twice with both hands, like he's laying claim to it. "The day I started expediting was the day I knew I'd become a real chef. Feels like a good night to get back to it."

I suck in a cold breath. Two chefs working together at the pass must remain in lockstep, inches away so they can match each other's movements. When I'm called, the Super Chef and I will be closer than ever. Closer even than we were in that limo. And it seems the closer I get to him, the more anger I feel, no matter how much I try to push it away. Worse still, the angrier I get, the more mistakes I make. This might be my longest night yet.

• • •

The fake restaurant we're cooking for doesn't have a name, but a couple dozen gorgeous menus have been printed for it—curling script, fancy descriptions. As they're doled out to our famous diners, Chef Wormwood gives us a crash course on the dishes. At the pass, the Super Chef chats up his fellow star chefs, providing entertainment until the kitchen starts churning out food.

After Chef Taylor asks Chef Dalibard to stand and raves about her work, the first orders, from the red table, arrive. The Super Chef carries the ticket forward. Taylor takes a deep breath. "Order up! Appetizers for red. Two scallop, two risotto, two ravioli."

All five of us respond with a resounding "Yes, Chef!"

Taylor glances at Pepper. "Chef Carmichael, why don't you join me up front this round?"

The rest of us start to cook, calling out ready times, Chef Wormwood coaching us if we seem out of sync. We're still working red's appetizers when the green ticket comes flying in.

The voice calling it this time is much higher-pitched. Pepper's. "Chefs!" she says, her puffy ponytail jumping against her back. "Pay attention! Order up for the green table: four ravioli, one risotto, one scallop."

"Yes, Chef!"

A new batch of appetizers and timing starts, even as the first are almost on their way to the pass. My head spins.

We're scrambling already.

I'm on scallops. Blocking out the crowd noise and, honestly, everything else, I manage to sear the first batch to perfection, then carry them toward Kiko. We work together to center them on top of the dollop of carrot cream she's prepared, along with a drizzle of herb oil made mostly from marjoram leaves. Kiko adds a rolled-up ribbon of pickled carrot soaked in rice vinegar.

"Go," she says as soon as she lifts her fingers.

"Walking scallops!" I yell. As I hurry toward the pass, I hear Joey shout, "Walking ravioli!" at the same time Bo cries, "Walking risotto!" They each stop at Kiko's station to add the garnish that goes with their dishes, all carrot based.

With the Super Chef watching her so closely their shoulders brush against each other, Pepper inspects the plates we bring like she's Mrs. Kadubowski back home, checking whether I've paid attention in class that day, done all my homework.

Chef Taylor, though, doesn't even glance my way when I slide my scallops onto the counter. He's all over Pepper, but just a few feet away I'm all but invisible to him. I don't even bother scolding myself for letting it steal my focus again. I just take a step back and wait. Joey and Bo do the same.

"What do you see, Chef?" Taylor asks Pepper.

She repositions the pickled carrot on my plate.

He smiles at her. "Nice adjustment."

Pepper touches the scallop to make sure it's cooked correctly. With a fresh spoon she tastes the risotto, and the Super Chef does the same. "Is it a little bit salty, Chef?" Pepper asks.

"A touch, a touch," Taylor agrees. "But not enough to send back. It's good work." He gives the waiter permission to take the dishes to his guests.

Once he's away with the dishes, Taylor turns around, meeting Bo in the eyes. "Watch the seasoning on those risottos, Chef Agosto!"

"Yes, Chef!" Bo agrees. He starts working a new pan of the rice.

We hurry back to our stations, but not before, behind me, I hear the Super Chef compliment Pepper. "Very good palate, Chef Pepper."

Is that the theme? Palate? Strong taste buds? Or does it have something to do with how we're coordinating on our end of the kitchen? And what do any of those possibly have to do with Chef Dalibard and her fancy desserts?

Thing is, there's no time for theme. We're in the weeds. Tickets are coming in fast and furious. I'm sweating bullets, but it's actually the perfect challenge for me tonight. If I'd been working alone, I might've frozen up. That's not even an option in this kitchen, though. I'm only one cog in a much bigger wheel, one with way too much momentum to stop rolling along.

Wormwood begins to rotate us through the stations, giving each of us the opportunity to prove we can handle fish, or meat, garnish, everything. One by one we're picked to help the Super Chef at the expediting station, too. Once there, each of us looks for imperfections in the arriving dishes, trying to intercept them before they make it to the guests.

Halfway through service, sweat raining off my brow, Chef Taylor calls on me. "Chef Pith!" I give my sizzling asparagus one last quick flip before looking up. "Please join me."

"Pepper," Chef Wormwood points. "Take over veg from Curtis."

We've moved from appetizers to entrées. When the slow march of my feet finally carries me to the service pass, the team is seconds away from delivering new dishes for the blue table. Chef Taylor repositions the tickets in front of him. "Pay close attention to what your friends bring," he warns me. "Our guests should receive exactly what they ordered."

He still doesn't look at me. "Yes, Chef," I say in a voice that sounds like a faraway echo. I raise my chin, gazing up at him, waiting hopefully for him to turn his attention to me. Instead he continues hurriedly organizing his tickets.

"Walking three New York strips," Joey shouts, and the rest mimic his call, bringing forward the other entrées for blue at the same time.

"Chef?" Taylor asks me as soon as the food lands on the pass. He's actually looking at me now, clearly concerned with my silence. *Work, Curtis.* It's food. This is what you do.

I start by touching each steak, comparing them against the orders on the tickets. The first two guests requested medium rare, and Joey's cook matches up. But the third steak is supposed to be medium well, and it isn't. It's barely medium. "This one is under, Chef."

The Super Chef squints at me, as if maybe he doesn't believe me. I grit my teeth and point at the ticket, sticking to my guns. "Order was for medium well, Chef."

Lucas Taylor touches the steak's surface. "You sure?"

I touch my middle finger to my thumb, then poke at the puff of skin at the base. Next I jab the steak again. "That's a medium steak." It's a trick I use. Well, not just me, a lot of chefs. The spot at the base of your thumb can tell you how done a steak is, if you know how to position your fingers just right to make the comparison.

"Very good," he says. The doubt shadow disappears from his gaze. It was a test. In the end, everything here is.

Taylor calls for Joey to refire. "On the fly," he shouts.

Seconds later, the red table's dessert ticket shows up. I walk with the chef toward the stations. He glances at the orders, then drops his arm to his side, calling out from memory like he's been doing all night. "Order up! Red. Desserts. One lava cake, two crump . . . two . . . the sorb—" The Super Chef raises the ticket again, makes a second attempt at reading it. "One lava crumble, two . . ." He shakes his head hard, like the words are stuck there.

"Sorry, Chef," Pepper says quietly. "Not heard."

Clenching his teeth, the Super Chef sends a pained expression toward the ceiling. His hand forms a fist, crumpling the ticket. He realizes what he's doing, straightens it again, and thrusts it toward me. "Curtis. Please." His voice sounds thicker than it should, heavy with . . . something.

I take the ticket and stare down at it. I've never done this before. When I lift my head and open my mouth to speak, nothing comes out. I catch Wormwood's eye. She stares at me, a new glower. But not an all-the-way glower. There's a pleading hidden in this version. Her expression, those wide eyes, seems to implore me. *Help him, Curtis. Please, just help him.*

There's a second where I wonder if I should. Who is this stammering man next to me? Is he the Super Chef, the hero I've idolized for years? Or the guy who suddenly can't speak right, walk right, whose hand is always shaking?

Is he Lucas Taylor, my father who never learned or tried to be a father? And what does that make him, anyway? Not a hero, for sure. And I guess if you're not a hero, then you must be a villain. But somehow that doesn't seem right, either.

I glance at the ticket again, lift my head, and speak as clearly as possible. "Order up! Desserts. Red table. One lava cake, two crumble, three sorbet."

"Yes, Chef!" the other chefs yell back.

I return to the pass and slide the ticket in front of the Super Chef, who's leaning with both hands out straight, his head bowed low. He doesn't look at me again, but through my side view of his expression, all I see is another pained grimace. It's like he just sliced his finger or burned himself.

But he isn't hurt. Not anywhere that I can see, anyway.

The Super Chef sends me back to help the others finish the final entrées, then the desserts. We pick up speed, probably because we're all on the same page as we work. No, not just the same page. We're different words in the same sentence. Five, working together as one.

Joey says, "Not yet," when Pepper's about to flip a piece of salmon too early. Kiko says, "Wipe the rim," as she notices me forgetting to clean my plate before walking it. There are "Careful, hot" warnings left and right.

It's amazing. For the first time in my life, I have a freakin' squad.

• • •

The apple crumble we're featuring in the dessert course is meant to be served warm. It comes with a scoop of vanilla ice cream that should be just beginning to melt when I bring it to Taylor.

Kiko and Joey announce they're walking three lava cakes just as I drop my scoop back into some warm water. I pick up my plate and follow them.

"Good, good," the Super Chef is muttering as he checks over their cakes first. "Where's my crumble?"

"Here, Chef." I squeeze past Joey to bring my plate up to the pass. The ice cream wants to slide, but I tilt my wrist, holding it in place.

The Super Chef swings his arm back, his face still turned forward. He crouches and checks the bottom of a cake by lifting it with a knife. "Excellent," he says, and both Joey and Kiko beam at his recognition of the perfection of their handiwork.

The finger on the end of the Super Chef's extended arm beckons me forward. I approach him, wedging my dish into his palm. The rest of his fingers close around the plate. I start to let go. But the dish teeters and, too late, I realize he doesn't have it all the way. It slips away and tumbles to the ground, ceramic splintering into a thousand pieces as it strikes the floor. Wet slices of apple spread out in all directions.

Everything is quiet for a few seconds. I almost expect

an eruption of shouts, screams, anger, but instead Taylor starts to laugh. It's not any laugh I've heard come from him before, though, not in six seasons. Almost a cackle— maniacal, filled with frustration.

"I'm . . . I'm sorry, Chef," I say softly.

"It's all right, it's okay," Wormwood is whispering as she rushes up, quickly starting to pick up the splintered ceramic pieces. "It's fine. Everything's fine."

His cackling dying down to an echo in the suddenly still arena, Lucas Taylor bends at the waist. He puts both hands on his knees like an exhausted member of the North Sloan Eagles, wondering when their coach will notice how tired he is. Like he needs to be taken out. Like he doesn't have the stamina to last another minute out on the court, in the spotlight.

When he finally lifts his face, it's to look straight into mine. He shakes his head slightly, clearly disappointed. But it was an accident, it could've happened to anyone. I was so sure he had it. The plate wasn't hot, it wasn't wet, it should've been . . .

"Stop. Just . . . stop it," Chef Taylor whispers, seem- ingly just now aware Wormwood's on her hands and knees cleaning up my mess. A few of the celebrity chefs onstage actually stand up to get a better look. One or two step for- ward, as if they're thinking of coming down to help. The audience in the balcony murmurs.

The Super Chef joins his sous chef on the floor. "It's not fine, Claire. Nothing's fine. Why can't you see . . . ?" He starts cleaning up the pieces Wormwood hasn't gotten to yet. A sharp edge slices into his hand. He grabs it with the other and stands quickly, wincing.

Wormwood wipes her forehead with her sleeve. She straightens, looking up at Taylor. "Just let me help," she says. "All I want to do is—"

The Super Chef's heavy panting picks up speed. He spins around, as if he's suddenly lost in his own arena. Takes the pressure off his cut. Fresh blood trickles toward his sleeve.

"I need a minute," he says, still breathless, gripping his hand tight again, blood squirming between his fingers. He backs away from the mess on the floor with a horrified expression, like there's a dead body there instead of just a bunch of ruined sugar and fruit and pastry.

Wormwood maneuvers away too, giving the black-shirts, emerging from the sidelines this time with brooms and mops, the room they need to take over the cleanup. She watches Taylor leave, and for a second it almost seems like she's going to follow him.

Then her face changes. Her features harden as she turns toward us. The Super Five are standing in a cluster, all of us staring down at the mess in shock. Neglected food sizzles at our stations. "Who told you to stop cooking? Our guests are waiting for their desserts." She claps her hands. "Let's go, Chefs, let's go! Finish strong."

The Super Chef still hasn't returned when the meal ends, but after they finish eating, the VIPs onstage give us a standing ovation. They remain at the tables drinking wine while the blue theme-guessing desks are brought out and set up in front of us. Little white card, new black Sharpie.

I have trouble concentrating. It's hard not to wonder where Chef Taylor is, to try to figure out what upset him so much. Maybe that cut was worse than it seemed. Maybe they had to rush him off to the hospital. I tap the black Sharpie onto the card, making a bigger and bigger dot, and force myself to come up with *something*.

We worked so well together, all the partnering up and helping each other on the line, but what seemed to be most important to the Super Chef was our time at the pass. And as much as I rack my brain for it, I don't see the connection between that and learning to make complicated pastries and cakes.

Time is running short. I take a stab at a guess, and I'm just putting the cap back on the Sharpie when Chef Worm-wood calls time. It's a commercial, and Wormwood and Graça take advantage of the break to disappear backstage. Just when I think they won't come back at all, that they've left for the hospital too, that the camera lights will turn red and we won't have any hosts, all three chefs reappear. The Super Chef is wearing that forced smile again. His hand is wrapped in white gauze.

Almost as if nothing happened, he announces it's time for the theme guesses. We raise our hands, turn over our cards. Somehow both Pepper and Kiko get ATTENTION TO DETAIL exactly right.

The Super Chef does his magical wave at the totals board, and it flashes new numbers the same way it has after every other challenge.

Pepper Carmichael	94
Kiko Tanaka	93
Joey Modestino	89
Curtis Pith	81
Bonifacio Agosto	80

Again Pepper's invited forward to receive her prize, passed to her by Chef Madeline Dalibard herself. A blackshirt brings out a sample tray of the chef's most famous desserts, and she spends some time explaining how precise cooks have to be with their recipes, how much attention you have to pay to all the details—sometimes temperature, sometimes speed, often the viscosity of the dough, always the specific order of the steps involved.

Attention to detail. Right. Knowing her specialties,

what the apprenticeship would almost certainly cover should've been obvious. If I could punch myself in the arm right now, I would.

The scoreboard, or whoever's been controlling it behind the scenes, wastes no time. The numbers flash again. Updated totals.

Pepper Carmichael	368
Kiko Tanaka	362
Curtis Pith	361
Bonifacio Agosto	350
Joey Modestino	347

And there it is: I've officially lost the lead.

It's not like it's a huge surprise. I'm lucky I didn't finish dead last. Dropping the crumble was bad, but now that I'm having a chance to review my performance, I messed up a bunch of other stuff, too. None of my scallops were quite as perfect as that first batch. I burned a pan of asparagus, and instead of doing my own quality control, I brought up the charred mess anyway.

I'm slipping, big-time, and I can't seem to fix it, not with meditation or promises to focus on only cooking. Nothing is working. Feels like I'm trying to scale a mountain covered in olive oil, my feet constantly sliding out from under me.

First came the epic fail during the one-on-one the other night. Now both Kiko and Pepper haven't just closed the gap on me, they've shot right past me, leaving me in their dust. One challenge left before the finale and my cushion is officially gone. I'm back to playing catch-up.

It might be less than ten actual points, but we're moving in opposite directions, and that makes it feel more like I'm hundreds of miles behind both of them.

A nother weekend blows into New York, our second one here. We spend Saturday working the food trucks again. From an entirely different city park, but I see a lot of the same faces waiting in line, pushing their shopping carts, wearing bulky backpacks, shrouded in blankets.

Graca, not Wormwood, supervises this time. He shows us how to pass a special cardboard tray down the line, filling one compartment with stuffing, another with sliced turkey, a third with mashed potatoes. Bo covers everything with a little gravy, careful pours to make it last, then dishes out a spot of cranberry jelly. Joey works the window, handing out our quick, five-day-early Thanksgiving lunches one at a time. He doesn't issue a single complaint, and it feels like we serve twice as many guests as last time.

On Sunday, we're expecting more homework catch-up, but it's a holiday week back home, and I guess our schools don't mind giving us a break. Instead we enjoy an almost-lazy breakfast. It's actually peaceful in the dorms until Chef Graca bursts in wearing the biggest grin I've seen on his jolly face, which is really saying something.

"Ah, the little chefs." He spreads his arms out wide, wrapping us up in a faraway hug.

"You're all mine today." He tries to say it in a sinister way, but I'm not sure Chef Gabriel Graca has ever achieved legit sinister in all his life. Besides, a day with Graca sounds great to me. I could use a break from the stress of being around the Super Chef.

"You know the drill. Everybody dressed and ready in one hour. Chef's jackets, please."

"What is happening?" Kiko asks.

"The last challenge is happening." Graca shares a grin with each of us. "Number five."

"But that's a day early!" Pepper shouts, raising the ever-present schedule in her hands and shaking the paper so it flaps and flutters. "This says challenge #5 is tomorrow. Monday." It's like she believes Graca is just confused and she can set him straight.

"Certainly nothing wrong with your reading comprehension, Chef Carmichael," Graca, still grinning, agrees.

"Can you also read those tiny words at the bottom there?"

Pepper looks again. "Subject to change?"

"Precisely. Now you know what today's subject is. Change." He laughs at his own joke, then turns for the door. "One hour, Chefs. Downstairs."

"I want you to make your signature dish, the one from your video," Graca says from the stage an hour later. "The same one that earned you a spot in this competition."

There's been no sign of Wormwood or Taylor. Kari isn't in the arena, either, but the camera people weave around us and a few black-shirts are visible in the shadows. It feels like a real episode. Or, I think as I realize how quiet the studio is, half of one, anyway.

"But I made two dishes," Pepper says.

"Then pick one, Chef Carmichael," Graca replies with a rare note of impatience. "Oh, and Chef Agosto? Since you took several days to make your mole but you'll have only one hour this morning, we're giving you a starter. I hope you don't mind using my recipe." Bo's eyes go wide, but Chef Graca shakes his head. "Don't get too excited. My mole starter is nowhere near as good as your family's. Actually, now that I think of it, maybe you can give me some tips." He chuckles. "Okay, let's get started. Each of you should find everything you need in the pantry—"

"What is this for?" Joey asks, eyeing the cameras. "Is

this a challenge? Are there points?"

Graca takes a deep breath. "Think of this as more of a . . . preparatory exercise."

"But it's part of the challenge?" Pepper asks.

"And we are on TV today?" Bo asks.

"Yes," Graca answers Pepper. Then, shifting his attention to Bo, "And . . . no." Bo scrunches his nose in confusion, and Graca notices. He looks up at the balcony. "No audience, right? We'll always have one if we're live. But we are taping, and we may use some of the footage tomorrow night, during the actual challenge. Depends on how things go."

"What kinds of things?" I ask.

Grace smiles back but doesn't answer. He tilts his head to the side, then straightens again. "Chefs, time's about to start. You need to be getting ready to cook. You'll just have to trust me. I've told you all I can. More than I was supposed to, probably."

All five of us glance around at each other, trading confusion. We've never participated in this kind of pretaping before any of the other challenges. But of course this is the last one before the Thanksgiving finale. Not so surprising they would change things up on us.

But . . . why do they want me to make my soufflé again? What's the point of that?

"Please cook your dish the same way you would if this

were a challenge," Graca announces. "Assume you're presenting it to a judge."

"Who is the judge?" Kiko asks.

Chef Graca shakes his head and smirks. "You know, Chef Wormwood warned me you kids ask a lot of questions." After that, he folds his arms across his chest and clams up.

Twenty minutes later, Chef G, who's been pacing on the stage watching us cook, checks his watch and says, "Chefs, I'll be right back. Keep working. You have forty minutes left."

"This is so insulting," Joey mutters as soon as Graca disappears.

Kiko takes the bait. "What is insulting?"

"This!" he cries, throwing his hands up. "You see what they're doing, right? Forcing us to prove we can make the dishes we submitted? They must think one of us had our parents do our homework for us or something. Like this is the science fair or a soapbox race where your dad builds your car for you."

Is that what real dads do? Build soapbox cars, help with science fair projects? Teach their sons to cook in restaurants their brothers own? Joey says it like it's something to be ashamed of, rather than stuff you'd give your left arm to happen just once.

"Yes . . . sí. I suppose you may be right," Bo says. He

focuses on his work, then speaks again while staring down at his quick-moving hands. "I don't understand it, though. Why would they wait until now to make us prove it?"

No one has an answer. We just keep cooking. Because Graca might've disappeared, but all these cameras are still watching. The eyes behind them are watching.

Another half hour evaporates quickly. We finish our efforts and bring them to the judging table. Eventually all five dishes are sitting in front of Chef Graca, waiting for . . . we have no idea what.

It's definitely weird city. Still no Kari, no Wormwood, no Super Chef. But once all five dishes are up front, the heavy clunk of a switch being thrown echoes in the empty arena and, to our left, the sensory deprivation booths light up again. Not sure when they added a fifth capsule, but it's there, squeezed in between the end of the row and the edge of the stage.

It will be Kiko's first time in a booth, so she gets the newest one. The rest of us are put in the same booths as last time. On go the headphones and blindfolds. The door clicks shut.

Everything descends into silent darkness once more.

Once again I have no idea how much time passes while I'm locked up inside this thing. I only know that, during almost all of it, I think about why I came here. How it had once seemed so clear. How murky it's become just a couple weeks later.

I wanted to win that prize money. Because I'd cost Mom her job, yes, but for deeper reasons, too. This was the last *Super Chef.* Ever. Where else could I ever go, what else could I ever do, that would give me a shot at that much money at my age? Doing what I do best? Where, if I'm honest, I figured I'd have an edge because I'm the main judge's son?

I warned myself to stay focused. Distracted Curtis equals Last Place Curtis. I learned that on my very first night in New York.

But I failed. During our only evening alone together, the one-on-one, I let too much old resentment bubble up to the surface and escape. Now look at the standings. I'm not all the way back in last place yet, but I feel myself spinning in that direction, so fast I don't think there's anything I can do to stop my fall.

Someone taps me on my shoulder, and I jump. Big hands lift the noise-cancelling headphones from my ears. Graca unties my blindfold and pulls it away. He smiles at me.

"Your turn, Curtis."

All five of our dishes are still up on the stage. My soufflé, Kiko's Wellington, Pepper's Jamaican Rundown,

Joey's stuffed squid, Bo's mole.

"This next part is simple," Graca tells me. I have one eye on him while the other tracks the cameraman on the other side of the table, positioning himself for the best shot, his red light already on. "Taste your competitors' dishes. Critique them."

I shake my head without meaning to. Because I couldn't possibly judge the rest of the Five. I'm hardly qualified for that. I mean, I may have been doing awful this past week or so, but one thing for sure hasn't changed. I'm *in* the contest, not *judging* it.

He addresses my doubts as if I voiced them out loud. "You'll need to learn to make honest comments about your colleagues' work," he says. "It's a big part of cooking, an essential ingredient to being a great chef."

I'm so used to racking my brain for theme possibilities, my mind auto-guesses. Honesty? But this isn't even the real challenge yet. There's no theme.

Even so, I'm positive I don't want to critique these other dishes. I'm thinking about what Kiko said. Everyone here is super talented. There's no reason for us to pick on each other. Not after we finally started to come together in the last challenge. But when I look down, I see a pile of dirty spoons and forks, including a few to the side of my soufflé.

Really strong Goldilocks vibes wash over me. As in, *someone's been tasting my soufflé.* I think of Joey, but then I see multiple spoonfuls are missing. *More than* one *someone's been tasting my soufflé.*

I glance over at the booths. All but mine are filled. It's impossible to tell which of the others were let out before me.

"Start here, please, Chef," Graca says, leading me to Kiko's beef Wellington. He's not going to give me a choice. There's no way out of this.

I sigh, pick up a knife and fork, and slice myself a piece.

When I finish tasting the dishes, finish making all my comments, all the while Graca encouraging me to "be honest," I'm returned to my booth. The headphones are snapped back over my ears, the blindfold tied tight to my head again. This time I'm grateful to descend into the depths of absolute quiet. It gives me a chance to calm down. Or try to, anyway. This is definitely the weirdest challenge yet. If this is actually the challenge. I'm still not sure I understand what's even happening.

What I do know is that critiquing all the hard work my friends did felt awful, as bad as cheating on a test or telling a big lie. Even though I didn't lie. The mushroom duxelles in Kiko's Wellington was a touch oversalted. Bo's mole was delicious, but the chicken was overcooked. Pepper's Rundown seemed way too spicy, and Joey's squid came out extra chewy.

Every comment I made was true, but I still feel slimy for

saying those things out loud. It's just . . . I know how much focus it takes to make a great dish. But in all the competitions I'd ever entered, I never realized how hard it was to be a judge, to say honestly what you really thought about someone else's food.

At least the other five were locked up in their booths when I said what I did. They couldn't possibly hear it. They'd never have to know. And I'd never have to find out what they thought about my soufflé, either. This whole exercise had for sure been what Joey thought it was—a way to confirm we could cook the dishes we'd claimed to make in our videos. Then they made us taste them to prove they were the real thing. Like Bo said, it's weird that they waited for nearly the end of the competition to do this, but at least it's over.

So it might not have been the best soufflé I ever cooked. It was a soufflé, and I did cook it. I showed whoever was asking that no one helped me the first time. I mean, *as if.*

The familiar tap on my shoulder comes once more. Same removal of blindfold and headphones. The only difference this go-around is it's a black-shirt helping me, and he's brought a laptop with him. He sets it up on a slim booth shelf I hadn't noticed before. Lifts the lid, nods at the black screen, then leaves me alone, this time with no blindfold, no headphones.

I swipe a finger across the touchpad. The computer

wakes up. A video's been started but sits paused. Chef Graca's smiling but frozen face fills up the entire frame. When I click the sideways play triangle, he comes to life.

"Hello, Chef Pith," the big sous chef says. "Here are today's results. Please listen carefully to what your competitors thought of your dish. Keep an open mind."

His face disappears, replaced by a wider shot of Bo issuing a reluctant stare down into my soufflé. My roommate reaches out with a spoon, dips it into my ramekin, tastes what comes back. His tongue flicks out of his mouth like a snake as he assesses my work.

I hear Chef Graca's voice in the background, even as the camera stays focused on Bo. "Well? What did you think? Be honest, now."

And Bo, just like I did, hesitates at first. But then, staring off into the distance, he tilts his head. He starts to talk, and each word he says shrinks my heart another size, until all that's left is about as big as one of those tiny Valentine's conversation hearts.

The saying written on the remains of my barely pumping muscle is the same as the one I got from Katie Wohlers in first grade, when she handed out a single candy to each classmate.

Mine had read, "Thought U Were Cooler."

"Rubbery!"

Joey makes one full lap around the sectional. Which takes a minute, it's a pretty big sectional. He stops and spreads his arms out wide, looking at us one by one— first Kiko, then me, next Bo and Pepper, never losing the shocked expression on his face. When none of us replies, his arms flap down to his sides again, hands bouncing off his hips.

"Rubbery!" he repeats, sounding, if possible, even more stunned. He starts another lap.

"Where's he going?" Bo whispers to me.

"Nowhere," I say. "None of us is going anywhere."

He looks up at me strangely. "I would like to be home by Thanksgiving."

"I know you would, Bo, I *know*."

But if he doesn't realize by now that's not going to be happening, there's no use in me being the one to break the news. Not when Wormwood's already done it. Taylor's already done it. Our printed schedule's already done it.

"I was just being honest," Pepper calls out in Joey's direction.

"It is very easy to overcook squid," Kiko tries from near the big windows. She twists toward us to make her comment. Before that, she'd been gazing out at the city with her arms crossed behind her back.

"Did you really think mine was too spicy?" Pepper, sounding horrified, asks, and I turn to answer her but she's talking to Kiko. "I swear I used the same recipe as always."

"Maybe I'm not very used to your dish," Kiko says. "It is my first time tasting this food."

Pepper's tone changes. "Oh, so you don't know what a rundown is supposed to be like. *That's* why you got it wrong."

"She wasn't wrong. The scotch bonnet is optional," Bo says. He pulls a chair out at the dining table and sits. "The rundown does not have to be so spicy as yours was."

"You do *not* make Jamaican Rundown without a scotch

bonnet," Pepper scoffs. She points at her feet, like she's letting us know she won't be moving from the spot she's standing in, at least not until we all agree with her. "Not in a hundred years you don't. My grandmother didn't, my father doesn't, and I never will."

"And salty?" Joey says. He veers out from his second rotation around the sectional, heading toward the kitchen. His focus is on Pepper. "My squid was rubbery *and* my filling was salty? That's your feedback?"

"Yeah," Pepper says, softly at first, but raising her voice with each new word. "That's my feedback. Problem?"

Pepper and Joey's shouting fills the room. I take slow, backward steps away from them, in the direction of Kiko. "So my soufflé was eggy?" I whisper from the corner of my mouth when I reach her. Last thing I want is to scream about it like Joey is.

I wish I'd tasted my dish when I had the chance. Maybe then I would know if the comments I heard when that video played—too eggy, overcooked, salty—were on the mark or not. But I didn't understand what recooking our entry dishes would eventually lead to.

I probably *still* don't understand what the whole point was.

If it's possible, Joey's voice grows even louder. Gazing around the room, waiting for Kiko to respond, I try to work out the real purpose of the exercise we just went through. So . . . maybe remaking our entry dishes wasn't about the cooking at all. Maybe the Super Chef *wanted* to cause all this arguing. But why tear us apart? Unless . . . what if he forces us to work together again tomorrow? And we can't, because of all this fighting still clouding our vision?

Wow. As each day passes, Taylor's seeming like less of a hero and more and more like that villain I wondered about.

"Guys . . ." Everyone stops.

Joey directs his harshest glower toward my interruption. He wouldn't be happy to hear how much like Wormwood he looks right now. "What, Pith? You have some *new* criticism?"

A pit in my stomach yawns open as I shake my head slowly. What if I'm wrong? On the one hand, it doesn't feel right to keep these guys in the dark and let them crash and burn. But a tiny part of me pictures the latest standings on the giant scoreboard, reminds me I've fallen behind again. Maybe if I'm the only one who sees Taylor's trap coming . . .

So in the end, I say nothing, and soon Joey returns his anger to Pepper.

Next to me, Kiko is looking out the window again, as if she'll find the answer to my question outside. New York's lights blink in tune with Pepper and Joey's rapid-fire shouting. "I did think so, yes." She pinches her fingers together. "Your dish was just a little bit eggy."

"Honestly? Only a little bit?" Because now that I've heard her reaction—and the others, too, she wasn't the only one who said that—and remembered my steps . . . well, maybe I did overcook it by a minute or so. Which meant it had probably been *super* eggy, not just a little bit.

This time she shrugs. "Perhaps . . . more than a little." She smiles nervously at me.

"Thanks," I say. "I mean, I guess."

I'm not sure if I'm happy to know or not. There's nothing I can do to fix it. Which means knowing I messed it up does me no good. Still, I'm somehow grateful for her honesty. She's only telling me the truth. That one minute. One stinking minute of lost focus.

Thing is, I've had way too many of those kinds of minutes lately.

Kiko doesn't seem to know what else to say. We just stand across from each other for the next few seconds. Behind her, I catch a glimpse of Bo scribbling notes into a pad.

Everyone else, though, continues reacting to today's exercise with raised voices. "Kiko, come explain to this dufus what 'salty' means. Your duxelles was the same. Why is this so hard to understand? Salty is salty."

Kiko takes a few steps in their direction. She freezes

when Joey starts shouting again. Pepper points a finger in his face and gives it right back to him. They're practically nose to nose.

The sound of the door opening interrupts them. Everybody stops and looks.

It's Kari. She glances around the dorm while biting her lip. She looks toward Bo.

"Time to get ready, Bo. I'll be back in twenty minutes to take you to your dinner. The Super Chef is really looking forward to spending some time with you tonight."

At the table, Bo's hand stops in mid-scribble, and his jaw drops open so wide I'm afraid he might've hurt himself.

Monday night, the cheering and crazy applause and foot stomping in the arena is louder than ever before. The five of us linger in our usual waiting area outside the double doors, not even lined up yet. Kari walks in, clipboard in hand, talking into her headset. She lifts up the top piece of paper to read something underneath, and the bold "*The Last Super Chef,* Challenge #5" text centered on the sheet she's bending back is as clear as day, even upside down.

For the first time, all five handlers are waiting with us. A few feet away from me, Brett and Bo are talking excitedly. It's easy to notice, because it's almost comical the way the farm-fed intern from Wisconsin towers over his Mexican assignee.

Ever since Bo came back from his one-on-one last night, he's been on cloud nine. Which is amazing considering how nervous he was when he left. As always we have no details on what happened. All we can read is the emotion. Joey's dancing, Pepper's smile. Kiko's quiet confidence. Bo's excitement.

I guess I'm the only one whose "Evening with the Super Chef" was more like "Nightmare with the Super Chef." *Awesome.* From across the room, Mel must notice my crestfallen expression. He approaches me and crouches down to my level.

"Hey," he says, wearing a rare concerned expression. "You okay?"

He's always been able to calm me down with that warm smile, those gleaming-white, Hollywood teeth. But now for some reason they seem fake. And it makes me wonder: How far does it go? How many of these people besides Taylor know that he's my father? Mel? Kari? Wormwood? Graca? Any of them? *All* of them?

"We haven't talked about your one-on-one the other night," Mel continues. "What happened out there?"

At this point, I'm about as interested in having a heart-to-heart with him as I was in having one with the Super

Chef, so I make an abrupt move to pull away from him. "We had our meeting. We ate Persian."

"I know," he says. "I was watching. 'Live,' remember? But that wasn't the Curtis I've gotten to know. Where'd you go?"

Kari suddenly bursts into action behind him. Someone must've warned her we're running behind, because she's wearing that panicked, everything's-about-to-fall-apart-but-at-the-same-time-I-have-it-completely-under-control look I see on her face often. "Okay, let's go. Let's go! Line up. Curtis, you lead."

Me?

She grabs my shoulders and starts guiding me toward the doors. Mel nearly falls backward in his hurry to clear out of the way.

"You got this, right?" Kari says into my ear.

Before I can answer, the double doors split down the middle, and the bright lights and cameras are on the Super Five once again. I'm pulled forward by the sheer momentum of Super Chef Arena.

"Welcome," the Super Chef says from the stage as we file in, "to the last challenge of *The Last Super Chef.* After tonight, we'll have just one more day of competition, Thursday's Thanksgiving finale."

He pauses, letting the information sink in that we're

as close to the end as we are. "The challenge we're doing tonight is close to my heart. It relates to some work we had our young chefs put in yesterday." He gestures toward the big screen behind him again. "Let's have a look."

My stomach drops at the thought of another video, flashbacks to the horror of seeing Pettynose's kitchen on this same screen. If it's possible, though, this film is even worse. Because it's us, all five of us, cooking our signature dishes for Graca, the cameras capturing it all—Joey's complaining, our snippy comments back at him. I catch movement in the corner of my eye and look over in time to see Pepper covering her mouth with one hand.

The scene changes to some of us tasting the other's dishes. Pepper puckers her lips in disgust after trying Joey's filling, Kiko frantically reaches for water after swallowing Pepper's on-fire rundown, Joey almost spits out my soufflé, crying, "Oh, man, way overcooked." I tell Graca that Bo's chicken is dry; Bo asks if beef Wellington is supposed to be so salty.

But the worst part is still to come. The arguments.

The screen changes again, and the aerial cameras in the dorm capture us shouting at each other, hanging our heads, making laps around the sectional. Pepper and Joey nose to nose. Kiko waving her hands as she joins their argument, Bo shaking his head at the table. Me, looking confused and mostly alone. Like I have no idea what I'm doing. Like I don't even belong.

Wormwood shakes her head. "Mmm. Hard to watch."

"I couldn't agree more," Chef Taylor says, his face twisted like his heart is broken over what ended up happening. As if he hadn't planned it from the very beginning of his and Graca's challenge #5 "preparatory" exercise.

"I say we give them another chance, though," Wormwood says, before holding up her index finger and glancing at the crowd. "I say . . . let's cook these dishes one more time!" With each word she points her finger higher in the air. Usually it's Joey behind me who groans, but tonight the sound comes from my left. Kiko.

The crowd erupts again, joining in with a booming chant. "One more time! One more time! One more . . . !"

I inhale, bite my bottom lip, fight back threatening tears. For the first time during an actual episode, I try to find Kari lurking offstage. Maybe she can help me drop out. Sure, it's live, yes, it would be embarrassing, but after last night's meeting, after the video they just showed, can I actually make *another* soufflé?

Chef Graca steps forward now, rubbing his hands together greedily, the same way he did yesterday. "You heard them, Chefs! Same drill! Into the pantry. Get your ingredients. Let's do these dishes over. By now you should be able to make them blindfolded."

Frantic, I scan the sidelines of the arena, looking for

the black-shirts to come pouring out of their secret doors with blindfolds. But nothing moves there; Graca was only kidding. Although now that I think of it, blindfolds might come in kinda handy.

Then I wouldn't have to actually witness what's about to happen.

We have one hour again, same as yesterday. Plenty of time to make another soufflé, as long as I can convince my brain to stop racing around the inside of my head like a salad spinner.

I'm only dimly aware of Joey and Kiko dancing around each other here in the pantry. Joey's hand darts in front of Kiko's face to grab the fennel he needs. He ends up stepping on my foot as he careens away from both of us.

The pain actually helps me focus, somehow reminds me of Tre and Paige circling the bonfire back home, Pettynose chasing them. I blink, breathe deep. Can't push Paige's smiling face out of my vision.

There's still time to win that money for her, still a chance, however slim, to give my sister the life she deserves.

I race for the cheese station and grab the best hunk of gruyère I can find.

Minutes later, I'm ready to slide my ramekins into the oven. Yes, ramekins, as in multiple. I'm determined to taste one this time. I've been careful with the salt and other seasonings. I took each step slowly, watching for mistakes. Every fold and whip and turn. Gently, I shut the oven door. Now, just like in Pettynose's kitchen, there's only one thing left for me to do. Wait.

I keep peeking through the glass window at my slowly rising soufflé, resisting the urge to open the door. Guess-timating. Praying.

The cameras have been swinging around us the whole hour, zooming in, getting different angles, but for now they focus on the other competitors, the ones still working. I have a rare moment to breathe easy.

Taylor and Graca stand up on the stage while Wormwood paces around the arena. I can't hear the Super Chef's hushed conversation with his old Portuguese friend. But just as Chef Wormwood calls out, "Two minutes. Two minutes remaining!" from behind me, I'm able to read the Super Chef's lips. Eyes on me, he leans toward Graca and whispers, "Overcooked."

I swear that's what he says. I'm as sure of it, suddenly, as

I am that I've overcooked my dish again, that my soufflé will be eggy once more. That all I've done with my slow carefulness over the last hour is verify my father's opinion of me. I don't belong here. I never did.

I wasted time cleaning up my station, looking around at the others, when I could've been . . . but there's nothing I could've been doing. Because a soufflé is a waiting game. Still, I can't shake this feeling that I've repeated the same mistake.

Rush to the oven. Open the door—too fast, probably—reach in to drag my soufflés out before they overcook again. Just before my fingers close around the first rame-kin, though, I hear Chef Wormwood tittering behind me. "Pith! No! Tut, ut, ut, ut—"

She slides on her knees, crashing into me. Grabs my arm, yanks it back. What's she fussing about? In answer, she pulls my wrist up, showing me my own hand. My naked hand.

"Potholder, Chef," she says, out of breath, fire in her eyes. Then Wormwood does something that doesn't seem very Wormwood-y at all. She wraps her arm around my shoulders and pulls me into a hug. Leans us away from the closest camera and microphone, whispers into my ear. "You've got to be careful, Curtis!"

The first time I burned myself, I was making soup.

More like helping Mom make soup. She turned her back for a second. One second. Long enough for me to grab the lid with my bare fingers. I could *hear* the metal singeing my skin. Mom hugged me close as she hurried me to the sink for some cold water. The whole way, she kept telling me the same thing, over and over.

"If you're going to cook, Curtis, you've got to be careful. Careful!"

I feel fresh tears threatening my eyes, but I grind my teeth together to stop them. I won't cry here, not in Super Chef Arena. There's no crying in kitchens, unless maybe you're chopping onions. Even then, blink a few times if you have to.

But how can I keep making these huge mistakes in front of all my heroes?

I shut my eyes hard, open them again. More blinking. Over and over, fast, until I'm sure the tears won't come. When Wormwood releases me, it takes a second to remember what I was doing and why. I stand. Reach for my potholder. Use it to pull the soufflés out as fast as I can. Set them up on my station.

Chef Graca yells, "One minute!" but I don't look up. I don't want to see what new disappointment Taylor might be beaming my way.

I'm just so glad I got my soufflés out. After giving them

a little time to cool, I grab a spoon, dip it into my practice ramekin.

"Thirty seconds!" Graca again.

I see my error as soon as I pull back the spoon. There's no need to taste it: the soufflé is close but it's soupy. Under-cooked this time. Under, and there's no time left to fix it. If I'd only trusted myself, if only I hadn't let the Super Chef's whisper change my plan, been so worried about his opinion of me. And am I even sure he said what I thought? I chew my lip, suddenly filled with doubt.

I was going to wait until the last ten seconds, then take them out. That extra minute or two would've made all the difference. If only I'd given that time to myself, to my soufflé.

If only.

It seems like those two words sum up my whole life lately.

"It was overcooked yesterday, wasn't it?" Chef Taylor asks.

I nod. I feel about an inch tall standing alone in front of the judging table. The Super Chef eyes my soupy soufflé with one arched brow.

It's not even blowing my chance at the prize money that has me upset anymore. It's that he's finally paying attention to me, finally seeing me here, and all I've given him to look at is the worst soufflé in the history of soufflés.

"Well, this one's under. That means you overcompensated, then, trying to fix yesterday's error. You can see that, right?"

I nod again, then gulp. "Yes, Chef."

But he straightens up. Smile replacing his frown. "Well, overcorrection is, at least, correction. It means you listened. Listening's a big deal, Curtis."

I trudge back to my station, as confused as ever.

Meanwhile, the rest of the Super Five, except for Pepper, do great. Despite last night's arguing, everyone seems to have made adjustments based on what they heard. Even Joey fixes the seasoning on his filling and cooks his squid better.

Bo, though, does the very best. He didn't argue with anyone last night. He just slipped off and started making notes. I realize now he was figuring out how to make the most of his time and the feedback he got, too. He took a whole new approach to the challenge, managing to elevate Graca's starter mole to better match his family's recipe while cooking his chicken perfectly this time. All because he focused on learning rather than being defensive.

Pepper, on the other hand, continues to use the scotch bonnet and pays the price for her stubbornness. "Yesterday your friends told you it was too spicy, didn't they?" Taylor asks her.

"I guess," she answers. "But that's not the way my

family makes a rundown. It wouldn't be right not to use the recipe they taught me."

"Here's the thing, though," the Super Chef says in a stern tone. "You're not cooking for your family right now. Maybe you're cooking for a restaurant full of patrons, or a whole audience of strangers." He gestures at the balcony. "Either way, you have to start being able to take in what's being said about your food. Don't let it be personal."

Pepper returns to her station with her head hung low. The blue desks are brought out next. LISTENING seems possible after his talk with both Pepper and me, but it doesn't feel right that it could be so obvious. I'm so turned around by my mistake with the soufflé, by trying to come up with a clever, not-obvious guess, that by the time the game show music stops, all I've written down is WORK.

Joey and Bo both nail HANDLING CRITICISM, and their already higher scores for the challenge shoot even farther ahead of the rest of us.

Bonifacio Agosto	93
Joey Modestino	90
Kiko Tanaka	84
Curtis Pith	76
Pepper Carmichael	72

Bo wins his first challenge prize, one whole week of access to the Super Chef, one-on-one, in one of his amazing kitchens, and I'm surprised at how hard my gut aches with jealousy. The screen flashes for the final time in a regular challenge and the new totals sparkle for the audience to ooh! and aah! at.

Kiko Tanaka	446
Bonifacio Agosto	443
Pepper Carmichael	440
Curtis Pith	437
Joey Modestino	437

Kiko never won a single challenge—except for the mise en place Takamura knife that first night, which wasn't technically a real challenge—but it's incredible what consistency can do, because there she is, at the very top again. And, despite winning teamwork and creativity, there I am at the bottom again, tied with Joey.

But it's close. We're all bunched together. I still have a chance.

"Wonderful," the Super Chef is saying again and again on the stage, applauding along with the audience. He stops and settles his feet, looking a little more serious.

"Chefs, I've really enjoyed this competition. Even more

than I expected to. You kids are—" He shakes his head. "Well, you're truly amazing. I'm so thankful you've given so much of yourselves to this competition. I know it's been very difficult. Tiring. Frustrating. Even a little scary, perhaps." He raises his voice further, gesturing around the arena. "Please join me in one more round of applause for the Super Five."

The audience just finished clapping, but they start in all over again. All three chefs spur them on, waving their arms up and down like football players trying to encourage the home crowd to make more noise. Soon another deafening ovation overtakes the arena. I feel my whole body almost lifted into the air by the crescendo, equal parts exhilarated and exhausted.

I can still win, I know I can. If I can just refocus myself by Thursday, stop thinking about weeks at Taylor House and lip-reading criticism, I can make a comeback in the finale. Mom's new house isn't that far away. Neither is that quarter of a million dollars.

"Don't forget about our finale!" the Super Chef cries, and immediately new tension locks up my joints again. "Thanksgiving Day! Three days from now. What better day to decide who will win *The Last Super Chef* than the national holiday that's always been all about food and family and gratitude? Am I right?

"Our Thanksgiving finale will be a two-hour special,

once again live. The first hour will air in the morning. We'll let you break and enjoy your holiday, but please! You *must* tune back that evening, after your dinner is over but before you fall into your turkey coma, for part two. I know you will! I know you'll want to join us to find out who *The Last Super Chef* winner will be!

"But I suppose we should find out who will have the edge—and when I say edge, I mean *edge*; it's a big one this time—heading into the finale. For that, we need to do one more thing."

The Super Chef issues another big-armed wave at the totals board, and the lights start blinking and flashing, the numbers scrambling into random dots and dashes.

"Our big board's adding in those one-on-one scores we've been hinting at, which were on a scale of one hundred like every challenge!" He shoots a grin at us. "Hope you didn't forget!"

Oh no. The night I couldn't stop thinking about. Storming out of the car, racing back into the dorms. Running away. All those one- and two-word answers. The way I felt, like I was guarding all my secrets. Like I was guarding my life with Mom and Paige. Like, in the end, I didn't want to talk about it so it wouldn't have to change.

But then, what was the point of coming here? Wouldn't all that money have changed everything anyway? Isn't that what I wanted?

It doesn't matter, because somehow I did stop thinking about my Evening with the Super Chef. Somehow, I *did* forget how badly it went, that those points hadn't been included yet.

I close my eyes, knowing the scoreboard will give me news I don't want to see. But I can't keep them shut forever. And when the crowd lets out a surprised moan, I open them.

FINAL CHALLENGE SCORES

Bonifacio Agosto	538
Kiko Tanaka	537
Pepper Carmichael	528
Joey Modestino	522
Curtis Pith	509

I want to puke.

At least before, I had company at the bottom. At least before I was in the ballpark. But my low one-on-one score—I notice the Super Chef spared me the embarrassment of revealing the exact details, but I don't need Paige for *this* math—now has me all alone in dead last.

Again.

Meanwhile, Bo tries to contain his excitement. He leapfrogged Kiko by a single point. Incredible. After all his bellyaching and wanting to go home, after seeming like the first chef who would break, Bo Agosto from Mexico City is in first place. He's actually the chef to beat.

"What did you mean by edge, Chef?" Graca asks Taylor, but I can tell from the giddy tone of the question that the sous chef already knows the answer. I can tell that, whatever it is, it's only going to make things even worse.

"Ah, yes." The Super Chef grins back at him. "The *edge*. It's so simple, but so huge. First of all, the good news for those behind in the standings." Does he look at me when he pauses? "The slate will be wiped clean. No matter what your previous scores were, the winner of our final battle will be the winner of the whole competition!"

The applause that follows isn't quite as thunderous as usual. It's more hesitant, calculated, like this seems like good news but also could be some kind of trick. The audience feels the same way I do, the way the rest of the Super Five must feel. What was the point, then, of all those challenges if, even from last place, I can just win Thursday and still become the champion?

"Ah, but now for the bad news." Taylor raises one hand, palm open, requesting quiet and patience. "For some of our competitors, anyway. Thanksgiving night, the final challenge of our last season here in Super Chef Arena, the chefs will have the normal one-hour cooking time. Well"—his hand closes into a fist, but the index finger remains extended—"one of them will, anyway. Chef Agosto." Hearing his name, Bo takes a confused step back from his station. "Each chef after him in the final standings must wait an additional seven minutes before they can start cooking. So, second place, Chef Tanaka, will have fifty-three minutes, third place, Chef Carmichael, forty-six, and so on."

The scoreboard flashes again. Taylor smiles and waits, clearly looking forward to the desperate details of what he just explained to hit us broadside.

THANKSGIVING FINALE—ALLOWED COOKING TIMES (minutes)

Bonifacio Agosto	60
Kiko Tanaka	53
Pepper Carmichael	46
Joey Modestino	39
Curtis Pith	32

I blink and shake my head, then look again to be sure I'm seeing what I'm seeing. But the numbers don't change. I'm reading them right.

They don't lie, either, and now the catch is clear. Sure, if I win on Thursday, I become the last *Super Chef* winner ever. But I have to do it in thirty-two minutes, which is barely more than half the time Bo will get. Half the time to make the most important dish of my life. It's not just impossible, it's . . . well, whatever's more impossible than impossible.

Maybe Joey had been right that first night. When I finished last in mise en place, maybe they should've just kicked me off like they normally would've in regular *Super Chef.* Because two weeks later, I'm down there all over again. Way down there.

It would take a Thanksgiving miracle for me to win *The Last Super Chef*, to bring home that money to Mom and Paige.

And miracles are more of a Christmas thing, right?

FROM CURTIS PITH'S RECIPE JOURNAL
(Back pages)

Super Chef Lucas Taylor's
Five Keys to Becoming and Staying a Great Chef

1.   Teamwork
2.   Creativity
3.   Multitasking
4.   Attention to Detail
5.   Handling Criticism

On Tuesday no one comes into the common room to blow whistles or shout for us to line up. There are no doughnuts or bagels. Not a single croissant or slice of bacon. No surprise challenges.

And the Super Five—some of us not feeling very super at all anymore—sleep half the morning away.

When we finally emerge from our rooms yawning and stretching, the common room is empty. No clothes rack with cleaned chef's jackets, no assistants, no handlers, no chefs. Just a dorm-shaped ghost town.

"There is a note," Bo says, standing on his toes and sliding a folded piece of paper across the kitchen island. He starts to open it, but Joey snatches it out of his hand, only to have Pepper grab it from his fingers and give it back to Bo.

"You should read it," she tells our smallest competitor. Turning to Joey, she adds, "He's the leader now."

Joey frowns at her while Bo unfolds the note and starts to read it out loud.

> *Good morning, Chefs!*
> *Today is your official day of rest. No need to worry,*
> *we promise there will be no challenges or tests or surprises.*
> *Later on, we'll give you another chance to chat with your*
> *families. Otherwise, please just relax! You've earned it.*
> *I'm so proud of all of you,*
> *LUCAS TAYLOR*

Proud. Even after everything that's happened, ending up in last place, feeling like a complete failure, waffling between being ready to go home and still battling a desperation to win, seeing that word in my father's handwriting makes my heart skip a beat. Seriously? Proud? Of *me*?

Bo sets the note back on the island. "Perhaps we should cook the breakfast?" he says.

"Whose turn is it?" Joey asks.

"Let's all do it," I suggest. "We should make pancakes and waffles—"

"And eggs and bacon and—" Pepper says.

"Grits!" Kiko yells. "Does anyone know how to make good grits? I have always wanted to try them."

We're still cooking when Mel and Brett carry the giant television in. As they're setting it up, Joey wanders over and hugs the box, then asks what channels we'll have.

"No channels, I'm afraid," Mel says. "Live TV might still influence the finale." Just then Ashley and Renata walk in with armfuls of DVDs and books. "No internet access, either. But you'll have all these. Take your pick."

They drop the stacks near the television. There are all sorts of great movies—all the Harry Potters and the Pixars, Star Wars, Hunger Games . . . and books, too. Classics like *Charlie and the Chocolate Factory* and *Alice in Wonderland.* Tons more.

"You kids have some fun," Renata says in her Italian accent.

Joey starts to paw through the piles. *The Incredibles* in his hand, he gestures toward the assistants, catching them before they leave. "Hey, you guys have been really cool this whole time." He points at all the action in the kitchen, the rest of us jumping behind and around each other, pans clanging. "We basically cooked the whole fridge. Want brunch?"

● ● ●

All five of our assistants enjoy brunch with us. We're forced to round up extra chairs from all around the dorm, even the assistants' off-limits back room. It's my first time in here. The walls are painted a soft blue, a completely different color from the greens and beiges that decorate the rest of the place. The huge window faces the totally opposite side of the building from the balcony.

Joey and I are snagging the desk chairs from in there when we notice a phone on the bedside table. It's bright red.

"Oh man!" Joey cries. "There was a phone in here this whole time? Bo could've called home? He's gonna freak."

The discovery makes me think of something else. I scan the ceiling. No cameras. Maybe the rules are different for the college-aged kids. Maybe they didn't sign a contract that said they agreed to be watched the entire time. Probably not. They're older. Seems like older people always have more rights.

"Actually." Mel's voice comes from behind me, humorless and deep. "That phone goes directly to either security or another room downstairs where the rest of us assistants tend to hang out. You know, in case we need anything while we're stuck up here babysitting y'all." He winks at us. "You can't call out with it. It's more like the Bat-phone, a direct line."

I exhale, louder than I mean to.

"Don't worry, there are more supervised calls this afternoon. Your families can't wait to talk to you guys again."

After lunch, Paige is much more subdued over Skype. Even Mom seems low-key compared to the last time. Don't get me wrong, she sounds concerned again, but not over how I'm being treated. It's clear she's a lot more worried about how I'm holding up.

Ugh. She saw my train wreck of a one-on-one. And the rest of the competition, too. She knows what a disadvantage I'm at for the finale. I mean, I knew she would, but the impact hadn't really hit me until I see both their expressions.

"Tough meeting last week, huh?" Mom asks. Last week. Seems more like a lifetime ago.

"I guess," I say, scratching my cheek.

"Only a couple days more, Curtis. Hang in there."

"You're doing great!" Paige adds, giving me a thumbs-up, but I can tell her enthusiasm is fake. Last Tuesday I was in first. Now I'm dead last. She must be so disappointed, even if she doesn't want to say it out loud or talk about the competition at all.

Instead Mom tells me what's been happening at her job. It's great they keep finding stuff for her to do and extending her time there, but in the end they're still a bunch of boring law office stories. Paige talks about school, when last time she thought I was crazy for asking about it.

They both tell me they love me, that they miss me, before Skype auto-ends the call right at the twenty-minute mark.

Harry's teaching defensive magic to Dumbledore's Army in the Room of Requirement when Wormwood pops her head into the dorms that evening. Ever since our family calls ended, we've been on a total Potter binge, skipping around the movies to everyone's favorite scenes.

We all sit up straight when we see the sous chef checking on us. She walks in. "You guys rested?"

Our only response is Kiko pressing pause on the movie just as Harry's about to kiss Cho under the mistletoe. Wormwood smiles at our stunned expressions. "Tomorrow," she continues. "Please dress ready for spending a few hours outside. Coats, hats, scarves."

"The food trucks again?" Joey asks, and this time there's no complaint in his words.

"Just be ready, Chef," Wormwood says.

Taylor's longest-running sous chef doesn't say anything else. She just takes one last, long, completely glowerless look at the five of us, then leaves. Kiko restarts *The Order of the Phoenix*, and we're all mesmerized by Harry's first kiss again.

I wonder if any of them are thinking what I am, noticed what I did.

That was the first time Wormwood called any of us "Chef."

Out of all the wild guesses we make, none of us imagine anything close to where we end up spending the day before Thanksgiving: watching the Macy's parade balloons being inflated, an actual New York tradition. But that's exactly where Wormwood and our handlers take us. Taylor doesn't join the field trip, and even though I'm excited, I find myself wondering what he'd rather be spending his day doing.

At first we move slowly around the tarnished, silver barricades guarding the balloons, the workers inflating them ignoring us, treating us like any other kid in the crowd and not the famous Super Five. I keep peeking between the mass of people and into open backs of running trucks, half expecting someone—maybe even the Super Chef himself—will pop out, surprising us with yet another cooking challenge. Every glimpse of bright silver makes me think I've spotted part of some stainless-steel kitchen appliance hidden among the colorful plastic balloon characters, when it's really just an air tank or a pole holding up a tent.

Soon we realize there's no trick coming. This is really and truly a day off. The only job we have here is to be kids, to race around pointing at Kung Fu Panda and Kermit,

Papa Smurf and SpongeBob. Mel and the rest of the handlers' breathing comes in cold, cloudy exhalations as they struggle to keep up with us.

We wind around the city streets until we've seen every single character worth taking in. And when we finally make it back to the van, out of breath but humming with excitement, we feel the best kind of sweaty cold. It's the kind that always comes with a day outside in winter, sledding or having a snowball fight. Most of our cheeks and noses are rosy, and some of us are sniffling, but all of us are laughing and reminding each other which balloon was our favorite.

It's not just us, either.

Because when we hop up into our seats in the van, Wormwood standing off to the side, counting us off to ensure we've all made it back, I catch a little something kinda foreign on her face.

It takes me a second longer than it probably should to recognize her smile.

eriously, how could I sleep? Sure, I was super tired after our day out, but for me Thanksgiving Eve had become the opposite of Christmas Eve. Where the night before the big December holiday has always been full of excitement and eagerness, this year the night before November's celebration is consumed with worry and dread.

Tomorrow's my last chance to do what I came here to do. I'm at a huge disadvantage, for sure, but I have to believe it's still possible for me to cook a better meal than the other four members of the Super Five. Even if I have only half the time.

I mean, I don't *have* to believe it, but I'm certainly trying really hard to make myself believe it. Which means . . . not sleeping. Nope, not one bit.

Lying awake in bed, the slightest glimpse of the city lights reaching me through a gap in the blinds, I wonder, since it's Thanksgiving, if the challenge might have something to do with the holiday itself. That's when an odd memory pops into my head: Mom talking about Thanksgivings when she was young. Which was always weird, because she hardly ever talked about her past, almost like she didn't have one.

Her mother would wake up at some crazy time, like five a.m., to start prepping their huge turkey, which apparently matched their huge family. The story always made me wonder how many hours my grandmother—it's a weird word for me to think, since I never met her, or any of my grandparents—had to cook this mythical, giant bird, but of course Mom could never remember what the weight was.

I try to picture her now, this grandmother I never knew, alone in her kitchen in the fading gloom of early morning, working on a meal for her whole family. No crowds or cameras. Nothing super. Not a contest.

Alone at five a.m., worrying about making sure everything would go right for the people she loved most. Awake like I am now, at two in the morning. Thinking about Paige, about Mom, about how badly I've messed up. About how, for me, everything did not go right. Not at all.

When I used to have trouble sleeping when I was little, Mom would make a glass of warm milk for us. Us, because of course Paige, who sleeps like she's in some kind of coma every night, had to follow me into the kitchen and drink a tall glass of it, too. Because little sister. Because copycat.

I haven't had a warm glass of milk in years, but maybe tonight it would do the trick. Worth a try, anyway. I'm hot, I'm itchy, and I'm awake. I throw off my comforter and pace out into the common room. Bleary-eyed, I stub my toe on a stool but resist crying out. If I wake everyone else up, this night will only get that much worse.

When I open the fridge, cool air washes over me, and I start to feel sleepy already. I take out the milk, set it on the counter, close the door. But somehow I'm still feeling that chill. I trace it to the sliding-glass door leading out to the balcony. It's open. I look that way in time to see the Super Chef and Mel coming back inside, their dueling shadows blotting out the city lights.

Mel's wearing a robe and pajamas, but Lucas Taylor's still dressed for the day—no winter coat for out there on the frigid balcony, either. The only difference between him now and when he's standing in front of us on the arena stage is his tie is loosened a little.

Mel steps forward, but Taylor stops, waiting in the open doorway. I guess he's as surprised to see me as I am to see him. My handler senses his boss's hesitation. He looks over his shoulder at Taylor, then back to me. "How about I give you guys a minute?"

Taylor nods, and Mel tugs at the collar of his robe to warm up, then takes his time closing and locking the sliding-glass door at the top and bottom. He tosses the keys into the air, catching them in his opposite hand, tucks them into his robe pocket. Finally he disappears into his room.

When the door closes behind Mel and we're alone, Taylor moves for the first time, pacing toward me and the kitchen. I haven't budged. Neither has my milk, the carton sweating dew on the counter.

"I needed to clear my mind," he explains, nodding toward Mel's closed door. "Mel there was kind enough to sneak me out to my favorite spot. It's where—"

"You stared at the city trying to decide the winner in the last episode of season one," I say. "And where you and Wormwood—" I gulp, then correct myself. "*Chef* Wormwood argued about how tough you were being on the competitors in season three."

He stares at me, his lips slightly parted.

"Episode seven," I finish.

Chef Taylor smiles. "So I take it you've watched the show, then?"

We share a quick smile.

He points at the milk, changes the subject. "So . . . late-night munchies?"

A little part of me still wants to hold back, say nothing, but maybe I'm too tired, because I do answer, and what comes out is way honest. "More like late-night nerves."

He exhales, then nods. "Yeah. We've been kinda tough on you guys." There's an apology in his stare back at me. At least, I think that's what I'm seeing. "So . . . let me guess. You're about to try warm milk? Something your mother taught you?"

It's the first time he's come within a thousand miles of directly mentioning Mom. Not sure I can handle that on what's sure to be my last night here, so I turn away from him without responding, reaching up for a fresh glass.

"Ever try walnuts?" he asks, stepping toward the fridge and yanking it open. "And pretty sure we have some of that tart cherry juice in here." His voice floats back to me because his head is leaning all the way in. "They both have melatonin in them. Good for sleeping."

He finds the juice and pulls it out, then nods toward the stools. "Have a seat. I'll pour you some. And a little dish of walnuts. I'm sure we have those, too. Somewhere."

"They're in that pantry," I say, pointing. I'd noticed them the other day when I was fishing around for some cornmeal for that night's dinner.

"Right." He wanders in that direction. "I do miss this place. I didn't realize how much of a touchstone it had become for me during the competitions. After the long days in the arena, I always used to crash up here."

"You didn't have to give it to us."

"I really did. We had to make sure you guys would be safe. Guarded."

The Super Chef holds his open hand toward me, and I pass him my still-empty glass. He brings down a small bowl for the walnuts. He fills both and serves them to me across the island. "Try this combo." He winks. "A secret I learned in Tibet."

"Really?"

He laughs. "No, actually my grandmother taught me. In a hotel in Nebraska, I think." A distant look crosses his face. "Maybe Oregon . . ."

His grandmother, when I'd just been thinking of mine. Lucas Taylor's grandmother, who would be my great-grandmother. Who I've never met either, never even seen a picture of. I'm suddenly filled with a desire to know everything about her, but he asks another question first.

"Why the nerves?" He pops a single walnut into his mouth.

Because I've blown the biggest opportunity I've ever had in only two weeks? Because the father I've never really talked with—that I so badly want to somehow be able to talk to—is mere feet away, telling me he wanted to make sure I was safe, and I still can't decide if he's my biggest hero or my oldest nemesis?

I chew a few of my own walnuts, a delay tactic. So I don't have to talk, because I can't decide what I would say if I did open my mouth.

"Listen, Curtis," the Super Chef starts. "It's true our meeting didn't go that well, but that score's been posted. It's over. You're still here, aren't you? Everyone who's still here has a chance. Tomorrow is like starting over."

I shake my head. "But we're not starting over. I'm in last place. I've deserved the scores I've gotten. I . . . and . . . that wasn't how I wanted our meeting . . . no."

Wow, Pith. *Super smooth.*

"Okay," he says slowly, clearly processing my jumbled comment. "So what happened that night?"

What happened? Part of me still wants to force him to explain all his life choices, to justify every decision he's ever made. Most of me isn't sure there's a point to that, though. In the end, I just stare back.

"Tell me," he presses. "What happened at Colbeh's?"

I shrug. "It's not really important. I wasn't brave enough." *I'm still not brave enough.* "Too scared, I guess."

"Scared?" he says, alarmed. "Of what? Me?"

The walnuts are good. Fresh, crispy. I keep crunching, because that way I don't have to talk, to admit things I'm still not ready to admit. I tilt the bowl so the last couple drop into my hand. Still stalling. Because . . . was I scared of him? No, that wasn't it.

I think I was scared of chasing something I'd secretly wanted without totally knowing it. And it wasn't money. Once what I wanted was right in front of me, though, once I could reach out and touch it, I guess I was afraid that, if I stretched too far, I would get burned. And there was no Mom or Wormwood to pull my hand back for me, so I did it myself. I pulled my own hand away from getting to know my father, told myself he didn't deserve to meet the real me.

I push the empty bowl back toward him. He reaches out for it with his left hand. Something changes in his face, and he pulls it back, extends the right one instead. It makes me remember the cobbler mishap, the dessert falling to the floor in slow motion, the way he got so frustrated when the apples splattered all over the clean arena.

I need a change of subject anyway. "Sorry about that cobbler," I say, nodding at his hand, still wrapped in gauze after the plate shards incident. Thinking how weird it is he'd rather pick the bowl up with his injured hand. "Is it any better?"

"A little. And please . . . no. That wasn't your fault. That accident was all me. My hands . . ." He opens his left one and stares at it, open-palmed, like it doesn't belong to him. Like it's some other thing, not connected anymore.

"I make a point of never reaching for anything with my left hand," he continues. "I think I got so wrapped up in the challenge, I just forgot. That's what happens. Sometimes I forget. But it doesn't last long. What I have . . . it always seems to find a way to remind me it's there."

I take a sip of the juice. It's really sour; my lips pucker. "What you have?"

Chef Taylor inhales. He looks toward the balcony, then back at me. Holds my gaze for a second before his eyes change. They focus in, like he's made an important decision. "Have you ever heard of Parkinson's disease?"

"Kind of."

"It's a nervous system disorder. Makes your hands shake, gives you a funny walk, turns simple things like grabbing plates into difficult tasks."

Like someone hit the rewind button on my brain, the images of all his strange walking and hand shaking and buttons not done up right on chef's jackets flash through my head, so fast they become a blur, and I realize I've noticed a lot more of them than I understood. All those things he was doing that weren't Super Chef–like. That weren't cool.

"So you have that? Parkinson's?"

He smiles a little, dips his head. "I do. Found out last year."

"How do you get it?" I'm whispering. Why am I whispering?

"No one knows for sure," he says. "There's a chemical

your brain needs. It's called dopamine. People who have Parkinson's, we don't have enough of it. So . . . let's just say our brains start acting funny." He glances at his left hand again. "Then we do, too. Might start with a trembling hand, or a shuffling foot, or a shaking head. And then . . . off we go." He swipes his bandaged right hand through the air, like it just rushed down a world-class water slide.

I take another gulp of cherry juice, because I'm not sure what to say. He's leaning on the counter with his head down. I've seen him do it a bunch of other times. All those times he looked hurt, but I never saw a single cut or bruise or burn. Not on the outside.

"How do you get better?"

He jerks one shoulder up. "There are some great medicines. They help a bunch, actually. But get better? You mean, like, cured?"

I nod.

"You don't, not really. There isn't . . . there's no cure. At least not yet."

A bunch of LEGO-shaped pieces snap into place in my head, the full picture in front of me for the first time. "So that's . . . all this . . . it's why you're ending *Super Chef*?"

The Last Super Chef.

He bites his lip. Nods agreement. "Yes, Curtis. It's exactly why."

"It was just time, that's all. This disease, Parkinson's, there's no manual for it. It's different for every single person who has it. Nothing is normal. I can't." Taylor holds up his empty hands again. "I can't master it. It isn't . . . predictable. There's no recipe.

"And it's only going to get worse. Eventually Parkinson's steals everything you've taken a lifetime to build, all your skills. The simple stuff, like tying a shoe, buttoning a shirt, getting dressed. And the kitchen stuff. Oh, the kitchen stuff. That's been a revelation. You know, Curtis. You're a chef. All these skills we build up, the ways we use our hands. All the stuff I need to be what I am. I can't be the Super Chef when I can't even carve up a chicken."

The way he stepped aside and let Wormwood do it. The week before he announced *The Last Super Chef.*

"You know," Taylor continues. "A few weeks ago, I missed the last step into the arena." He nods toward the door leading to the stairway down. "Fell flat on my face. At first I worried someone would stumble upon me lying there. So embarrassing. And, depending on who found me, potentially hard to keep quiet. I told myself to hurry. Get back up. But I couldn't. And eventually I started to wonder: What if I just . . . didn't? Thought even, maybe, I shouldn't. It might be easier to stay down. Not just for me. For everyone else, too."

Still turned around, he sighs. "I've had some doubts now and then during this competition, wondered whether I was doing the right thing, but at that moment, I knew for sure. I can't wait around for my disease to get so bad that worse things start happening on TV." He stretches his neck, eyes on the ceiling. "You know, though, the time I've had has been so wonderful. I would never say different. This thing—cooking—it's all I ever wanted to do, ever since I was little. Chef is all I've ever wanted to be."

Yeah, I know *that* feeling. "That's why you wanted to pick a kid and not another adult."

He turns around to face me. "Yeah. I guess . . . I've heard a few times this idea I'll be the last great chef. Which, of course, is simply preposterous. There will always be a next great everything. Chef, basketball player, physicist . . ."

"So Bill Nye the Science Guy's not always gonna be the GOAT?"

He snorts. "Let's hope not." His expression flattens again. "I love this show. I love being the Super Chef. But if it has to end . . . I didn't want it to be a sad ending. I really didn't. I wanted *The Last Super Chef* to be about the future. I wanted to show it could be shiny and bright, not depressing and dark. I wanted to make sure no one would call me the last Super Chef. I wanted that to be someone else. Someone who would be around for a while."

Taylor takes a deep breath. "That could only happen with kid competitors."

He pauses and stares at me, as if he's waiting for agreement. "Makes sense," I say.

"Claire—Chef Wormwood—she thinks I should wait. That I can get by for a while with a little help. Like this is a—" He bites his lip, and I can tell it's because he almost cursed. He lowers his voice. "Like it's a Beatles song and not my actual life. But she *knows* how I grew up. With a single parent, just my father, traveling all around the world with his mother, my grandmother, who was very sickly, me taking care of her all that time . . . I'm used to a lot of responsibility. I'm used to doing things on my own, being self-sufficient. I can't . . . it doesn't make sense to suddenly . . ."

"Did your grandmother have it, too? Parkinson's?"

"No. Not hereditary." He lays a hand over his chest. "She had trouble with her lungs."

I've heard the stories. More like lived and breathed them. How he learned to cook traveling the globe with his family. But now I realize no one ever said what his "family" was. I always figured it was him with his mother and father. Even the other night, in our meeting, when he'd agreed with me that "three's a good number." Sure, because his family was three, too, but like mine, not the three you'd expect. Not one child, one mother, one father. Maybe not that many families are that way anymore. Maybe there's no such thing as normal when you're talking about families. They are what they are.

"I've been thinking about her a lot lately, actually," the Super Chef says. "Wishing she were still here. I'd love to ask her if I'm making the best decision."

"I think it's working," I say right away, before flicking my eyes toward both closed doors of the dorm, girls and boys. "All these guys you picked . . . they're amazing. They've definitely shown me the future of cooking. I'm sure everyone else has seen the same thing."

"Thanks, Curtis. That's . . . That means a lot." Again he holds my gaze a moment. "Don't forget yourself, though. That okonomiyaki was out of this world. And your scallops, your soufflé . . ." He trails off.

"Only the first one," I say, wondering if he's just being nice. "These last two . . ."

"Must've been pretty scary to get thrown onto national TV like you've been. So maybe there've been a couple of missteps here and there. Overall, you really did great."

I cast my eyes downward. I don't want to admit how difficult or scary these past few weeks have been, not even to him. Or maybe *especially* not to him.

"You know, the truth . . . Curtis . . ." The tremor in his voice makes me look up again. "The truth is, sometimes I'm pretty scared, too." He taps his temple. "Scared and really, really tired."

His trembling voice grows thick. He turns around again, facing the sink.

With every movement he's made, each word he's uttered, I've understood a little bit more. About him, and about this competition.

Not being able to cook like he's always cooked, losing his knife skills? And talking weird? Walking weird? Falling? Shaking all the time? Plus, it's going to get a lot *worse*?

I can't imagine getting as good at something as he has, then having to stop being that good. Reaching your dream—for me, for both of us, the *only* dream—and then seeing it end because of some disease, one he doesn't even understand where it came from.

Part of me wonders why he's told me all this. Why not

Joey or Pepper, Kiko or Bo? But of course I know why. None of them are his children. Whether he's ever going to admit it out loud or not, he's telling me all this now because I'm his son. Maybe this is his apology, his explanation for all our lost years. The best one I'm going to get, probably.

I feel a door slamming shut in my mind. Behind it are all the times I questioned whether he was my hero or my nemesis. Good guy or bad. Because he's none of those things. And he's all of them, too. In the end the Super Chef's just a person, like me, dealing with his own problems.

Maybe he doesn't deserve all the admiration I've felt for him all these years. He probably deserves none of my resentment. Well . . . okay, maybe a little bit of it.

The fact is, I don't want to know or talk about the years behind us anymore. Not when his future has such a dark cloud over it. I don't want to do anything to make the struggle he's facing even harder. If I say something, it should be to help him. But what? What could I, a kid, ever say to make the actual Super Chef feel a little better?

He said tired. Scared. I've felt both for almost two weeks. For him, it's been more like a year? *Man.*

"Maybe we can be scared together." I spit the thought out without thinking about whether it's the right thing to say or not.

He turns around. The Super Chef. Chef Lucas Taylor. My father turns around, his face lights up, and he smiles at me. "You know what? I think I'd like that, Curtis."

As if that were some cue they agreed to, Mel's door quietly opens, and he emerges from his room. Like twins, he and the Super Chef glance toward the clock at the same time.

"But right now," Chef Taylor continues. "It's getting late. You've got a big day tomorrow." He exhales again. "I really hope you're able to get some sleep for it, Curtis."

"You too."

In bed, as I feel my eyes growing heavier, the whole conversation replaying in my mind, I have this idea I understand so much more about Lucas Taylor, about my father, than I did only one hour ago. There's just one thing that keeps bothering me, one thing that I keep trying to run through my brain like potatoes through a ricer to get them as smooth as possible.

Why would the Super Chef think the future of cooking has to be about just one person?

On Thanksgiving morning, we stand around the common room in our chef's jackets, watching the seconds tick toward eleven a.m. No one talks. There's hardly any eye contact. Just five kids with growling stomachs, waiting for the start of the day that would change one of our lives forever.

No one volunteered to cook a group breakfast. Kari warned us that the morning part of today's finale involved brunch. We'd be eating it, we knew that much, so none of us wanted to fill up on a big meal, then push *Super Chef* food around our plates on live TV.

I'd gotten maybe three hours of sleep last night, even after the walnuts and tart cherry juice. All the things

Taylor confessed to me across the kitchen island bounced around in my head for another hour, as if the Super Chef had whipped a super ball into my brain, just to see how fast it could ricochet across the inside of my skull and knock over everything inside it.

Parkinson's disease. Little puzzle pieces had been falling from the sky since I heard those two words, locking together neatly as they landed. The reasons why this contest existed snapping into the reasons why the five of us had spent over two weeks in New York, perfect matches for how Wormwood had been behaving. And Taylor, too.

"Chef Wormwood and your handlers will be back to pick you up a little before eleven." Those were the last words Kari spoke before leaving the dorms a couple of hours ago. What was "a little before"? 10:30? 10:45? All of us grew paranoid, so what we did eat, we ate super fast, just toast or energy bars, then got dressed and, one after another, assembled in the common room. We'd been waiting for a half hour or more, pacing, sitting, then standing, picking at threads on our jackets, doing one final check that turned into ten final checks of our hair in the mirror. Anything but actually talking to each other.

Last night, Taylor said that Wormwood hadn't wanted him to hold this contest at all, that she thought he could continue being the Super Chef if he just accepted a little more help from the people around him. Like a ghost, I feel her hand squeezing my shoulder the other day, pulling me close, protecting me from getting burned during the Handling Criticism challenge. And that's when I realize it: that scowl she's been sporting for two weeks hasn't been about the Super Five.

Wormwood's not against *us*. She's against this *contest*. And I'm not sure she's wrong.

"Where are they?" Kiko asks, and it's maybe the first time I've heard that level of impatience in her tone. "How long do we have to wait?"

It's like her voice doesn't just break the silence in the room. It tears down the wall of thoughts stuck inside all of us.

"And what're we going to eat?" Joey asks. He rubs his stomach, then looks longingly toward the fridge.

"All I know is they better not make us critique each other again," Pepper says.

I want to tell her they'd never do that, but then they repeated mise en place, didn't they? And I made that soufflé how many times? Could it have been only three? Felt like a thousand.

But the words seem trapped behind my tongue. Or maybe locked up behind some door in my brain. It makes me think about the Super Chef flubbing that dessert order the other night, having so much trouble coming up with the words right there in his hand.

One lava cake, two crump . . . two . . . the sorb—

I'm still thinking of it when the door bursts open. Not the door in my mind, the actual one, to the dorms.

When I turn that way, though, there's no Wormwood in sight. It's only our handlers—Mel and Ashley, Brett, Renata, and Craig. "Everyone down there is ready," Mel says. Somehow he looks excited and very serious at the same time. "Let's go."

Super Chef Arena is reconfigured yet again. The biggest change is up on the stage, where one long dining table with about twenty chairs sits waiting. Places are set at each seat—candles, plates, glasses, napkins. It looks like the Thanksgiving dinners I see on TV, how the really big families decorate their fancy holiday tables. I've never seen such a thing in person before. Mom used to make it a point that we sit at our kitchen table for any once-a-year dinners, but the last few Thanksgivings we've eaten in our laps on the couch, like almost every other meal.

Our stations are set up in the normal configuration again, so when we stand at them, we'll be facing the stage. The audience is back up top in the balcony, too, cheering and stamping their feet. I've learned to ignore them so well, I don't even bother looking that way. We march in like Kari taught us, and I wonder, as I split off from the line at the right time and land at my station like a seasoned

TV star, if it's for the last time.

"The Super Five, ladies and gentlemen," Chef Taylor announces, encouraging another shower of applause from the balcony. The Super Chef, this time instead of becoming more animated with the power of the cheering, flattens his expression. "I want to thank each of you. You kids have sacrificed so much. So much. To be apart from your family for weeks, and now, to be here on this holiday, ready to cook again, willing to miss your loved ones on Thanksgiving. Another big sacrifice."

Even from one row behind and on the other end of the stations, I hear Bo's deep sigh at the mention of the word "family."

"It's frankly too much to bear. For you, for your families, and for us." Taylor gestures at Wormwood and Graca. "Even the audience can't stand it!" Laughter from above. "But!" He raises a finger into the air. "Maybe a few members of our crowd can help the situation."

I look up for the first time. There's a lot of shuffling in the balcony. A few audience members turn sideways to make room for others to move forward. Still, I don't get it. How can the audience help? I don't understand at all until I hear Bo's shout. "Mamá! Papá!"

The paths between the people in the crowd widen, clearing the way for Mr. and Mrs. Agosto to separate from the throng. They weave their way toward the stairs, then start to carefully lumber down them.

Next to me, Kiko shouts something in Japanese and points to the opposite side of the balcony. I follow her finger to find her parents up there as well, along with both sets of grandparents. There's a moment of wild, back-and-forth shouting in rapid Japanese.

That's when I get it. That's when I understand.

Our *families*. We've been so focused on when we could get back to them, longing for the distant contact of those too-far-between Skype moments, that none of us thought of the opposite happening. It never occurred to us—not to me, anyway—that the Super Chef would bring our families here, to us, on Thanksgiving.

My eyes hunt the balcony. It's like an awful game of *Where's Waldo*. Somewhere in this sea of faces, they have to be here. They have to be, but as I search with no luck, I get a sinking feeling that my family are the only ones who didn't make it. That you had to pay your own way or something, and Mom couldn't afford it.

Joey shouts recognition, then Pepper. I don't follow their pointing, though. I'm too busy looking for Paige, for Mom.

I squeeze my eyes shut and tell myself to slow down. When I open them again, there they are. Right in the center of my vision, under the giant arena clock.

Mom wears a fancy green dress I've never seen before,

with heels and earrings. Everything looks expensive. She's smiling, but when our eyes meet, she starts laughing. Some tears escape her eyes. At her side is Paige, wearing a nice skirt for the first time since Mom's work friend got married a few years ago. She's giggling too, so hard her tongue pokes out of her mouth, caught between her front teeth. I recognize them both, but then again they seem different. Paige looks older, like she's grown a whole foot. Mom seems to have aged too.

They both start to push their way through the crowd. People pat them on the shoulder, or just squeeze against each other to make room for them to pass.

I race to the bottom of the steps, passing Kiko hugging one of her grandmothers, Pepper showing her parents her station. I hear Joey talking a mile a minute with his uncle and father, gesturing toward the pantry, showing them where the sensory deprivation booths were. Bo's in a quiet group hug with his mom and dad that looks like it will go on forever.

One of Mom's heels clacks onto the concrete floor of Super Chef Arena. I hear the sound of it echoing, as if it happens in a completely silent stadium, even though it's as noisy with excitement and cheering here as it's ever been. Mom steps down with her other foot at the same time as Paige hops down with both of hers.

Then Mom's bending and reaching for me. She wraps

me in a hug so strong I catch my breath. She lifts me up and swings me into the air. I have a weird thought, some sense that not so long ago, I wished that the Super Chef, my father, would do exactly this someday, but why? How many times has Mom lifted me into the air just like this? Tons.

But not for a while now. A couple years ago she started telling me I was getting too heavy. I didn't realize how much I missed it. Now I understand I don't need anyone else but her doing it.

Even if Mom hadn't told me over Skype, I knew somewhere deep in my heart that she must've been missing me as much as I missed her. But I had been trying not to think about it. When she whispers it into my ear, though, it slams into me, sends a tingling from the top of my head to the bottom of my feet. "Oh, Curtis. We missed you *so* much."

Paige is tugging at my chef's jacket, talking a mile a minute, even though I can't hear her words. Mom squeezes me tighter, like she'll lose me if she allows her grip to loosen.

There's no crying in kitchens, unless maybe you're chopping onions. Even then, blink a few times if you have to. But just then, when I start bawling in Mom's arms as she keeps telling me over and over how she missed me, how I should never go away again, as everything that's happened in the past two weeks runs through my head, ending with last night's talk with the Super Chef, my first truly private talk with my father, the news that he's sick, the reason I'm here more clear, the moment all my anger and resentment melted from my body like butter in a pan, I finally understand those contestants I used to make fun of. Because it doesn't matter if I'm in a kitchen or not. I couldn't stop crying if I wanted to.

Maybe I was wrong about crying in kitchens. I think, maybe, I was wrong about a whole bunch of things.

The long stage table turns out to be for us. Us, meaning the Super Five and our families. Now I get why they'd told us we'd be eating brunch. The Super Chef announces there's no challenge or cooking during this first morning segment. He just wanted to give us a Thanksgiving reunion. Live on TV.

We surf a wave of humanity toward the stage table. Joey's crew arrives first, snatching up the chairs near the head, where the Super Chef sits. Kiko's family, all seven of them, take up a bunch of seats next, near Chef Graca in the middle. Then come Pepper and her parents. Bo's group and mine end up completely opposite from Taylor, on the other end of the table, where Chef Wormwood joins us, seated at the foot.

Paige is still talking a mile a minute, recounting the details of every episode while surveying the arena. "Oh, and over there is where you guys waited in the booths, right? Oh my gosh, there's the scoreboard, and the pantry, and the—"

She's the same Paige she's always been. Almost. Oddly, her hair is stringy, flying all over the place, like she's been electrically shocked. It makes her look sort of tired.

Immediately I assume it must somehow be my fault. "Paige, I'm so sorry," I whisper.

Shocked, she clamps her mouth shut. "Sorry? For what?"

"Doing so bad. I'm in last. I have no chance tonight, not with just thirty minutes—"

"Bad? Bad?!?" she cries, and I actually have to check around to see if everyone's staring, but there are so many loud conversations going on at once, no one seems to notice her raised voice. "Are you kidding? It's been *incredible*. They wouldn't let us say much on those calls, but when you did that pancake, I mean, OH-EM-GEE, and how you guessed three out of the five skills, and—"

"Indoor voice," Mom reminds Paige, but when I peek at her, she's not looking at us. Instead she seems fascinated by the fancy place setting in front of her. Watching her rearrange the silverware absently, her guard down, I notice the dark circles under Mom's eyes, how her head droops slightly to one side. If I saw her at home like this, I'd know it was time to shut down the TV and let her turn the couch into a bed.

Maybe Paige is tired, but my mother? She's completely *exhausted.*

It's been less than fifteen minutes since she's been here, but it's like this place, this arena, has already sapped her of all her strength and energy. Maybe it isn't the place, though. Maybe it's the person who runs it, who created it, who's draining her emotions. Come to think of it, I haven't seen Mom glance Lucas Taylor's way, not one time. He isn't looking at her, either.

Seriously? They haven't seen each other in how long? Years, right? They can't even acknowledge one another? Does Mom know Dad is sick? Does she care?

And what're we doing all the way on the other end of this table? Shouldn't we be right next to him? Or is this just a new way for him to engineer the same distance he's always wanted to exist between him and us?

Scared together? Wasn't that our agreement last night? Then why are we so far apart?

Suddenly I see his promise for what it is. Empty. Completely.

"Curtis," Paige says, pulling my attention back to her again. "You didn't do bad. You were awesome. Kids in school are asking for my autograph, just because I'm your sister. Oh, and watch parties. There've been a ton of those. Plus Tre! You know he's set up a table at the last couple of Eagles games to sell blown-up, signed photos of you and him from his birthday party last year?" She giggles. "His sign says, 'Meet Curtis Pith's Sue Chef!'"

"He spelled it S-U-E, didn't he?"

Hearing my best friend's name, I stop glowering at Taylor long enough to glance at Paige. When our eyes meet, her giggling picks up speed. "Totally."

I should be laughing with her, but I can only stare, openmouthed. It's like she—and Tre and the rest of North Sloan, apparently—only watched half of each show, the parts I did well in. Didn't they see all my mistakes?

A bellowing shout and hoot pulls my attention back down to the other end of the table. It's Joey's dad, tousling his son's hair as they laugh together.

Kiko's family joins in with them, enjoying whatever story Mr. Modestino's in the middle of telling. Her father pulls her into a tight embrace I'm guessing he's done hundreds of times back home in Japan.

Meanwhile, my own shoulders feel cold. Empty and alone.

Watch parties. Signed memorabilia. It's hard to believe all of that's been going on. There was a time I wondered if anyone in North Sloan besides Mom and Paige was paying attention at all. If my family had even been allowed to keep their apartment. But Mom had already assured me there'd been no issue with that. In fact, she was surprised I even asked. Instead it seems almost everyone back home has been rooting for me. Well, maybe except for Pettynose.

But what about the people here? Did I ever have a chance with them? I look down the table at Taylor again. He glances up. Our eyes meet. His widen; he shifts his gaze away quickly.

I sense Mom watching me. My exchange with Taylor. She looks down at him, then back to me, down at Taylor again. She's concerned. Of what? Is she afraid I'll blurt something out with Paige sitting here? Seriously? After I stayed quiet for how many years?

Why does it have to be a secret, anyway? Stay a secret? For weeks I've worked my butt off, trying to impress the Super Chef, and it still hasn't been enough. Because after all that, including last night's confessions, he's still making sure to sit very far away from me on Thanksgiving—the "national holiday that's always been all about food and *family* and gratitude."

Maybe for everyone else. But not for me. Not for us. We're apart, not together. Again.

It's the same as every other holiday, isn't it? I love my sister, my mom, I'm so grateful to have them. But why does being Curtis Pith's father have to be some kind of ugly badge no one wants to be caught wearing?

And hold on . . . is that what I've spent my time here doing? Trying to *impress* Lucas Taylor?

A lot of good that's done, when he hasn't lifted a finger this whole time to try to impress me. Sure, maybe he finally let me into his life last night, but was it too little? And way too late?

Look at all these other families. All the moms and dads, together with their children. Heck, some even have extras. Besides her two parents, Kiko has four grandparents here, too. Four! And Joey has his uncle Frank, the big restaurant owner.

I feel tears pushing their way forward from the back of my eyes. I lean my face into Mom's shoulder to try to keep them at bay.

Last night, after hearing about Taylor's Parkinson's, I decided to forgive him, to go back to seeing only the chef who's helped me learn to cook for all these years, the man who finds himself in so much trouble he's ending the show he loves. To see only the person he is, just a man with flaws and challenges like everyone else, like me, like Mom.

But seeing Mom looking so defeated by her trip here, defeated by the Super Chef, knowing I've already been beaten by the same forces, too, it's just too much. There's no possible way for me to forget who Lucas Taylor really is. Chef—that's only what he does. Father—that's who he was supposed to be.

Father is who he never was.

"Curtis?" Mom asks, gripping my shoulder, hugging me closer while at the same time prompting me to sit up. "Everything all right?"

Still pressing into her, I look straight up into her eyes. I should answer the same way I've always answered that question. *I'm fine.* But my neck feels red and scratchy under the collar of my suddenly heavy and hot *Super Chef* jacket.

"He's tired," Wormwood says. "I'm afraid all these kids must be." She reaches over and pats the back of my hand. "Stay strong, Curtis. It's almost over."

Almost over? As in, "It won't be long until you lose officially" over?

I dig my head deeper against Mom's shoulder. A recipe pops into my head. French onion soup. It's what I do, what I've always done: think about cooking when I don't want to think about what I'm really thinking about. Find comfort in food.

Purposely distract myself with menus and measurements. I try to let it happen now, because I know I should.

2 cloves garlic, minced

3 pounds sweet onions, sliced

¼ cup . . . ¼ cup . . .

I should. I should. I should. But I can't. I can't. I can't.

"Why don't you talk to him?" I ask Mom, quickly pulling away from her.

I point at Lucas Taylor. At the Super Chef. At my father. "He's right there, but you haven't even looked at him since you got here." Now I direct my gaze down the table, raise my voice. "And what about you? Why don't you say something? Do you hate each other that much?" I gesture toward Paige. "Do you hate *us* that much?"

I'm not even sure which of my parents I'm more angry at, because I don't even know why they're not together. That story's always been *the* big secret, hasn't it? More like the big lie. The biggest one of my life.

The entire table is staring my way now. All the cameras trained on me. But this time I'm not afraid of face sweat. Maybe I'm finally not afraid of anything anymore.

I stand up out of my chair, backing away. The Super Chef's jaw drops low. Mom hisses at me, "Curtis! What are you . . . ?"

"Did you know he's sick? That's why this is all happening. He's sick, and you come all the way here and don't even say two words to him. Maybe he needs help."

I switch my rage to Taylor. "Can't you see how tired she is? This was my only chance to . . ." Tears sting the corners of my eyes. I swing my arms, pointing to every corner of the sparkling arena. "Look at this place!"

Chef Wormwood inhales sharply. "Chef Pith! Sit down!"

Paige looks up at me like she's watching the final scene

of some scary horror movie. Eyes wide, breath held.

Scared of what? the Super Chef asked me last night. *Me?*

"You don't know, Paige," I try to explain to her. "You just . . . you can't understand. He's our father." I point at the Super Chef again.

"Lucas?" Chef Wormwood. A tense whisper, full of alarm and shock.

At the same time, Mom bolts up from her chair. "Curtis!"

My name leaves my mother's mouth differently than I've ever heard it before. A short, completely shocked bark. She does a double take between me and Taylor. If it's possible, when she speaks again, her surprise comes out even greater. "What?"

A wave thick with her clear disappointment washes over me. My lips stop working.

She shakes her head vigorously, and now she's beginning to cry. "Curtis, I . . . I don't understand where you're . . . ?"

My heart drops into my stomach at the same time my hand drops to my side. She *still* won't admit it? "You told me. In second grade. Don't you remember? Y-you said . . ."

Mom inhales, fighting tears, panting. "No. Curtis, no, I don't remember that. Just . . . listen to me. Your dad, he's someone . . . someone who wasn't ready to be a dad. He's still not ready."

"No . . ." As I try to order my thoughts, the tears I'm unable to hold back any longer start to roll down my cheeks. "When I came home on career day, when I made you tell me who my dad was . . ." I'm heaving heavy sobs now, almost so hard that I can't speak through them. Backing away one more step with every other word. "You told me he was a great chef. The S-Super Chef was on. You p-pointed at the TV. You pointed . . . at him." I raise my hand toward the Super Chef a third time. My finger shakes and, stupidly, I tell myself I shouldn't have used my left hand. Because I'm confused. More confused than I've ever been.

"This is all just a misunderstanding," Mom explains to the room, trying to regain some of her composure even as her face turns as red as boiled beet juice. Even now, she's worried about what everyone else thinks. What they see. "Can we . . . ?"

The Super Chef finally finds his voice. "Oh my. Of course. Yes." He glances up. For the first time I realize the usually murmuring audience has fallen completely silent. Taylor points at the nearest camera, the red light seeming brighter than ever. "This is . . . Can someone please?"

All at once, the camera lights blink out. So we can hide from the truth for a little bit longer. But the truth isn't something you run from. It's always there, right behind you. Waiting to dive at your feet and drag you down just before you reach the goal line.

"You're lying!" I shout at Mom. "You just don't want everyone to know. You've *never* wanted people to know."

Mom shakes her head. "Curtis." She comes toward me and grabs both my shoulders, lowering herself to my level. "I don't know how you . . ." She shakes her head. "That doesn't matter. Listen. You have to believe me. I swear I'm telling you the truth." She sniffs. "I'm not . . ." She glances back at Taylor. "We're not . . . Chef Taylor is not your father."

Amid the silence, someone else sniffs. It's Paige, choking back ugly tears. My little sister, the only person in the world who's always looked up at me with anything close to the admiration I've always felt for the Super Chef. Until now. That trust she had in me, that belief I could do no wrong—it was one of the things that allowed me to believe in myself. But the vacant look in her eyes tells me even that's gone.

I turn back to Mom. Her expression remains flat, her face open and covered in tears. How did we all end up crying?

I'm desperate for her to admit she's lying, but I can see that she isn't. And it's all too much. I can't even remember why I thought what I thought or how it all started. Five minutes ago seems like a lifetime ago.

The Super Chef is not my father.

Which means . . . I wasn't born to be a chef. I wasn't

born to be anything. I'm in last because I was meant to be in last. I never had a chance to be anything else. Because if I don't have Lucas Taylor's talent running through my veins, then what do I have?

Nothing, that's what.

I want to run somewhere. Anywhere. I start to wander backward again, directionless. Mom reaches out for me, but I dodge away from her grasp, jumping back quickly, knocking my chair over. It crashes to the floor, the sound echoing throughout the eerily quiet arena.

"Leave me alone!"

The words come out as a scream, and it actually takes me a second to understand that it was me. I screamed. All my feelings poured into a single response, a focused desire. To be alone. To escape all these unblinking eyes.

The Super Chef bursts to his feet, but stumbles before he takes a step, and I don't know how to feel about his Parkinson's disease or this whole contest anymore. I just want out.

I race away from the table, heading up the stairs. I hear a bunch of voices call "Curtis!" after me. Paige, Mom. All the chefs. But I don't stop. I take the steps two at a time until I hit the dorms, then slam the door behind me.

I slam the door on anyone who might've followed me.

I slam the door on everything I thought my life was before today.

I head for the handler's room. Because I know from the other day there are no cameras in there, and the last thing I want is for the Super Chef or anyone else to be able to watch me falling to pieces right now.

Someone will follow me, I'm sure of it. Probably Mom, maybe the Super Chef. Could be Paige, or one of the sous chefs. Maybe Mel. No matter who comes, though, there's another reason to be back here. The second door provides an extra layer of protection. I turn the lock and back away from it, like I'm in a game of hide-and-seek.

I slump to the floor, my back propped up against the bed. I drop my head into my hands.

The Super Chef is not my father.

So who is, then?

It's hard to remember all the tiny details of a conversation that happened when you were seven. I know it was career day. I know *Super Chef* was on. I remember Mom avoiding the question for a while, until finally my tears got to her.

I swear she pointed at the television, at the Super Chef, when she said my dad loved to cook, that he was really good at it. But maybe she didn't.

I'm one hundred percent sure the actual words "The Super Chef is your father" left her lips. Or at least eighty-five percent sure. Fifty? Okay, maybe . . . maybe my mind somehow twisted what she really said into something else. Something I wanted to hear.

Something I wanted to believe.

I hear the common room door beep open, and I focus my attention on the doorknob, waiting for it to turn, for Mom or whoever to try to force their way in here with me. I consider propping the desk chair against it, but I don't want to make noise.

Someone calls out "Curtis?" but I can't figure out whose voice I'm hearing. There's a commotion on the boys' side. More on the girls'. Finally rushing feet stop outside the door I'm staring at. The knob turns, but it stays locked. It must be Mom. Did she bring a key?

But the shadowed feet remain outside. "Curtis? You in there?" Is that Pepper?

"Come on, dude, open up." Joey?

"*Por favor.*" Bo. Definitely Bo.

I push off the floor and inch toward the door, pressing my ear against it to make sure I'm not hearing things. That the people who followed me are ones I didn't even consider in the possible list.

"We can see your feet," Kiko says, and her voice is low, like she's dropped to the floor and is looking under the door.

I put my hand on the knob and breathe in. Turn the lock, open it. I wasn't wrong. The rest of the Super Five are standing there, all four of them, like a team of superheroes gazing down at the defeated villain, waiting for him to confess his plan. But I had no plan, other than escape.

Joey's in the lead, the others flanked behind him. "Hey, man," he says, locking eyes with me and taking a quick breath in. "You wanna talk about it?"

"So all this time," Kiko says. "You have thought Chef Taylor was your father?"

We're sitting in a circle on the floor of the back room. The door is closed and locked again. Everyone is cross-legged except for Kiko, who sits on her knees with her feet tucked under her. They've already explained that they convinced the adults to let them come talk to me. Apparently Paige was so distraught it took both Mom and the Super Chef to calm her down. I didn't think I could feel worse, but the idea of making my sister that upset does the trick.

"Why didn't you say something earlier?" Pepper asks.

I shrug and stare down at my hands. "It never seemed like the right time. I thought I could do it during the one-on-one—"

"That is when I would have done it," Bo says.

"But the camera, all those people watching. My mom, Paige. I couldn't."

"That is seriously messed up," Joey says, and Pepper smacks him in the arm. The surprised expression he sends her clearly asks, *What did I say?*

"The worst part is, I thought I was a chef. Can you believe that? I actually thought I had Lucas Taylor's talent, that it would me give a fighting chance against all of you."

"Curtis," Kiko says. "You are one hundred percent a chef."

I look around. Everyone's nodding with her. My eyes land on Bo last. He raises both eyebrows. "*Muy bueno.* After all, you taught yourself, isn't that correct?"

Pepper scooches closer into the circle. "Your mom didn't . . . ?"

I shake my head.

"A grandfather? An uncle?" Joey asks.

"Nobody."

Bo gives me a thumbs-up. "*Definitely* amazing."

Is it? Guess I never realized. Besides, does it matter?

"Thanks. But I still managed to ruin this for all of you. I know how important this contest is for you guys. It's just, I think I came here with a lot more pressure on me than you did."

Pepper starts to chuckle. Before long she's laughing so hard she falls backward. It's kind of scary, like it's the Joker or something across from me rather than a ten-year-old.

"What's funny?" Kiko asks her. She leans away, frightened by Pepper's sudden, wild cackling.

Pepper straightens up again. "Just . . . sorry, Pith, but I'm not sure you know what pressure is. You know how good my parents are at *everything*? You know how hard it is to try to live up to that? I'm running a business!" She throws her hands out. "Why am I running a business? I'm ten. You don't think I'd rather spend time doing normal kid stuff?"

"Yeah. Like hanging with friends," Joey agrees, nodding. "I kinda wondered."

"I wish," Pepper says softly. "I . . . The thing is, I don't really have any. I'm too busy for friends." Her eyes glisten, and her hand shoots up to one as she sniffs. "I know way more about balance sheets and marketing plans than video games."

"Well, I pretend everybody in school is my friend. Most people can't even stand me," Joey says, looking away from her.

"That cannot be true," Kiko says.

He shrugs. "It's mostly true. A few dudes hang around me because my family has a lot of money. I can get tickets to stuff. Take them on trips. My uncle and dad go on a lot of trips together." He glances toward the big window. "You know, it's weird. All I really want is for my dad to pay attention to me, but instead he spends all his time with his brother. They're inseparable. He admires him so much for all the restaurants and everything . . . that's actually why I started cooking."

"What do you mean?" Pepper, still wiping at her eyes, asks him.

"I just thought, maybe if I got good at it, as good as my uncle Frank is, my dad might pay as much attention to me as he pays to him. Spend as much time at home as he does at all my uncle's restaurants."

"But your dad is perfect," I say. "When you got your certificate, he was so happy for you. He lifted you into the air, hugged you."

"I guess," Joey says. "That's what I mean, though. I did something he could admire, finally. And that made him happy." After a momentary pause, he sniffs, too, but just once. "It's not perfect, trust me. I don't even *like* squid."

"That is seriously messed up," I say.

Joey laughs with me, wipes his sleeve across his eyes. "You know what's even weirder, though? Even with all that, I still just want to go home. I don't even want to win stupid *Super Chef* anymore."

"There is no other location like the house," Bo agrees, nodding seriously.

"No place like home," Kiko corrects him. "You mean there's no place like home. I miss mine, too."

"Can I make a confession?" Bo asks. The rest of us wait quietly. "I thought this was my big dream. To be on *Super Chef*. To win it, maybe. But since the day I got here, going back home is the only thing I have wanted to do."

The rest of us shout, "No kidding, Bo!" at the same time. Pepper reaches up and grabs a pillow, wings it at Bo's head. It hits him square in the face. He somersaults backward.

When he untangles himself from the pillow, he looks around at all of us in shock. "It has been so obvious?"

"Dude, you've only said it like a hundred times," Joey tells him.

"Maybe a thousand," I agree. We laugh some more. I start to feel a little better. Everything isn't so . . . heavy.

"But it's why we love you," Pepper adds, crawling over

and side-hugging Bo, then reaching around him to snatch the pillow she threw. "Sorry," she says, gesturing at it. "Couldn't help it." She shimmies back to her spot.

"I have six parents," Kiko says. "You are talking about pressure from your families," she explains. "I have it, too. My family works so hard to give me the best opportunities. Not just my parents, my grandparents, too. Everyone is living for me, to make sure I make it further than they did. It is very hard to be as perfect as they want me to be. To always win first place."

"Bet you still want to go home, though," Joey says. "Even with all that waiting."

Kiko nods slowly. "I guess I do."

"Weird, isn't it?" he says.

They're not so different from me. Their families aren't as perfect as I assumed. And maybe . . . maybe I didn't get a father out of this whole thing, but I do think I found a squad after all. At least, I think I made some new friends. Kids my age, who love the same things I do.

"Doesn't seem to matter if we have six parents," I indicate Kiko. "Or one." I tap my own chest. "Everyone has a ton of pressure at home, but we all still want to go back there." It isn't really a question, but all four of them nod with me.

"So, does anyone even care anymore? About winning, I mean?"

The nodding stops. All four heads shake instead, a lot of mumbling joining the motion. Several *not reallys* and a few *not sures*. A bunch of *I don't think sos*. I'm the only quiet one.

"What about you?" Pepper asks me.

I think about the original reason I came to New York, all that money, how much it would've helped Mom, Paige, us. But then I also think about why the Super Chef is quitting, about Wormwood. How I came into this room to make sure no cameras caught me falling to pieces, and yet Lucas Taylor has felt like he's been doing it in front of a live audience for weeks now. Months, even. In the past hour, I'd gone from forgiving him to not forgiving him to realizing there had never been anything to forgive him for in the first place.

"I guess I . . . I'm not sure it would be right to win anymore."

"What do you mean?" she asks. "You've stopped wanting to be a chef? You don't want to represent the future of cooking?"

For the first time in years, I wonder. For the first time in years, I consider that maybe I could grow up to be something else besides a chef. Maybe.

"It's not that," I say.

"So what, then?" Joey asks. They all lean forward, waiting for me, gazes intense.

I take a deep breath. Then, leaning in to match their

posture, tightening our circle, I start speaking in hushed tones.

First I tell the Five about my conversation with the Super Chef last night in the kitchen. I tell them about his secret, why he's even holding this contest. His Parkinson's.

Then I tell them what I know about Wormwood, what she thinks about what Chef Taylor is doing. How wrong she believes it is.

Then I tell them my plan, because all of a sudden I have one.

head over to the bedside table and pick up the red Bat-
phone. There are two buttons—line one and line two.
My finger hovers over one, then the other. I can't decide.

"Line one would be the security one, I think," Kiko
says over my shoulder.

"Are you sure?"

She chews on her thumbnail. "No."

I trusted her okonomiyaki idea. I trust her again now,
pressing down on line two. It rings once, twice, three
times before a confused voice answers. "Hello?"

I think I recognize it. I hope I'm right. "Mel?"

"Curtis?"

I sigh out relief. I picked the handlers' hangout room,

and not security, like I wanted to. "Yeah, it's me. It's us. We . . . um, we need your help," I say, then quickly add, "but you can't tell anybody."

I explain some of our plan, then hold my breath. This is an internship for him, it's super important to his culinary career. He's old enough to have decided it's what he definitely wants in life. We'd argued about whether he—or any of the assistants—would take such a huge risk to help us, but it's our only shot. What we want to do, we can't do on our own. I hear Mel covering the phone with one hand, then whispering. I can only hope it's to the other handlers and not the Super Chef or Mom.

He returns to the line. "We're in."

"You're . . . you are?"

"You kidding?" Mel laughs. "This whole farce has been a house of cards from the very beginning. Half of us have taken bets on when it would topple over. Waited to the last possible second, didn't you?"

"I guess."

"Well, as far as we're concerned, you little dudes are the bravest kids we've ever seen. And you're the ones who've had to go through all this these past few weeks. I figure it should end however you want it to end.

"Besides, if what you just described happens, pretty sure Craig owes me fifty bucks."

• • •

I return downstairs with the rest of the Super Five. Taylor and Wormwood and Mom and all the other parents and families are waiting near the bottom of the steps. They look at me expectantly.

Kari is the first one to approach. "Okay," she says, kneeling in front of me and taking one of my hands in hers. "Everything's arranged. You and your family can head straight to the airport. There's a plane ready to take you home—"

I pull away from her. "No."

Her eyes widen.

"No," I repeat. "I came here for *The Last Super Chef.*"

"Of course. Of course you did. We all understand that, Curtis. But under the circumstances we would never force you to finish the competition."

"You're not forcing me. I'm okay. I'm staying."

She locks eyes with me. "You're sure?"

I nod.

Kari stands up and paces over to where the Super Chef and Mom are talking. They hold a low conversation, during which Mom starts shaking her head almost immediately.

She looks around Kari at me. "Curtis, I'm sorry, but no. We're going home."

"Not yet, Mom. This isn't over yet."

The Super Chef puts a hand on Mom's shoulder and

whispers to her. She nods. He separates from the others and comes forward.

"How are you doing?" Lucas Taylor asks, crouching in front of me.

I try to keep the emotions out of my expression. It's hard to shake the idea I'm not looking into my father's eyes. That I'm just talking to a famous chef whose show I watch a lot. Chef Taylor could be Chef Graca or Chef Wormwood. Any of the other celebrities. *Not* my father.

"I'm fine."

The Super Chef inhales once, quick and sharp. "Well . . . okay. If you say so." His voice lowers even more, to something below a whisper. "Listen, I'm sorry I dumped all that on you last night. That wasn't fair. I don't know what I was thinking. It obviously wasn't the right—"

"That's not . . . That had nothing to do with it," I interrupt him to say. "I'm okay. I'm the one who should be sorry. For messing everything up."

"Oh, no, you didn't—" The Super Chef sighs.

He stares into my eyes, as if he has some power to detect the truth. "So I guess we know why you had such a hard time talking with me at Colbeh's." For the first time, he smiles a little.

"Guess so."

"I want you to know, I've never met your mother before today. If we . . . if I ever . . . I would never . . ."

"Yeah," I say, nodding a little. "I get that now."

"Listen, why don't you give yourself a break? And your family—your mom and sister are worried to death about you. They love you so much. Kari's got it all worked out. You can go home. And you don't have to worry." Now he's downright whispering. "They'll be taken care of. You all will. Promise."

The thing is, it's not about the money anymore. It's not even about my family. Me and Paige, Mom . . . we're gonna be fine. We've always *been* fine. But if I just go home, I'll be stranding the rest of the Super Five here. That's not what he taught us. The very first challenge, Lucas Taylor taught us teamwork. Sure, some of them can be kind of annoying—*cough*, Joey—but they all love cooking as much as I do. They're as good at it as I am, too. I could never leave them here on their own.

So, no, it's not about me. It's about the Super Five. And it's about the man in front of me, too. The Super Chef. I can't leave until everybody gets what they want. Or at least what they need. Even if I'm not sure he knows what he really, truly needs yet.

"I'm a chef," I tell him, raising my voice so the rest of the people in the room hear me, including Mom. "I came here to cook. I came here to win. I read the fine print. You can't kick me off unless I request it. I'm not asking."

Taylor hangs his head in defeat.

"I'm not leaving until this is over."

The Super Chef meets my eyes with his. He tries to keeps his expression unreadable, but I quickly recognize the hint of a smile behind those definitely-not-hazel peepers.

"Yes, Chef."

Chefs Wormwood and Graca pace around the arena, supervising the finale. The audience is strangely quiet. I could probably hear a pin drop. Maybe the same pin I used at brunch, the one that seemed to deflate the excitement from this whole competition, as if I'd popped one of those Macy's balloons we saw yesterday.

For the first half of the cooking time, I have to wait. My penalty for finishing last in the challenge round, and it's agonizing. Not just because I want to be out there cooking with the rest of the Super Five. It's also because I have too much time to gaze around the arena. A watched pot never boils? Well, a watched plan, especially when it's pretty much all your idea, is the opposite. It makes your insides bubble over way faster than you expect.

Twice I see Mel whisper into the ears of one of the shadowy black-shirts. Too many times I catch sight of the rest of the Five exchanging glances that are a bit too meaningful.

There's no turning back now. Not that I ever thought

about it before this lonely half-hour wait started. Even so, the butterflies in my stomach double. Just before they triple.

Finally, with precisely thirty-two minutes left on the clock, I'm allowed to rush to my station and join the cooking. The pantry had been restocked with the best produce and meats we've ever had access to, and we all responded by challenging ourselves with complex, unique dishes that even a lot of adult, professional chefs might be afraid to attempt on live TV.

I work hard, but even as my hands move as fast as I can make them go, my mind is consumed by our scheme. The hours between the end of the morning brunch and this eight p.m. final had passed slowly, but we used them to finalize the details. Hushed whispers the microphones in the dorm couldn't possibly pick up, manufactured reasons to sneak into the back room and have longer conversations that weren't being recorded at all.

Mel had been useful for that part, coming upstairs a few times to fake-ask for help that required me to join him in the handler's room. There he would ask a question about some aspect of the plan he didn't understand completely. Once or twice, he whispered an idea for improvement from one of the other handlers. "What if we . . . ?"

For the first time, our families are in the balcony, watching us work the challenge like any regular member of the audience. Every once in a while I peek up at them. More often than not I catch Mom and Paige looking concerned rather than cheering me on. It makes sense, they're worried I'll snap again, that the pressure of this contest has been too much for me. It's not like my behavior since they arrived has given them much cause for optimism, after all.

I try not to think about any of that. I just cook the best meal I can.

Even if I know what I'm making will never be judged at all. At least not by the Super Chef.

ucas Taylor never appears during our cooking time,
which ends with another ear-piercing shriek from
Chef Graca's whistle. There are probably a hundred possible reasons why, but of course I assume it's because of what
happened at brunch. I figure he doesn't even want to be in
the same room with me anymore.

For my plan to work, he has to show up eventually, but
I try not to worry about that. In the meantime, I just cook.
I can't waste a second of this precious half hour if I want to
finish a presentable dish in time.

Finally, when our time is up and the cooking is over
and the judging is about to begin, the Super Chef returns
to the stage with his two sous chefs by his side. I hope he

doesn't notice my sigh of relief.

Each of us waits at our stations, our now-covered, waiting-to-be-revealed dishes sitting in front of us. Taylor reminds the audience of his announcement the other day: the winner of the finale will be the winner of *The Last Super Chef*, regardless of the scores accumulated during the challenge round. The slate's been wiped clean.

There's no theme this time. It's just cooking. Just food, and whose dish tastes the best. That's the idea, anyway.

"All right," Taylor says, looking at us with sad eyes and no smile. "Bring them up."

The front row goes first. I follow Pepper and Kiko with my dish in both hands, carefully setting it on the judging table when I get there. Behind us, Bo and Joey are next. Soon all five covered dishes are waiting in front of the three judges. We take a choreographed step back.

"There was some marvelous cooking going on this past hour," Wormwood assures the Super Chef. "Truly amazing." She eyes me. "And resilient."

"Absolutely," Graca agrees.

"Well then, let's see these incredible dishes," Chef Taylor says. And, as we step forward, he adds, "No matter what happens, kids . . . thank you. I'm honored to have met you and watched you cook these last few weeks. We had some ups and downs, for sure, but I think we did what we set out to do. I'm sure these final dishes will once and for all demonstrate the true direction of the culinary world, and the part our final winner can play in it. You've done so well and learned so much."

You can say that again, I think to myself.

"Now, please. If you would."

Placing our hands on the dish covers, we look down the line at each other—Pepper all the way to the left, Joey all the way to the right, me in the dead center. Nodding, we lift and step back.

The Super Chef looks down at our dishes, scanning from one side to the other, then back again, his head moving faster as his shock grows.

Because all of our plates are the same. Every one of them is empty. The overhead lights reflect off the spotless white ceramic, as if to highlight the missing food.

"Where's your food, Chefs?" Chef Graca asks. "The dishes you cooked?"

"Yes, what is the meaning of this?" the Super Chef asks in a loud, panicked voice.

The five of us stand stock-still. No one answers yet.

The Super Chef can't hide his confusion as he states the obvious. "There's nothing . . . These plates are empty."

"This isn't what you prepared out there," Wormwood agrees. "I watched you." She looks at Graca. "We both did. Kiko, you had a filet. And, Bo, that beautiful snapper. Where . . . ?"

"Did their dishes go?" It's Mel, emerging from the side-lines, stepping under the studio lights for the very first time. The Super Chef's bewilderment switches rapidly between my handler's unexpected appearance and our empty plates.

Mel points at the big screen behind the Super Chef, the one that before has always been under only the big boss's control. "Have a look."

The scene that flashes into view is of a soup kitchen. I didn't know there was one so close, but Mel did. Two of the other handlers, Renata and Brett, stand in the serving line, helping each guest. I recognize some of the people waiting, including Sam, Chef Taylor's friend from the food trucks. He holds out his plate. It shakes wildly.

Renata helps him steady his dish so she can serve him. He stares at the food she places there. The camera closes in on his face.

"Thank you, Lucas," he says, raising his plate to his chin. "You always think of us."

And if you were one of the millions of viewers at that particular moment, watching on the whatever-inch-your-family-could-afford screen, if you were looking closely as the camera zoomed in, you might see something else besides a Thanksgiving Day slice of turkey and hunk of mashed potatoes. If your screen was whatever-inches big enough, or maybe if you were just paying the right kind of attention, you might have seen the hand-basted red snapper cooked by Chef Bonifacio Agosto, hands down the best kid chef in all of Mexico.

"You gave it away," the Super Chef says, his voice full of disappointment. He sounds like he's watching his life go up in smoke. But it's not his life; it's just his plan. It had to die so that mine could live.

Man, I hope this works.

"Whose idea was this?" Taylor demands, anger overtaking some of his surprise now.

"Yours," answers Joey right away. "We learned it from you. Food-truck Saturdays."

Wormwood looks away from the screen, down at the empty plates, then at the five of us. Her shock starts to fade. A smile creeps across her expression. "You swapped them," she says, glancing at the anonymous black-shirts, the ones who had such quick hands during that last commercial break.

It was too risky to include her in our scheme, but since I'd uncovered why she felt the way she did about this competition from the very beginning, I'd hoped she'd be smart enough to recognize her opening when it arrived. "You cooked for the challenge," she continues slowly, working things out as she talks, "to make it look like you were competing, but what you made is gone. And you're presenting . . . this? Nothing?"

Graca seems to catch on quickly too. "Clever," he mutters.

"What do you mean, swap?" the Super Chef asks, still confused. "Clever? How are we supposed to judge this?" He gestures wildly at the plates again. "What *is* this?"

"It's teamwork," I say.

"Creativity," Kiko adds.

Joey glances at his dad and uncle, then says, "Attention to detail."

"Multitasking," Bo, starting to laugh, adds.

"All the things you taught them, Lucas," Wormwood says, fully on board now. "In only a few weeks." She takes in our straight, perfectly spaced *Super Chef*–compliant row, a far cry from the haphazard organization of that first night, when she wondered aloud if we could do anything right. "Seems they learn faster than any of us gave them credit for."

Taylor shakes his head. "You can't . . . You're ruining . . . Do you have any idea what kind of mistake this is? You signed a contract . . . and the grand prize . . ."

"We knew you'd be mad," Pepper says. "But it's okay. You taught us to handle criticism, too. Remember?"

The audience murmurs, and the Super Chef notices. His left hand starts to tremor. "How in the world . . . ?"

"We had help," I say, nodding in Mel's direction. "Sometimes you need it."

"Then," Taylor huffs, shaking some more. "Then . . . then none of you will win. We'll have to have another competition. Different kids."

"We're hoping you won't," I tell him. "We're hoping you'll take a second to rethink this whole thing."

"We're hoping if you think about it, you'll see the same thing we do," Pepper agrees.

"And what," the Super Chef asks, "is that, exactly?"

"You wanted to hold a final *Super Chef* competition," I say. "Why? So you could pick a last winner, show everyone a bright future. As if the future is something you can control."

"But," Pepper says, "well . . . it worked, actually. This contest has shown *us* the future. A different one, one where you're the only Super Chef the world needs."

Lucas Taylor opens his mouth to respond, but nothing comes out.

"They're right, Lucas," Wormwood issues a surprised half whisper to Taylor. "If you let us help you more . . ." She squeezes his shoulder hesitantly.

"You were the first Super Chef," Joey says.

Without missing a beat, Bo picks up his sentence. "And if you're the only one—"

"Then you should be the last one, too," Kiko finishes.

Chef Taylor exhales, and it seems like it's not just air that releases from his body. The way his shoulders tighten up, then droop, it's like everything else he's been holding in comes out, too. Fear and stress and exhaustion.

He and Graca exchange a glance. Graca nods meaningfully at his boss.

Still, the Super Chef shakes his head. "I don't know . . . I'm not sure I can . . . not anymore."

"You said there's no recipe for what you have," I call out. "But isn't that when chefs like us are at their best?"

Chefs like *us*. Because I'm a great chef, too. Nothing from the past two weeks has changed that. Nothing ever could've. Winning this contest, not winning it. Who my father is, who he isn't. None of that decides who and what I am now. Or what I'll become later. I'm the one who gets to do that. *Me*.

I hold his gaze for a moment. "The best chefs blaze new trails. We figure stuff out that hasn't been figured out before. You wanted to see the future, but . . ." I hesitate and shrug, unsure I have the right words to finish.

The Super Chef comes to my rescue. Now he's the one working through his thoughts as they come out. "It's . . . not . . . possible to know the future. You . . . just . . . adjust as you go. When the world takes away the ingredients you expected to have . . ."

"You figure out a way to make okonomiyaki anyway," I agree.

"Or when you have only sucky ingredients," Joey starts.

"Inexpensive," Kiko corrects him, but it's with a smile.

"You make the best kind of bread pudding you can," Wormwood finishes. "Even if it's out of English muffins and plain white bread."

"And when you need a little help from your friends," Graca says.

"All you have to do is ask," Wormwood finishes again. This time, when she's done, she and Graca both hug the Super Chef, sandwiching him between them. He shrugs at first, resisting them slightly, but they press against him harder, refusing to let him escape.

Finally, the Super Chef relaxes. He lifts he arms around each of his sous chefs' shoulders. This time it's him who pulls them close. "You're sure?" he whispers.

Both Graca and Wormwood nod emphatically. Then all three of them start to laugh in celebration, and soon the Super Five join in. Maybe I learned just this morning that it was okay to cry in kitchens, but it's definitely a whole lot better than okay to laugh in them.

The arena had been quiet, the confused onlookers attempting to process our back and forth, to make sense of all the unexpected surprises. They're still confused. Of course, they don't know about the Super Chef's Parkinson's.

But I suspect they'll find out soon enough.

Finally Lucas Taylor looks up, noticing their silence for the first time. He pulls his arms from his friends and steps forward alone, shouts toward the unsure crowd at the top of his lungs.

"Well? You heard them! We're not done after all. I'm not done. So make sure you come back for the NEXT Super Chef!"

Though they might not completely understand why yet, once the crowd comprehends the news that their beloved show won't end after all, they erupt into the wildest cheering yet. The applause and hoots fill the entire arena, growing louder and louder and louder.

I'm not sure how long it lasts, but there's a lot of laughing and clapping and high-fiving, between the Super Five on the floor, and the chefs up on the stage, too. In the crowd, on the sidelines. Everywhere.

Eventually, the whole arena still thundering with activity, the red camera lights wink off.

Kari jogs out from her secret side door so she can hug us one by one. Mel and the handlers are right behind her.

The studio lights dim.

The crowd makes its way to the exits.

The Last Super Chef ends, but only so the next one can begin.

Two Days Later

Tre's waiting in Josh's car, exhaust floating into the air, when the limo pulls up to our apartment building and drops us off. After we help Mom carry the suitcases upstairs, Paige, Tre, and I go for a walk up the street, even though it's kind of freezing outside. After all the excitement of the past few weeks, it feels awesome to be back home. So good, I start noticing all the things that make North Sloan a much better place than just about anywhere else I can think of. Even New York.

That piece of sidewalk jutting into the air. The corner market. Even the high school basketball team everyone seems to care so much about.

My best friend. And my sister, too.

Tre spends the first half of the walk telling us about all the people who paid for autographs, and how cool watching the competition on TV was. "There's one thing I don't get, though," he says. "If you thought the Super Chef was your father all those years, why didn't you say something?" He sounds a little hurt.

I glance at Paige. "I was protecting my little sister. She didn't know about it, and I thought it would bother her if she did."

"I've known who our father is for years," Paige says matter-of-factly.

We all stop walking. I gawk at her. "What?"

"Yeah," she says. "I found some old photos and letters in Mom's closet. Figured it out pretty quick." She counts off her discoveries on one hand. "They worked together at Murphy's. It was a burger joint. Doesn't even exist anymore. There's a taco place there now. You know, Seven Burritos? Anyway, when it was Murphy's, our dad was the cook. His name was Terry. Timmy? Something like that. Mommy was a waitress." She pauses, and her next words are whispered. "I don't think he's coming back any time soon, though. And, personally, I don't think it matters, either."

"You're right," I agree. "It doesn't matter. But I don't get it. Why didn't you tell me?"

"I was protecting my big brother. I mean, had I known

you thought the Super Chef was our father, I probably would've said something." She shakes her head, exhales. "I just figured Mom would tell you eventually."

"That's what I thought about you."

We grin at each other.

Tre gags. "Okay," he says, marching ahead. "I don't care what you say, Curtis. I need to hire one of those sous lawyer people. You guys are breaking about four hundred and seventeen brother-sister laws right now." He breaks into a run for a nearby swing set, one of our favorites going back years.

When he's far enough away not to hear us, I turn to Paige. "Is that why you didn't come up when I ran off on Thanksgiving?"

"With the Super Five?" I nod. "I guess. I felt so bad. It . . . Listen, Curtis. I had no idea that you thought all that. For all that time. If I had just told you what I knew—" Tears pool in the corners of her eyes.

"Paige, stop. It's okay." I step in front of her and face her. Pulling my sleeve over one hand, I wipe her eyes dry. "Seriously. Totally not your fault. You have no idea how much I missed you."

She leaps into me, hugging me hard. With her face still pressed into my chest, she whispers, "Curtis?"

"Yeah?"

Paige pushes away and looks up at me. The admiration

I thought I'd lost, it's right there. Back, like it never left. Maybe it didn't. Maybe it was just my imagination. Seems like a lot of things were. "Did you really think you had to become a chef just because the Super Chef was your father?"

I look down at my feet. "Guess so."

"Must've been a lot of pressure to put on yourself."

I shrug. "Sort of."

"Isn't it great, then?"

"What?"

"That you don't have to worry about being the Last Super Chef, or the Next Super Chef, or any Super Chef at all." She kicks my foot with hers. "For once you can just concentrate on being the First Curtis Pith."

Seven Months Later

"**W**elcome, students, to the first annual Super Chef Culinary School for Kids," Chef Taylor announces. It's summer. We're standing in a gleaming kitchen in New York. Not Super Chef Arena, a new building. The school the Super Chef opened shortly after we left in November.

Because why would the Super Chef think the future of cooking has to be all wrapped up in just one person, kid or not? Even if you can't control the future, if you want to shine a light on its potential, why not use a whole army of helpers to make the bulb as bright as possible?

I didn't do an actual head count before we lined up, but there must be twenty-five eager kids here. The Super Five plus a couple dozen others. We, the veterans, make up the entire first row. After all, we're the only ones in this bunch to survive the actual show.

Taylor surveys the class, taking a deep breath before turning his attention to us—me and Joey, Pepper, Kiko, and Bo, right in front of him.

"Well, Chefs? Any suggestions for our first lesson?"

We turn our heads, looking at each other, grinning at each other. And we don't use any secret signals, and we didn't plan this at all, but I guess someone must've taught us teamwork somewhere along the way.

Because we straighten and speak at the same time. And we all say the same thing.

"Mise en place."

ACKNOWLEDGMENTS

There's no one, single test to tell you that you have Parkinson's disease. Instead, the way the doctors figure it out is by first eliminating all the other possibilities. Which means getting tested for everything else, and when all those tests—some of which are a little bit scary—come back negative, you're left with Parkinson's as the answer to the weird things you've been noticing about the way you're walking or how much harder it is to suddenly find the sleeve of your shirt with your arm.

When I first accepted that I had Parkinson's disease, I probably spent too much time thinking about all the things I loved that I might have to stop doing. Trying to figure out a way to control my own future. I struggled with the idea that what I thought I was destined to do and be had suddenly shifted, taken a sharp left.

Eventually, though, I righted the ship. I found out that I'm pretty stubborn, so I ended up working really hard to keep that list of stuff the disease forced me to give up or change as small as possible. I refused to let it control my life in the way I feared it might. I mean, it's true that a lot of things have gotten much harder to do with Parkinson's, but just because something is more difficult doesn't mean you have to quit doing it. What I do next is up to me, not Parkinson's, I realized.

I started thinking, though, about other people who suffer from the same disease I do. Maybe some of them aren't as stubborn as me. Certainly all of them have different challenges from me—one of the odd things about Parkinson's is that it affects each person who has it a little bit differently. What might it be like, for instance, for someone with a job working with their hands a lot more than me? Someone who relied on the precision of their fingers, someone who might even be in danger if their hands were as unpredictable as mine sometimes are? Might they throw in the towel before realizing that maybe they didn't really have to?

These "What Ifs" were the starting point for the character that became Lucas Taylor, the Super Chef. Not long after, Curtis Pith arrived in my imagination. I knew right away that Curtis had inside him that stubbornness, that same refusal to give up on his dreams, no matter what might stand in his way, that I had recognized in myself.

I started to see how Curtis and the Super Chef were

connected to each other, and how they weren't, too. I glimpsed a future where they might be able to help each other get through their very different challenges.

Speaking of connections, our ties to each other are really important. They're what make us . . . well, us, and it's often other people who help authors turn their disorganized thoughts and ideas and feelings into actual books. That happened with this project, too, and it means I have a ton of people to thank for making this story real.

First and foremost, my editor, Elizabeth Lynch, who shaped this book into what it needed to be through several revisions. I often hear stories from writers who struggle with their second book, but Elizabeth made finding the core of this story easier than I would have expected. She told me openly when I was saying too much, or too little, or not being as clear as I needed to be. She zeroed in on these characters and their stories in a way that I never could've done on my own. I'm forever grateful to have been able to work with her on this book.

The rest of the team at HarperCollins as well—especially Chris Kwon for another fabulous book design and Chelen Ecija for her unparalleled artistry on the cover, front and back. I can hardly verbalize the wonder an author experiences when something entirely in our heads—like a TV set for a made-up cooking show—is turned into a real visual on a cover that will forever live alongside that story. Not to mention Jill Amack, Laura Harshberger, Jacqueline Hornberger, Vaishali Nayak, and Mitch Thorpe for all their amazing and priceless contributions.

Thank you to my agent, Alyssa Jennette, who is always beside me at just the right moment, pushing me and my stories in the proper direction. I couldn't do this work without your constant and treasured guidance.

I shared early chapters with a couple of different critique groups, to make sure I was headed in the right direction. Thanks goes to the Forsyth Public Library Writing group, led by Kim Ottenson and including Michelle Tompkins, Toni Bellon, Nicole Collier Harp, Heather Elrod, Justin Joseph, Leo Penha, Meg Robinson, and Rich Smith, among many other rotating members. You gave me the confidence to know I was off to a good start.

Thanks also to my other chapter review group, consisting of JD and Ellie Jordan, Emily Carpenter, Jane Haessler, and George Weinstein, for listening to and commenting on early chapters of this project. One of my favorite memories of starting this book is when I left chapter one at JD and Ellie's house and they shared it with their daughter, who returned it to me with an "A+" slashed across the top. There is no better salve for the inevitable imposter syndrome a kid lit writer fights than getting a good grade from an actual young person who is at the right reading age.

To my constant support group, my Rojo squad, Becky

Albertalli, M.J. Pullen, Emily Carpenter, and George Weinstein, thank you so much. Most of the time I have no idea how I ended up writing books or surviving the publishing industry, but anything I do know is because of meetings with and advice from y'all.

Special gratitude goes to Ivy Knight, food writer extraordinaire and former chef, who read an early version of this book and helped me get all my food- and cooking- and chef-related problems fixed. Any remaining errors are definitely because that stubborn part of me didn't listen to her, which makes them entirely mine.

To all my family, who I cannot name here but many of whose names I try to include in the pages of these stories, thank you for being the reason I can write inspiring family books for kids.

My mother Joyce continues to be my number one fan, and I so appreciate her for it. This book is dedicated to you, not because you were ever a single mom, but due to my father traveling so much when we were very young, I know you had to do lots of single-mom-ish things. I hope when you read the scenes between Curtis and his mother, you can see how I'm trying to thank you.

Speaking of my dad, I do wish he could've read these stories, too. I think he would've liked them.

Lastly, thank you to my wife, Mary, for her constant love and support. This book is about not giving up, about looking forward to your own future and not fearing it, even if you can't predict what's to come. It's about diving in with two feet when you can't see the bottom. In that sense, it was easy to write, because it's what we do every day, together.